ACROSS THE DEEP

LISA McGUINNESS

bonhomie  press

AN IMPRINT OF MANGO PUBLISHING

Published by Bonhomie Press, an imprint of Mango Publishing Group, a division of Mango Media Inc.

Cover design: Hugh D'Andrade

Cover illustration: Hugh D'Andrade

Layout & design: Tracy Sunrize Johnson

For permission requests, please contact the publisher at:

Mango Publishing Group
2850 S Douglas Road, 2nd Floor
Coral Gables, FL 33134 USA
info@mango.bz

For special orders, quantity sales, course adoptions and corporate sales, please email the publisher at sales@mango.bz. For trade and wholesale sales, please contact Ingram Publisher Services at customer.service@ingramcontent.com or +1.800.509.4887.

Across the Deep: A Novel

Library of Congress Cataloging-in-Publication number: 2020940939

ISBN: (print) 978-1-64250-391-3, (ebook) 978-1-64250-411-8

BISAC category code FIC019000, FIC044000, FIC042000

Printed in the United States of America

For my husband, Matt McGuinness.
Thank you for traveling through life with me;
for being fun, smart, kind, incredibly supportive, witty,
and the best person I know.

Also for Kate Canova and Jeff Reed:
the most inspirational and encouraging writers' group
anyone could ask for.

Suda

AT FIRST HER EARS AND EYES were acutely attuned, hoping that if she focused intently enough, she would be able to make out something—anything—in the pitch-blackness. Suda's ears took over the work of discovery when her eyes could only fail at their task. She tried to determine the significance of each creak and rumble as the ship's huge engine roiled to life. The vibration it caused matched the accelerated beat of her heart. Her hands traced the perimeter of the four-foot by eight-foot steel box that surrounded her. Trembling palms touched cans she assumed contained food, and her fingers scrambled birdlike through the box until they alighted on a can opener. In one corner sat a case of water bottles, and in another, a bucket. She dropped to her hands and knees and found the tattered mattress she had seen before the door had slammed shut. It took up most of the floor space, which was good. It would keep her from banging onto the ridged steel during the unexpected but inevitable motion of the ship.

As days passed, she stopped treating the darkness as an adversary and accepted it as her companion. She was relieved it protected her from knowing the extent of her filth. The fetid bucket had slopped over when a great wave rocked the ship. The smell at first intolerable was now a simple fact.

She had never before known the fear that came with complete isolation. Her childhood family had been small but close. She and her brother, Asnee, had been free to roam the village, exploring in the safety of a tightly knit community. And later, at least she had been with other girls. But now, in the dark, cold, uncomfortable container, the shock of being completely solitary was almost as difficult to bear as the fear of her unknown future.

Outside, the deep blue water pitched and churned— as if expressing distress while simultaneously protecting the ship's hidden cargo. Desolate and lonely, only the sounds of seabirds and crashing waves kept Suda company—and even those were muted by the steel cage of her shipping container tucked among many on the outer deck. The wind, which began as a warm breeze against the ship at the port of departure gradually turned cold and howled as the days passed, allowing both the metal and the ragged girl to become chilled. It finally stilled just before the ship reached its destination. Weak with hunger and deeply fearful of what was to come next, Suda's journey across the deep ocean from Thailand to the docks of San Francisco was complete.

In the dark and lonely hours, Suda's mind drifted back to her untroubled days, when she was a little girl, before her life had taken its dark turn. When she closed her eyes, she could see the details of that time—sun shining on the verdant hillsides of her village after the rain, her brother laughing, her parents sharing a look over their children's heads. She suddenly could taste the mangosteen fruit eaten on special days and the sweet sticky rice with mango her mother made when the crop had been good.

Suda simply meant "daughter" in Thai. But her mother, smoothing back her little girl's silky black hair and braiding it into an intricate design in the back, insisted her name was special because she had always wanted a daughter and finally had one. She kissed Suda's soft tawny cheek and pulled the worn, faded orange tee shirt down over the girl's head.

"There you go, little princess. You're ready for the day." She smiled at her daughter whom she could already tell was quick witted and sharp.

Suda didn't know her hillside village was poor. To her, the dirt floor of her small house was normal, and rolling out blankets to sleep each night was how it was done by most of the families who inhabited the hills. The soft, brightly colored blankets were beautiful and meant rest. Her family tended coffee trees, an endeavor much less lucrative than the poppies many others in the nearby villages grew to supply the heroin trade. But her parents wanted no part of drugs, even though it meant remaining poor.

Now, as Suda's legs cramped in the cold-dark prison of the shipping container, as she lay hour after hour on the hard mattress, she allowed her mind to visualize her life back then. Her earliest memory was of running; she saw her little, skinny legs confidently hurrying along the thin, rutted dirt paths in her village. The view of lush green hills, covered in rows of trees, peeked through the leafy plants along the path and between the small houses that made up her rural community. Her feet, heavily callused from never wearing shoes, knew each narrow track in the hillside, though the paths twisted out from her home like the roots of an old teakwood tree. Her mother sent her out many times each day to transport one thing or another.

"Bring lunch to your brother," her mother pressed a circular bamboo container of rice fried with eggs into the little girl's hands, knowing she would carefully deliver it to her brother, Asnee. Upon her return, her mother thanked her and called her "precious jewel" or sometimes "her joy," and Suda drank in the praise, not understanding it was rare and would be fleeting.

By the time she was six and ready to go to school with her brother, her hillside village was as intimately known to her as her own body.

"Are you excited, Suda?" her father asked her that first school-day morning.

Suda nodded in response as her mother finished brushing and braiding her hair.

"Stay with your brother and be respectful to your teacher," he reminded her.

"I will," she nodded, an earnest expression on her young face. Her mother smiled at her daughter's seriousness.

"I'll miss you and Ploy," Suda looked at her baby sister asleep in the scarf her mother had tied around her middle.

"You'll hardly miss a thing," her mom patted Suda's cheek.

"Tell me if she does anything new," Suda visualized Ploy sitting up for the first time or developing some other new skill while she was away.

"Off you go," her father said, steering his children toward the door.

Asnee obediently took Suda's hand as they left but dropped it and ran ahead to catch his friends as soon as they were out of their father's sight.

"Hey!" Suda yelled after him, but he didn't turn back. She looked around, momentarily fearful and alone, but the excitement of being included with the other children walking to the nearby school overrode her apprehension. Her slightly-too-large uniform had been handed down from an older girl in their village. The short-sleeved, pale blue top wasn't crisp and spotless like those of some of the other students, but it was hers. And she had her very own navy blue skirt in place of the pants she usually wore.

Suda loved school, but her favorite time of the day was when she returned home, burst through the front door, and found her mother and Ploy there. She went straight to her baby sister, picked her up, and held her while her mother quizzed her about what she had learned that day.

Once Ploy learned to walk, she and their mother sometimes strolled a little way toward the school so Suda and her brother could join them along the way home. Suda could hardly wait for the day Ploy would be old enough to go to school with them.

"A few more years," she told her. "Then you will get to go to school, too."

"You mean have to go to school," Asnee corrected. He, at twelve, was just counting the days until he could stop going to class and start working the land with their father full time.

The monsoon season that year hit early, hard, and fast. That day, clouds and humidity had been building throughout the morning, and then torrential rain was unleashed midday while the students were at lunch. Immediately soaked, they scrambled back inside the class-rooms and then sat, doing the rest of the day's lessons in damp clothing that clung to clammy skin. Once released, Suda and Asnee ran home through the rain as quickly as they could, occasionally slipping on the muddy paths along the way but laughing as they splashed through the streams of water. They knew Ploy and their mother wouldn't meet them in the wet weather, but they didn't expect their little house to be empty when they arrived home. Suda made them a snack, and they did their home-work while they waited, but even as the dark evening fell, their parents and Ploy weren't back.

Finally Suda started the rice they always ate for their evening meal while Asnee went out to ask after their par-ents and Ploy. The rarity of being alone in their home felt strange to Suda—especially with the pouring rain slam-ming against the metal roof. Her stomach clenched with anxiety. They should be here. Why weren't they?

The water boiled, and she added the white kernels to the pot. Soon the scent of jasmine rice wafted into the room. It momentarily comforted her, but when her brother hadn't returned by the time all the water had ab-sorbed, she knew there was something seriously wrong.

Time passed, and then more time slipped by before the front door swung open. But it wasn't her parents, Ploy, or Asnee who stood on the threshold, but her Aun-tie Pakpeo. Suda looked at her warily. She had never liked her auntie. Her mother said Auntie Pakpeo had been nice at one time, but when her husband died, she turned bitter and mean.

"Come with me," Auntie Pakpeo gestured toward her.

"Did you see Asnee?" Suda asked about her brother. "He's out looking for our parents and Ploy. Do you know where they are?"

"I saw him. He came to my house, and I told him to wait there. Now you come, too."

"But, what about . . .?"

Her aunt seemed annoyed at being questioned.

"Put the rice in a bowl and bring it." She gestured toward the pot Suda had been stirring when her aunt entered. "No reason to let good food go to waste."

Suda obediently began scooping the contents into a bowl, hungry and desperate to slip a spoonful into her mouth but not willing to incur Auntie Pakpeo's anger.

"Have you seen my parents and Ploy?"

Her aunt made no attempt to soften what came next.

"They were on the hill when the rains came," Pakpeo told her matter-of-factly. "The water was rushing. Ploy slipped. Your parents went after her to try to stop her from being swept away . . ."

"Ploy?" Suda's voice quivered.

"They're all gone, Suda." Her aunt put out her hand, gesturing Suda to come with her, but Suda was frozen. She couldn't understand what she was saying.

"All gone?" she stammered. A terrible vision of her parents and Ploy being swept away in a flash flood raced across her mind. "But . . ."

"Come," Auntie Pakpeo said gruffly and put out her callused hand toward Suda, who placed her own small hand inside.

Their deaths had been years ago. The loneliness that had never left her after that day had become something Suda had gradually come to accept. Yet, being trapped in the container had brought back memories of the freedom she had felt as a young girl. She longed for humid fresh hillside breezes and imagined inhaling the moist warm clean air into her lungs, now clogged with fetid smells and air that had been entombed with her on her ocean journey. She rested on the bare mattress, arm across her face as she visualized her past. How different her circumstances had become.

By the time the ship's huge engines slowed, Suda already suspected they were close to land. The water sounds had changed. The waves felt less ferocious, and the rocking had stilled. Deep, low blasts of noise seeped through the metal that separated her from the outside world. She later learned they were foghorns, but from inside the inky blackness, they sounded as if the earth was weeping. When the ship thumped against what she imagined must be a dock, Suda—half delirious—knew it soon would be time to enact the plan she had devised. Muffled shouts reached her ears, but it sounded like gibberish, and then a certain stillness came stealthily with deep night and the wee hours. She slept on and off, her tongue dry and her stomach gnawing painfully—having consumed her last can of food at least two days before. Her foggy brain dozed until abruptly awakening to the rumbling of heavy machinery and a shocking, loud clang of metal reverberating against her container. The box that had become her prison rose into the air and assumed a swinging weightlessness as it was transported through the air before it thumped onto land. Although she had tried to brace herself, the motion threw her against the side—the impact adding another deep bruise to her already-battered body.

Again quiet; eyes once more staring into darkness, ears keen; waiting . . . waiting until finally muffled footsteps approached.

As the door slowly opened, a sliver of light hit her eyes like a blow across the face. Her eyes, as dark as bitter chocolate, closed against the pain, but she forced them open so her target would be visible as her shaking arms threw the bucket's contents toward the silhouetted figure at the open door. Her plan was simple: hurl her own waste at whoever opened the door and then run.

Her weakened arms visibly trembled, but she cocked the bucket back and heaved its contents with what little strength she could muster.

"Ahhh!" a man's voice yelled. In her weakened state, most of it had slopped on the floor, but Suda thought at least some had met its mark. It was her chance to escape, and her wobbling legs slid past him toward the door. She was almost through when his strong fingers wrapped around her bony arm. She tried to wriggle free, but her strength was too depleted. She dropped her head in abject defeat: just like that, she had so easily been caught.

She reversed directions and scrambled back into the container, trying to get away from him, even if for a moment, but her body was wheeled around in the man's firm grip, and his voice whispered urgently in accented Thai. He held his face close to hers, intently talking, talking faintly and somewhat unintelligibly. He put his finger to his lips, but she wouldn't have been able to speak even if he hadn't told her to be quiet. Her mouth was achingly dry. She was trapped, and they both knew it.

He smiled at her and waved his hand toward the door, trying to coax her to go with him, but she clenched her jaw and went limp, refusing to help, so he was forced to hold her upright and pull her, feet dragging, through the door. Her cracked lips puckered to spit at him, but there was no moisture in her mouth, so she simply stared at him defiantly. Was he Thai? She couldn't entirely tell. His face held a hint of hill tribe, but his eyes were too round. Had she journeyed for days and days only to end up back in Thailand? It didn't make sense.

"It doesn't matter," she tried to say, but no sound came out.

She breathed deeply, experiencing this fleeting moment in the cool morning sunlight, proud to have survived the journey. The hope of fresh air and sunlight had sustained her for weeks, and her lungs inhaled the scent of the brackish water. Her face tilted to the sun as she tried to hold onto it, to savor it, but instead she felt her consciousness slipping away and embraced the darkness.

Suda heard the honk of a horn and the distant sound of a siren. Her frail weight was stretched across a battered leather seat and covered by a blanket that smelled faintly of grease. Her bruised limbs were tender, but she came to understand that she was, in fact, still alive and now in the back seat of a car. The man who had taken her from the container was in the front seat, hands gripping the steering wheel until his knuckles looked white against his skin. He looked over his shoulder, changed lanes, and then glanced back at her before turning his head to face front again. His window was open wide, but the blanket was tucked around her, keeping the chill at bay.

She wanted nothing more than to simply stay in that cushioned space, warm and comfortable at last. Heavy eyelids closed again, but they snapped back open moments later when the tires tapped a curb and the door was flung open.

"You're going to be all right. I've got you," the man said in English. Then catching himself, he repeated it in Thai, even as her sunken eyes told him she wasn't really listening.

He lifted her and then gagged as the smell of her was too strong to ignore. The blanket fell away, and foggy air blew against her. Frigid and damp, she both couldn't get enough of its freshness and wanted it to stop because it was painfully cold against her skin. This air smelled different from what she was used to—sharp like exhaust and something tangy. Where was she?

Through her haze, she saw that they were on a narrow wooden stairway that creaked with each step the man took. Held tight in his arms, Suda felt helpless. As they ascended, the expanse of crisp white walls was broken by a series of large black-and-white photographs of flowers. The focus was close, showing the speckles of nectar on the petals of one and raindrops on another. The peacefulness of the photos lured her in, and she wished she could stop and look more closely—but they went by quickly as each step carried them to the next level of the building. Against her will, her eyelids dipped closed again until loud rapping knuckles jerked her awake. The closed door in front of them was the green color of a young mango, waiting to ripen. Her stomach growled at the thought. A woman, young, with pale skin and hair the color of teak wood opened the door just enough to peek out. The woman's eyes were light green with a yellowish iris circling her pupils. Her face registered shock—or maybe it was horror—at seeing the two of them on her on her doorstep.

Still, she threw open the door to let them in, and even in Suda's weakened state, she thought she saw the woman's expression change from caution to compassion before she pressed her forearm against the lower half of her face to shield herself from the smell.

"What's going on? My God, what's happened?" Simone instinctively whispered. She recognized the man as a regular customer from the bakery on the bottom floor of her building.

"I'm sorry to show up like this," the man began and held out his hand while still supporting Suda with his arms. "I'm Chai," he introduced himself and began explaining even as he cautiously pushed past her, gently barging into the room as if he'd been there many times. "I can't take her to the hospital or to the police. I'll explain later. For now, I need you to try to get her hydrated and fed—not too much, something easy to digest or she'll vomit—and I'll be back as soon as I can."

Simone's eyes widened, but she found herself imme-diately moving forward to help the limp, filthy girl. Her fingers brushed the phone in her back pocket, checking to make sure it was there in case she needed to call for help.

"I'm not the one who hurt her," he said reading her look. "I'm trying to save her."

"Here," Simone grabbed a throw blanket and laid it across her couch. "Set her here," she was frowning at him but wasn't willing to tell him to leave when a young girl's life was clearly in the balance.

He gently laid the emaciated girl onto Simone's couch. "Here's the thing, Simone. I know this is a safe house. And I know you can handle this."

"I've never told you that," she replied guardedly. "How do you even know my name? What makes you think this is a safe house?" She gave him a blank, noncommittal stare, but her eyes darted to the door as her mind imme-diately began calculating whether this man posed a risk to the other girls who were staying there.

He had been a regular customer at Hope Bakery for some time, but aside from general pleasantries while Simone made him a latte or bagged a croissant, they'd never even crossed paths. Simone guessed the man was a police officer or a detective or something with the San Francisco PD because he sometimes wore a badge on a chain around his neck, but that wouldn't make him privy to the fact that this was a safe house; would it?

"I know this seems crazy, and I'm sorry to drag you into it." He spoke rapidly. "As I said, my name is Chai. Chai Swatangsatian. I'm police . . . undercover. I can't get into what's going on right now. I've got to go, or I'm going to be in a bad situation. Do you understand what I'm saying?"

"Yes," Simone waved her hand as if shooing him out the door. She could make a good guess because by now, she'd heard pretty much everything in the book when it came to undercover police and prostituted women. "Go." Her eyes moved toward the door.

He hesitated at the door.

"Go," Simone repeated more emphatically than the first time. "I'll take care of her, but come back as soon as possible. It looks like she needs a doctor." She hoped she wouldn't regret taking him at his word.

"If you think she's worse than I suspect, take her to the hospital, and I'll worry about the consequences later. We can't let her die when was she clearly so determined to stay alive."

"Got it," she was already moving to the sink, wetting a cloth and filling a glass with water.

The front door clicked closed, and Simone paused for a moment, thoughts reeling. Just a few minutes earlier, she'd been binge-watching *The Great British Baking Show*, and now she had an extremely needy girl laying on her couch. Her days of rescuing girls off the street had ended years ago. Now it was mostly official placements from either social services or even the FBI, if young women had been moved across state lines.

Her eyes took in the emaciated young women, and she shook her head, a cross between heartbreak and fury rising in her chest.

Suda

Earlier, Chiang Rai, Thailand

WARM NIGHT AIR SAT HEAVY AND STIFLING in the small room. Loud, pervasive inescapable music thrummed, as it had all evening, even into Suda's sleep. Her stomach ached with hunger, yet the very thought of food sent waves of nausea through her. Wafts of lemon grass, garlic, and too many people in a humid room choked the air, and her breath felt stifling and tight.

Young men, old men, foreign men, cologned men, unwashed men, an occasional woman.

It hurt between her legs. Her small breasts were bruised. The back of her head throbbed because the last man had repeatedly banged it against the wall when he was done with her, just because that's what he liked to do.

But it didn't matter as much as it used to. She met the eyes of the men in the bar with an alluring look. At least that's what she always tried for because she knew it would go better for her if the boss, Gan, thought she was putting in effort. If he saw her looking away or trying to disappear into the corner, she paid for it later. But, really, either way was bad. Just a different flavor of bad.

Suda was fairly certain she was fourteen when she had started at the karaoke, but she couldn't be sure. She had been born in the hill country where documentation was sparse at best. Small, skinny, and underdeveloped, she had looked more like she was about ten. And that, in turn, made her more valuable to the men who liked the girls young.

Four years had passed since she had come to the karaoke, and she was used to the routine. At the moment, she was a little bit drunk, which helped. She both hoped and feared being chosen. The small amount she earned helped keep her brother alive, and at least that was something.

Suda despised the word *karaoke*. For Americans, she now knew, the word brought to mind funny drunken singing, but in Thailand the word *karaoke* was a code word for brothel. More often than not, that brothel was a dingy one.

She smiled at the men in the bar but felt the weight of weariness inside at the thought of her body being used again. A bleak sense of hopelessness ached in her very core. She was a commodity, nothing more, and certainly less valuable than the wallets and iPhones she observed the clients so carefully guarding.

Her tired eyes took in the grimy linoleum floor. Cigarette smoke had gradually stained both the walls and the floors a sickly nicotine brown. Loud music pressed in on her from all sides; raucous talking and a brash clinking of barware created a din in her mind.

She saw Aanwat, the young man who helped the boss, subtly frown and then accept money from one of her regulars. He turned and met her eyes, an unspoken apology held deep within his own as he nodded to her. She stiffened at the thought of what that particular man would want from her. Usually with men, she could imagine she was somewhere else, but with this one, the mental escape was more difficult because he liked to bring her back to the moment by inflicting pain.

When Suda was a young girl, her family had taken a trip to a beautiful botanical garden. She often thought of those colorful flowers and of the small, red bridge that had delicate gold swirls etched into the rail as this particular regular, with his protruding belly and brown teeth, did with her what he wanted. The garden had an entire section devoted to orchids, and she loved those flowers the best of all. Some had seemed to grow straight out of trees, the small white blooms peppering the foliage with their elegance. There were pretend *tuk tuks*—small motorized vehicles—decorated with bright blooms. She could almost feel her mother's touch as she had lifted her onto the seat of one, and she laughed with delight at her little girl surrounded by flowers—her dark hair shining in the sun. Images of her mother's smile and of her brother joyfully running across the expansive lawn exploded into the moment, and she smiled at the memory.

"You like that; do you, baby?" the man asked, mistaking her smile at the memory for a smile of pleasure. It didn't matter. She didn't understand him because he spoke another language and the syllables he uttered sounded unintelligible to her. She nodded in an effort to hurry him along.

And then her reverie shattered as he touched the searing tip of his cigarette against the back of her knees. She braced herself and sucked in her breath, but held her scream. That would have given him what he really wanted. More than sex, he derived pleasure from her pain. He wanted evidence of the agony he inflicted, but she refused to give him the satisfaction. Her pain was the one thing she kept for herself.

A sense of deep separation from the world crept into her heart. She was no one. She was lost.

"I'll be back for you in an hour," Aanwat had whispered to her when he had shown the man to the door of her tiny bedroom.

She would try to stay alive that long. After all, what else was there for her to do? Her hope for salvation had died a long time ago.

"Do you think you can bring some dumplings for me when you return?" she had asked him under her breath as the door was closing between them. The sweet dumplings were the only food she could stomach anymore, and she was so very hungry.

The men and occasional women who visited the karaoke sometimes bought her food so they could feel as if they were all friends out for fun, but eating their offerings hurt too much because the little dishes they ordered tasted of despair on her tongue.

"I'll try my best," he had whispered, giving her a sad smile to show his regret at bringing that particular man to her room. She knew he would do what he could to smuggle the dumplings to her, but Aanwat couldn't always do so without calling attention to himself by giving her preferential treatment. Gan didn't tolerate Aanwat being soft with any of the girls.

Aanwat

AANWAT LAID BACK ON THE BED and stared at the hotel room ceiling. For the first time in years, he deeply craved heroin. It might not solve his problems, he reflected, but then at least he wouldn't care.

He thought back to the opium poppy farm where he had grown up. His entire village had been in the heroin business, and most everyone was using—even the children. The parents started them young to keep them complacent. He could see the faces of each of his siblings as they had been then. He was one of seven, and all but he and two other brothers were already dead. And those two were so deep into the drug trade that even he was afraid of them.

He sighed at the memory of his parents. Both were addicts, and he hated them. He hated all of it. He left in horror after his six-year-old sister overdosed. Even at thirteen, he had known he had to get away or he would be next. It had been difficult to get through those early days without the feeling heroin gave him. His body had itched all over from the withdrawal, and he had been sorely tempted to go back, but at that point, his poverty saved him. Because he had no money in his pockets either to get back home or to spend on drugs, he went through withdrawal alone on the streets.

He'd had a hard time finding a job, not only because he was a skinny, undernourished kid but also because helping on the farm wasn't a skill needed in the city of Chiang Rai. He spent more than a few nights hunched down in doorways, trying to remain out of sight. Then Gan found him sleeping outside of the karaoke one morning, and his troubles were over. Gan put him to work.

Aanwat pictured himself then, a scrawny kid, sweeping the floor and doing dishes. He'd been proud though. He had work. He earned some money, and pretty soon Gan let him sleep inside at night. And there were girls. Beautiful girls to watch. He didn't dare speak to them then. Their faces were prettier than any he'd seen. They wore make up and fancy clothes. They got to sit at tables and drink and eat with customers who came in. They sometimes danced on a small stage so men could see them and choose the one they wanted. Aanwat liked to take a surreptitious peek at them then. He would pretend he could choose one as well.

By the time he was eighteen, he'd moved from sweeping the floor to bigger and better things. Not only did he get to run errands for Gan, he got to negotiate the price with the customers who wanted to go with one of the girls. Over the years, he had come to recognize the regulars. And the girls openly talked about what the different men wanted from them. So, Aanwat knew when the men came to him for a price if he should charge extra for the kind of thing they liked. Not that it helped the girls, but Gan would get more for what they wanted.

Then one day in walked Suda. Well, *walked in*, he reminded himself, wasn't really the right way to put it. Gan had her firmly by the upper arm, but her feet were two paces behind, so she came in, but anyone could see that it was not what she wanted. And there was a sadness hiding behind her determinedly blank expression. He couldn't tell how old she was, but he could see that she was younger than most. She looked scrawny just like he had when he'd arrived. He guessed her to be around thirteen or fourteen. She was lovely even then, and he knew they'd get a high price for her first night. He realized he didn't like the thought.

The other girls had already been working when he'd arrived, and he hadn't really given their lives before they'd been there any consideration. He'd been happy to be able to work near them with their fancy high heels and short skirts. But Gan had been talking about needing more variety. Someone younger for the men who liked that. And it looked like he had found what he wanted.

"What's her story?" Aanwat had asked.

"Aunt needed some money," was all Gan said.

"Where's she from?"

"A hill tribe. Doesn't matter which one; they're all the same to me."

Aanwat clenched his jaw to make sure he didn't utter a word in response. Gan knew well enough that Aanwat, too, was from a hill tribe.

"How old is she?"

"No papers. She doesn't even know. Old enough, though, I'd say."

Aanwat looked down at the floor.

"She looks pretty young. Are you going to wait a while?"

Gan laughed and then said, "I need a return on my investment."

It was four in the afternoon when Suda had been brought in, and a few girls were milling around, having a drink before the evening got going.

"Nah Sa," Gan snapped at the one who made the most money for them. "Come." He waved her over. She got up and walked to them, looking curiously at Suda.

"What do we have here?" she asked.

"She's new," Gan gestured toward Suda, looking at her appraisingly. "She's skinny, and her clothes are ugly. Get her cleaned up."

Aanwat watched the new girl, and he noticed a tear slide down the corner of her eye.

"No crying, girl," Gan snapped at her. "You're lucky to be here. And you'll do what we say, or you'll be beaten so badly you'll wish you were dead."

Aanwat looked up at Gan.

Suda's eyes went wide, and Nah Sa took her hand. "Come," she said. "I'll get some clothes for you."

Aanwat's eyes followed them to the door that led upstairs. "How much should I ask for her?" he asked.

"I'll negotiate this one," Gan told him. "I have someone in mind."

"Who?"

"It's none of your business, who. You just need to make sure the bar is full and there are plenty of drinks on hand."

Aanwat went about his business with one eye riveted to the door, waiting for Nah Sa and the new one to walk back through. When they finally did, he could tell from the young girl's puffy face and red eyes that she had been crying. She was so small, she looked like a child to him. Her long hair had been taken out of the braid she'd been wearing when she'd arrived. It now hung below her shoulders and was curled at the ends. Her skinny legs were exposed below the miniskirt she now wore, and the tight top she had on allowed the eye to see that she had barely developed breasts. Her tiny feet were in high heels, and her instability revealed that she was not accustomed to walking in them. Her eyes were rimmed in eyeliner, and Na Sa had colored her lips a shade too red for her young face, making her look like an overly painted doll.

Nah Sa presented Suda to Gan, and Aanwat heard him question Nah Sa about her.

"Did you tell her what to expect?"

"Yes," Nah Sa assured him.

"Did you tell her what happens to girls who resist?"

"I did," she said, looking at the floor, remembering what had happened to her when she resisted the first customer who paid for her.

Gan turned to Suda and lifted her chin, "I don't want to have to beat you, but be assured, I will."

Suda tried to keep her eyes lowered, but it was difficult with him lifting her chin.

"Do you understand me?" he asked.

"*Chi*," Aanwat heard her whisper. "Yes."

Simone

SIMONE, WITH "TO DO" LIST IN HAND, clicked on one set of lights in the bakery's kitchen. The full force of having them all come on at once was a bit too much for her first thing, so she always eased into illuminating her space. As it was, she usually closed her eyes for a second or two against the glare off of the metal countertops. She would turn on the rest of the lights; after she had her first cup of coffee. Her ritual morning latte was more for the delicious taste and a sense of comfort than for a caffeine rush. Although her usual arrival time was 4:30 in the morning, she was used to the early hour, so her mind was already alert and reviewing the day's tasks. The hiss of the coffee steamer, the clatter of dishes, and the murmur of conversation were the sounds that formed the auditory backdrop to Simone's life. But for the first hour, she had the place to herself.

Now, first coffee of the day in hand, Simone mused about her routine, which was as consistent as the city's fog: In the morning, her neighborhood was usually shrouded in the misty condensation. That gave way to sunny afternoons, and in the evenings—whether in the form of wispy tendrils or a thick blanket—the fog rolled back in to chill the nights. The bakery was nestled in the Haight-Ashbury neighborhood of San Francisco. There, as part of Hope House, Simone took care of young women who were recovering from being trafficked and oversaw the bakery cum teaching school, waking before sunrise each morning to start creating yeasty concoctions that warmed the building and sent wafts of fresh bready scent drifting out onto the sidewalk. The aroma lured passersby inside for flaky croissants or peach muffins, which they then savored with their morning coffee or tea.

Above the bakery was her homey mess of an apartment, where Suda had been unceremoniously dropped off the night before. It was on the top floor of the same converted Victorian that housed Hope Bakery. The rooms, nestled on the floor in between the bakery and Simone's apartment, sheltered a constant rotation of young women. They lived with Simone and Grace while they worked on slowly regaining their health and the lives that had been stolen from them. This morning, as Simone gathered ingredients from the walk-in refrigerator's shelves and set them on the kitchen's long counter, her mind focused on Suda, who would be a particular challenge.

Simone kept a small, tattered wooden box full of index cards on a shelf in her apartment, tucked in among her favorite books and trinkets. Each card held the name of a young woman who had passed through the safe house under her watch. Simone wrote each young woman's name on a card when she arrived, and there the cards remained—even once the woman had moved on. Simone often sorted through the entire stack and prayed for each young woman by name, even after the woman had left the haven Simone had created.

Each girl traveled her own road; their journeys took them up and down through brokenness and healing. Some were success stories; others not. Or, as Simone liked to say, they were "not-yet-success stories." She still had hope.

That morning, before she went down to the kitchen, Simone had written "Suda" on a card, set it among the others in the box, and then placed the container back on the shelf. For now, she would have to think about Suda while she worked, because downtime was a luxury that she didn't have. She pulled her hair into a ponytail and reached for a large metal bowl.

The kitchen was large, industrial, and her favorite part of the safe house. She and Grace used it not only to bake goods to sell but also to feed the residents who lived in the house at any given time. In addition, it was a teaching tool; cooking classes were given as part of the regular curriculum so that each woman who left the program had a usable, marketable skill, and therefore was less vulnerable to ending up back in the untenable situation from which she had come. It was also the one place in the house where the residents were required to muster enough self-control to hold it together—especially if they were working the front and interacting with people who came in for coffee and the takeaway treats they made. It was all part of the program.

Still, in the beginning, nothing was required: no classes, no cooking, no helping out. Instead, Hope House was simply a place to feel safe, to sleep without being afraid, to feel nurtured and allow healing to begin. All the young women were given time, and when they were ready, they knew to come to Simone.

The corners of Simone's lips turned up into a small smile as she added flour and baking soda to the bowl and reflected upon how she had gotten to this unexpected place in her life. Truth be told, she hadn't intended to get involved in helping women who had been victims of forced prostitution. It had come about accidentally when she had witnessed an event that chilled her and then stayed in the forefront of her psyche.

When people asked her how she became involved in Hope House, her answer was usually the same: "An unexpected moment that altered the course of my life" is what she said.

She could still see it, if she let her mind drift back to that early morning: She had left early for work—which at that point was a marketing job for a Fortune 500 company. She was in desperate need of catching up on a few things that she could never seem to get to. The streets were quiet. It was a regular day; an ordinary, average, nothing-special moment. She got off the MUNI train in downtown San Francisco, grabbed her regular milky sweet latte at her favorite shop, and headed up Pine Street to her office.

The edge of her vision caught a man holding the arm of a young Asian woman—or maybe a teen. It had been difficult to know. She was scantily clad for a cold, foggy morning, her pale face radiated *despair*. Her black eyes bleakly sought Simone's gaze. Her beautiful young face was devoid of hope. The grip the man had on her arm was menacing and proprietary.

Simone gasped and looked around. Were others seeing this? It seemed to Simone that the girl was the man's captive. As if she had tried to escape but had been caught. Simone glanced around, looking for someone— anyone —to be a co-witness to this event. She wanted another set of eyes to meet in a quick joint assessment. But the early-morning street was empty except for the three of them.

Simone had felt a powerful urge to grab the young woman and wrench her free of the man's grasp. To run with her—but to where? She reached into her pocket for her phone to call the police because the hopeless look on the woman's face and the beseeching eyes intensely focused on Simone's own told her clearly that this situation was sinister. But her fingers urgently felt around first one empty pocket and then another. The vision of her phone still sitting on the table next to her discarded cereal bowl passed in front of her mind's eye.

Was she imagining it? No. She knew what she was seeing, and she understood her own powerlessness.

The experience had impacted her profoundly. It had shaken her. And changed her.

When she got to her desk that morning, she ignored the work she had come in to handle and instead Googled "human trafficking," a term she had been hearing more of lately in the news and in conversation. Even a cursory search brought up pages and pages of articles about young girls from impoverished countries being sold as sex slaves, prostitutes, and trafficked girls, often by their own families desperately in need of money, out of options, or perhaps simply overwhelmed by one too many mouths to feed. Simone scrolled through articles about boys, smuggled to the United States in hope of a better life, who instead ended up at the mercy of criminals who used them like commodities. They arrived believing they had legitimate jobs, and instead owed a debt that could be paid only in flesh.

Other links led to articles about local girls, who for one reason or another ended up on the streets: grabbed or lured with potent cocktails of feigned love and drugs and then compelled to do things they never wanted or intended to do.

Simone hadn't realized how prevalent the sex trade actually was. She'd heard of it, sure, but assumed it was something obscure and rare; not rampant in her own city. She'd been wrong. In fact, it was very much thriving in San Francisco, hidden in plain sight.

That day, Simone stepped away from her computer only to grab some takeaway chow mein from her favorite restaurant. She went right back to her search as she ate the noodles straight from the carton.

Her mind spun as she clicked on different sites. From her research, Simone learned that the city was home to many young women who were living trapped lives. Maybe if she helped one person to start, it would make a difference.

"I don't get it." Olivia looked at Simone over the teapot as she poured each of them a hot cup of English breakfast tea, her face open and her blue eyes curious. Olivia had been Simone's best friend since they were roommates their freshman year at college, "How are you going to help someone?"

Simone had broached the subject of getting involved over breakfast at her favorite diner one Saturday morning. Her French toast and chicken apple sausage steamed as she tucked into her food.

"I'm not sure," Simone confessed, pouring on syrup. "But I'm going to figure it out."

Olivia smiled and twisted her long brown hair behind her ear as she set the teapot back on the table between them. "I have no doubt you will," she said. She picked up her teacup and blew on the steam, looking at Simone over the top of the cup. "If there's one person who can get something done, it's you."

"Thanks, Liv!" Simone smiled and cut her sausage. "That means a lot to me. I appreciate you not just blowing this off as some crazy plot."

Olivia waved her hand. "I probably would if this was coming from someone else, but you're the type who will actually do something, not just talk about it."

"Nonetheless," Simone put out her cup and tapped it against her friend's. "Support gratefully accepted."

Gradually over the next few weeks, a plan began to solidify in Simone's mind. She began talking tentatively about the idea of taking in a girl from the streets. Her parents, and most of her friends—truth be told—thought she had completely lost her mind. Her mom was the worst. She was sure Simone would be killed.

"That's noble, Simone, but you've got to get real about this," her friend Justin advised, passed her a glass of wine, and led her to a couch where a group of their friends were snacking on cheese and crackers one Friday after work.

"It's not *noble*," Simone retorted, furrowing her brows at the slightly condescending tone. "It's just something I can do to help someone."

"Is she on this again? You're becoming boring, Simone," Justin's girlfriend, Pamela—who had always made Simone clench her teeth—felt compelled to put in her two cents.

Simone bit her bottom lip so she didn't blurt out something she would later regret and caught Olivia's eyes.

Olivia, gave her a look that said, "Ignore them. They don't get it."

Simone's widened eyes subtly told Olivia the message was received. Then she took a sip of the wine and smiled.

Another woman joined the foursome on the couch. Simone hadn't met her before, but something about the way she comfortably inserted herself into the conversation told her that this tatty-jeans-wearing, nose-ring-sporting, beautiful young woman had a strong sense that she knew a lot and was more than eager to impart wisdom to those around her.

"What's your training?" she asked Simone as if she'd been a part of the conversation all along. Simone noticed she was drinking some aggressive amber liquor on the rocks instead of wine, as if to show them all that she was more hard-core than they were.

"No formal training," Simone said. "I volunteer two evenings a week at a safe house in Oakland, though. I had to take a class they put on for volunteers before I could start, which helped."

"That's a nice beginning, but you're not a therapist, a social worker, or a cop. So, really, what do you have to offer?"

"Wow." Simone was taken aback. She took a sip of her wine, put up a finger to show that something was coming, and inhaled deeply, trying to quickly gather her thoughts. The entire group's eyes were focused on her expectantly. "What I have to offer is a safe place to live. Help. Kindness. If we never do anything that isn't a challenge, that's not out of our comfort zone, then we are going to live very small, extremely limited, and most likely fairly dull lives."

"You'll be in way over your head," said nose-ring girl.

"Probably. But I have some good friends and family to help me. Why are you concerned about it?"

"I'm not. Just playing devil's advocate."

"You were a business major and work downtown," Justin added, looking towards Simone.

"Listen, you guys, to a certain extent I can't disagree with you. I get that you think I'm crazy to want to 'take in some street waif' as I believe one of you said earlier," Simone swirled her pinot noir and looked at the rich red liquid in her glass. "Still, I feel compelled to do this, so you can either be supportive or you can think I'm nuts, but either way, I'm going to try to help someone. I have to try. Worst case scenario is that it doesn't work out."

"Uh, that's not the worst-case scenario." Nose-ring girl rolled her eyes. "The worst-case scenario is that some pimp shows up; you get beaten up, raped, robbed or what have you; he takes the woman you're trying to help, and leaves you for dead."

Simone looked at Olivia and raised her eyebrows. She had nothing to say to that.

"More wine?" Olivia asked Simone, who held out her glass.

"Yes *please!*"

After that evening, she found it was easier to either skip going out with her friends or to avoid the topic with them at all costs. Except for with Olivia, who she could always count on. Volunteering at the safe house had given her an inkling of what these young women were up against, and she felt a deep calling to move forward, even if she could help just one person, she mused. She could get that person on her feet and then after that maybe she could help someone else. The key was to figure out who was the right one. Simone prayed that someone would become the obvious choice. Finally she thought maybe she had found her.

"There's this girl I keep seeing," Simone was sitting on the couch in her apartment after she got home from work, laptop resting on her knees, tea on the coffee table when Olivia popped over to hang out after work. Without preamble, chitchat, or offer of a glass of wine, Simone cut straight to the chase.

"Really? Since when?" Olivia, asked.

"Most mornings when I get off of the train. She's sitting on the steps around the BART station. She looks haggard, overly alert, too skinny, too hardened for someone her age. Lots of makeup, but it's always smudgy, like she's been through a night. You know?"

"Yep, sounds questionable for sure. Are you going to talk to her?" Olivia asked.

"I think so. Maybe I'll buy her a latte and just chat with her for a minute."

"Be careful. Be discreet in case she's being watched." Olivia tossed her keys into the bowl they kept by the front door for just such occasions.

"Yeah, yeah," she smiled at Olivia, half exasperated that her friend was telling her what she already knew, half appreciative that she was looking out for her. She was grateful that Olivia, unlike everyone else, had never once tried to talk her out of her plan and instead had championed the idea.

"I'll be your sidekick. You know, the one to get the two of you out of scrapes. The one she can come talk to when you're being difficult and making her follow rules and such," Olivia had told Simone when she'd broached the subject back in its idea infancy.

"Do you think she's the one?" Olivia now asked, a noticeable spark of enthusiasm creeping into her eyes and voice.

"I have no idea, but I've got to start with someone. And something about her feels right."

"Exciting," Olivia walked to Simone's fridge and opened the door, peering in for something to eat. She grabbed some baby carrots and hummus, set them on the coffee table, and started nibbling while Simone talked about the desperate girl they would come to know as Grace.

The autumn morning she'd introduced herself to Grace had been six years ago. In the eventful intervening years, Simone had eventually dumped her day job and created Hope House with the very young woman she'd seen on the steps. What had begun with her impulsive dream had gradually expanded until inviting strays off the streets had filled her apartment to overflowing and gotten her into more than a little trouble with her landlord.

Once Grace had been rescued, she had never left. Others had been added, sleeping here and there until the apartment was bursting.

"Wow," Olivia said one day when she stopped by after work. "There are mattresses everywhere." She stepped over one to get to the kitchen.

"I know," Simone shrugged, having stopped trying to keep the floor clear of the makeshift beds. She looked around but tried to think of the mattresses as little "cocoon havens" rather than "disorder" and smiled. They were all tidily made up with sheets and blankets, but she knew it was time to expand to a larger place.

In addition to too many beds and not enough space in her home, Simone found that too much of her workday was taken up trying to rustle up pro bono therapy for her "foundlings" as Olivia affectionately called them.

Simone sighed and added "carrots," "tomatoes," and "pasta" to the grocery list. The food bill was getting ever larger in spite of her creative menu planning.

"You've got to get a grant or something," Olivia leaned against the counter after filling Simone's teapot with water and putting it on the burner to heat.

"I know but it's hard to find the time to research them let alone write the applications."

"I'll help."

"Really?" Simone's tone told the story of just how much she would appreciate it.

"Yes, really. And you should check in with your church. I bet they have some sort of missions funds or something."

"Great idea. Why didn't I think of that?"

"Because you're too busy just trying to keep your head above water."

The whistle blew on the kettle, and Olivia poured a cup of tea for each of them. They both leaned over the steaming mugs and inhaled the fragrance of dried jasmine.

"Cheers." Olivia tapped her teacup against her friend's.

"Cheers is right," Simone agreed, her mind already spinning with the thought of talking to the pastor.

"We'll tag team it," Olivia told her, grabbed her laptop from her bag, and set it on the counter in front of her. She opened it and typed "charitable grants" into the search field.

Olivia's idea worked. Simone had thrown her monetary plight to her church and had been relieved to get a bit of help there. And together she and Olivia clicked away on their keyboards late into the night, working to get a grant and actual funding. Bleary eyed, hair stuffed into messy ponytails, the two often munched on the food Grace tried to cook as they filled out forms.

"Sorry," Grace often said before setting her barely edible meals in front of the two.

"Are you kidding?" Simone said, gamely sticking a fork into the overcooked penne. "I'm so grateful you're even trying."

"Seriously," Olivia added, smiling through a mouthful of the too salty meal, "It's delicious."

"Shut up. I know you're just saying that."

"No, we're not!"

"I'll get better," Grace said, almost spitting out the food onto her own plate, but hiding her secret pride in the fact that she was learning her way around the kitchen.

—

Their efforts had been labor intensive but fruitful. Then one day the fact that this was a 'God thing,' as Olivia called it, was confirmed when a man from Simone's church—who conveniently happened to be a serious tech guy—decided more substantial funding was in order and wrote a check for more than she could have ever imagined. Once that ball got rolling, she quit her day job and never looked back.

That's when Simone and Grace had conceived of Hope House and its bakery filled with aromatic loaves, croissants, pastries, tea, and coffee. The top floors had been renovated to house Simone in a tiny apartment at the top; the middle flat comprising four bedrooms for Grace and the residents. Simone started before the crack of dawn each morning to get the bakery going; Grace cooked meals, coordinated group therapy sessions, and drove the girls to appointments. They often switched up the tasks so neither of them burned out, and Olivia—always upbeat and ready to pitch in—sometimes helped after work—but more often than not, she just hung out with everyone.

"Hey," she said in greeting when she popped by a few days after Suda arrived. "I'm Olivia," she reached out her hand in greeting and did her best to mask the shock she felt when she saw the condition of the hollow-eyed, emaciated young woman.

Suda

SUDA AWOKE WITH A START, the dream of being in the container again searing her sleep. She looked around, heartbeat racing. The dark was different here. Not so black. Ambient light shone on the bed at Simone's.

"I'm safe; I'm safe," she whispered every night when she crawled into bed, repeating the mantra in her mind as she drifted off. But as soon as sleep found her, she was immediately back in the inky dark box, heart racing, feeling terrified and desperate to get out. Her eyes had flown around the metal space in the few seconds they'd given her before the heavy door creaked shut and she was engulfed in an impenetrable black.

In her dream, the space was even smaller than it actually had been. Standing straight was impossible; her back had to be hunched over; her eyes were blind. Screaming to be let out and pounding until her hands were too sore to make contact with the metal walls, her cries gradually became a whisper. She was afraid she would suffocate.

"I'm not there anymore," she whispered to herself from the sanctuary of Simone's warm bed. She wondered whether Aanwat had stood on the dock in Thailand and watched the container as it was lifted and secured in the stack of others on top of the deck, locked into place with containers of other goods. His eyes had been unreadable on the way to the port, but his agitation had been obvious. Had he known what was going to happen to her? She thought he must have.

He'd warned her. She couldn't deny that. He'd whispered that she was getting skinny, ugly, and undesirable and told her Gan had threatened to ship her off to the United States where things would be much worse for her. He had told her to eat. Had told her to smile. He had told her to stop fighting. She hadn't.

At the time, she'd thought, "How much worse could my life be?" and brushed off his threats with a defiant lift of her chin and a dream of escape.

But when the container door closed and she was sealed in, she realized that her life could in fact get worse. Or could at least become a different kind of horrible.

"It's over now," she told herself again and pulled the covers up over her shoulders. But at night, even in a warm, clean bed, it all came flooding back. The stench, the pain, the terror. Her rage at Gan was constant and palpable, but it felt even more inescapable in the dark. Just one more reason to use the night-light Simone had given her when she realized Suda was terrified of the dark.

"But it *isn't* over," the small voice reminded herself.

Chai had broken the news to Suda earlier in the day: He had managed to get to her before the smuggling ring he'd infiltrated had, but there were unexpected repercussions. Gan, the man who ran Suda's brothel back in Thailand, wasn't happy that his cargo had escaped, so he was sending his right hand—Aanwat—to find her. The local affiliate didn't know what she looked like, but Aanwat did, and he was charged with getting her back.

Aanwat

"I SEE TALL BUILDINGS," Aanwat's young seat companion intoned excitedly to his exhausted mother as she gathered the detritus of a fourteen-hour trip into a large straw bag. The boy clutched his stuffed elephant and held him to the window so he too could see the view.

Aanwat also looked out the window of the plane and saw the expanse of the city as they made their descent. The topography of San Francisco was very different than that of Thailand. There was no lush green to be seen. Just a sprawl of buildings, roads, houses and then the bay beyond.

When the plane doors opened, he was expelled into a cacophony of foreign languages spoken by the tapestry of humanity found at San Francisco International Airport. It had been his first plane trip and, if he didn't figure out what had happened to Suda, it would be his last. And beyond that, he was pretty sure he would end up in something worse than a shipping container. He would find her. He was determined. Gan had saved his life when he was a boy, so he would do what it took to make things right for him now.

The only information they'd received was that, upon arrival, she was not inside the closed and locked container. The food and water were gone, shit covered the floor, but Suda was nowhere to be seen. The door had been shut and locked when she'd left; he'd seen to that himself. And from the description, she'd been in the container for the entire trip. So what had happened to her? There was no evidence of tampering; how had she gotten out? And once free, where had she gone? That's what he had been sent here to learn, but he was completely out of his depth. This wasn't just arranging a price for an hour of pleasure with a karaoke girl. It was organized. International. He hadn't even wanted in initially, but Gan had, and now here he was: searching for Suda in San Francisco, California. He had thought California was supposed to be full of surfers and hot weather, but this city was cold and foggy. Just his luck.

Although his English wasn't at all fluent, he had picked up enough from tourists over the years to help him get by in basic conversations, but he didn't know how to read a word of it, and the alphabet was indecipherable. In addition, it appeared that there were no *tuk tuks* for hire to get him to his hotel.

Claire

"CLAIRE," SIMONE CALLED UP THE STAIRS to the whip-thin, damaged young woman who, until Suda had appeared in the night almost two weeks ago, had been the newest resident of Hope House. Both Simone and Grace despaired that this beautiful girl, whose rare smiles never reached her eyes, wouldn't be able to heal until the impenetrable shield she had erected around herself softened. For almost four months, she had stonewalled kindness and eschewed the advice of her therapist.

"You're late for the bakery." Simone was careful to keep her tone soft. She climbed the stairs to see what was keeping her. She peeked into Claire's room and saw her standing in front of the mirror above her dresser, dragging fingers through her straggly blond hair. She twisted it into a knot on her head and secured it with a pencil because she couldn't find a hair elastic in the chaos that was her room. That morning, Claire didn't have the energy to wash her hair—or even comb it if she was honest with herself. Or maybe she just didn't feel like it. Either way, Simone made her keep it pulled back when she worked in the bakery, and it was her shift, so up it went.

Claire knew she had to work with the new girl that morning. She couldn't figure that chick out; aside from the language barrier, Suda kept to herself, and Claire found it boring.

Claire could tell that Simone was becoming frustrated with her, especially when Simone closed her eyes for a long moment after Claire instigated something or another. She breathed deeply and then purposefully redirected Claire as if it wasn't obvious what Simone was doing. Claire's therapist had told her to focus on her own healing and not interfere with the mechanisms others use to cope, but whatever. She needed to keep things interesting in one way or another.

Grace was the only one here who really understood her moody behavior because she had been in the same situation. Now she constantly hugged Claire, encouraged her to just hang on, and told her that things would get better. That had better happen soon, Claire thought, because she missed the content feeling that she got when she was taking the Percocet. She missed it a lot. In fact, she could really use one now.

"Yeah, I'm coming," she muttered to Simone, as she slouched past her and went down the stairs into the bakery's kitchen.

"Great," Simone followed her downstairs and then handed her the cappuccino she'd made before she'd come upstairs to track her down. It was just the way Claire liked it; milky and sweet.

Claire grunted her thanks but made sure Simone didn't think she felt all warm and fuzzy toward her just because she gave her a coffee.

She saw Suda tying on her apron, her long black hair twisted into a tight braid at the back of her head. She was still too skinny and small, but she was looking healthier these days, Claire had to admit, although her eyes still got a weird vacant look sometimes.

Simone passed Suda a Thai tea, and Suda pressed her palms together.

"*Kap khun kha*," she said.

"Fuck," Claire mumbled under her breath and shook her head. She hated it when people were all gracious to each other.

"Hey, no swearing," Simone reminded her.

"Sorry," Claire said half-heartedly. She knew the rule just fine, but swearing was one of her ways of keeping things lively around here.

"So, what's on the list this morning?" she asked with a dry, subtly snarky tone.

"Croissants. Lots of croissants." Simone answered.

"Ah f . . .," she started to say again.

"Claire!" Simone gave her a look.

"I know; I know," she answered. "But I hate making croissants. They're so labor intensive."

"You can hate something and still be polite," Simone said. "Besides, it's a good skill to have," she countered. "If you can make the perfect buttery, flaky croissant, you'll be set for life."

"If you live in France, maybe."

"Ha," Simone countered. "Croissant makers are a dime a dozen there. Here's where the skill comes in handy."

"Yeah, whatever," Claire said, downed her cappuccino, and tied on her apron.

Even though she missed the Percocet and hated getting up early, she did appreciate the feeling of safety and having her own room that she knew wouldn't be breached. She was sheltered, secure, and getting three square meals a day without having to put out—at least not sexually—she told herself as she reached for the flour. Baking bread was a better deal than that, she had to admit. And now Simone and Grace were starting to prattle on about her going back to school so she could earn her high school equivalency. She hated the idea of being stuck in night school with a bunch of losers whom she had run academic circles around before everything happened, but on the other hand, books and learning were her bag, so to speak.

"Simone, when do I get to work in the front of the house again?"

For now, Claire was still working in the back of the house, as Simone called it. Baking bread, croissants, scones, tarts. It wasn't Claire's favorite way to spend the wee hours of the morning.

"When I feel confident that you won't yell at some poor schmo who just wants to compliment you on your gorgeous blonde hair."

"My hair is no one's business."

"I get it, Claire. I absolutely do, but you can't call a customer an 'asshole' because he tells you you're pretty."

"I know. I know," Claire held up her hands in surrender, but Simone knew if she let Claire work in the front at this juncture, it would happen again. It had happened the last two times Claire had sweet-talked Simone into letting her try working the register. For now, Claire couldn't help it. One questionable comment from someone she didn't like the looks of, and that was it. Simone didn't blame her. She had been subjected to too many comments by too many johns over the years. She'd lost the ability to differentiate between a suggestive comment and a simple compliment. And her pretty face and blonde hair were compliment magnets, as much as she tried to hide them behind her baseball cap and large, black-framed glasses.

She was getting more patient, though. Claire could feel it when she was in group therapy and some annoying chick was blathering on. She used to storm out, but now she sat there and listened. She sometimes even threw in a helpful comment or two if she was feeling generous.

And now here was Suda who looked as if she'd been through the ringer worse than any of them. She was so skinny that she looked like she could have been blown away by the slightest breeze those first few days. Claire had done her best to overhear as much as she could from the snippets of conversation circulating. Although she didn't have the whole story, the words she had en-countered most were "storage container" and "hiding," and surviving that, she must admit, did instill a certain amount of respect for the young Thai woman in their midst.

When Simone showed Suda around after she was strong enough to get a tour, the young woman had paused at the threshold of Claire's room, taking in the shelves and piles of books, and Claire clearly detected a hunger in her gaze. Maybe she was a kindred spirit when it came to reading, Claire thought. She would have to wait to find out, because as of now, they couldn't say two words to each other.

Suda

WHEN SHE WAS FIRST UNLOADED like a sack of dry goods onto Simone's couch, Suda was alert enough to be terrified, but her body wouldn't get up and run as she was instructing it to do. She laid there, limp. After that, she didn't remember being asleep or waking up, exactly. It was more like floating in a warm sea. She was weak and famished, and either she was hallucinating it, or someone was gently spooning chicken broth into her mouth. It tasted nourishing and slightly salty, and she felt her body respond to each small amount. Some of it dripped down her chin, and even that felt good. It warmed her for an instant before someone wiped her face with a cloth. She couldn't remember being treated delicately since she was a small girl, back when her parents were alive. She wasn't sure how long she'd been there, but at some point, the voice of one woman was joined by another, and she felt their arms lifting her and placing her in warm water, all the while talking to her in smooth, calm voices in a language she couldn't understand. The water felt silky and primal. Floating, floating—just living and nothing else. Breathing in; breathing out. Neutral.

Although she wasn't sure why, she trusted the women. Eyes closed in the warm bath, she felt gentle hands shampoo her hair; their fingertips tentatively scrubbing her scalp clean. They used a bath sponge to rub off layers of dirt, gently cleansing her skin, bruised from rough encounters with ridged metal, having been tossed against the floor and container walls by surging waves. Her body had long ceased being her own, so any sense of modesty she'd had was long gone. Her nudity was inconsequential to her, so she simply embraced the cocoon of warmth.

As the water became tepid, she was helped out of the tub and into warm pajamas, then tucked into a bed—the blankets unusually heavy on her delicate frame. Her fatigue was so deep she felt it down to her bones. She hoped more broth would be spooned into her mouth again soon. She would figure out a way to escape later, she decided, and allowed herself to sleep.

Hushed voices inside, street noises outside, and another language being spoken entered Suda's consciousness. Car horns and the distant wailing of a siren jarred her further to the surface. For weeks she had heard only the wind's shrill call and the creaking of the ship; now this. She sensed that she was in the midst of a city at night; there was that certain undercurrent—a muted symphony of sounds that indicated being surrounded by vast, yet mostly sleep-quieted humanity and the strum of their machines. She remembered the sensation she'd experienced when she arrived in Chiang Rai in contrast to the quiet hillside where she had grown up. The sounds and smells had overwhelmed her at first, but then they had gradually dulled—like an overloud auntie whom one learned to tune out. She turned over and allowed sleep to envelop her once more.

When she drifted up from sleep again, the sounds were not distant and indistinct but, rather, were voices close by. She recognized the unique accent of the man who had brought her here. He was with the women now; both were speaking in hushed tones. She couldn't understand what was being said, but she felt less foggy, more alert, and she assumed they must be speaking in English. She had heard it spoken plenty of times in the karaoke, but she never had learned many words beyond, "Do you like this?" She didn't think that would help her much now and regretted not trying to learn more. She listened intently to the tone. They didn't seem angry.

The memory of how she had gotten into the warm bed had blurred. The images of a car, stairs, and the bath were a kaleidoscope of memories. Who were these people, and why had they captured her? The fear she had lost while she was semiconscious slammed back into her chest and squeezed. What should she do? She looked around for an escape and saw a window.

Simone

AFTER CHAI HAD FLED BACK OUT THE DOOR, promising to return as soon as possible, Simone allowed her eyes to take in Suda more thoroughly. It seemed that every rib was showing through her threadbare, filthy tee-shirt. *Her arms look like sticks*, Simone thought when she saw the young woman's elbow joint jutting out too visibly under the skin. Tears threatened to slip down Simone's cheeks as she thought about how hungry she must have been. Her bruises were in various stages of vivid purple, red, and faded yellow. Her eyelids looked paper-thin and— Simone hesitated, standing over her. The fact that she was not actually conscious came with its own concerns.

Simone's hand reached out to touch her, but she pulled back, hesitating. She didn't want her to feel further violated by a stranger touching her. She bit the nail of her index finger, contemplating the next move. She was loath to call for medical help because the look on Chai's face had been clear. He was deeply undercover and couldn't risk this young woman being discovered. She sighed, making the decision to honor that to the best of her abilities, but she also wasn't about to deprive her of medical care if it was needed. If she thought she required a doctor, Simone would take her and worry about the consequences for the cop later. He could take care of himself.

Her initial thoughts were dehydration and malnourishment, so she did what people throughout the ages and across the continents have done: made chicken broth. In her case, it involved opening a can and pouring the nourishing golden liquid into a saucepan. While it heated, she picked up her phone and called Grace. The two had been inseparable since Simone had sat beside her on the steps outside the BART station those many years ago. That morning, Simone had carried two lattes in her hands. One she had sipped; the other she had held out to the straggly young woman. Simone's first success story.

Grace was on her doorstep before Simone hit the button to end the call.

"What's going on?" Grace threw open the door without knocking, saw Simone kneeling next to her couch, and gagged. Throwing her arm across her face to block her nose, Grace moved next to Simone and looked at Suda. "What the hell, Simone?"

"I hardly know what's happening myself." She recounted their customer-police officer unceremoniously arriving on her doorstep and leaving her with this young woman.

"He said he's undercover," Simone emphasized at the end of her explanation.

"Do you believe him?" Grace asked.

Simone shrugged. "It seemed legit."

They both looked at Suda.

Simone went to the kitchen, picked up the warmed broth and poured it into a bowl, snatched a spoon from the drawer and knelt beside Suda. She gently raised her head and attempted to spoon the warm liquid into her mouth. Some dripped down Suda's chin, but some stayed in.

"She does seem to be eating the broth." Grace looked encouraged.

"Yeah, I think so." Simone nodded and spooned in a few more mouthfuls.

"Let's try giving her some water." Grace went to the cupboard, filled a glass and brought it over. She handed it to Simone who tilted it to the woman's lips.

"I think she's drinking it!" Grace said, avidly watching Suda swallow little sips.

"Thank you for not thinking I'm insane for believing him," Simone looked from Suda's face to Grace's.

"I do actually think you're a little bit insane," Grace smiled. "But that's been the case since long before this," she gestured toward Suda lying inert. "You know I would never leave you to deal with this on your own after what you've done for me."

Simone met her eyes, remembering the tentative, nervous smile Grace had given her when Simone handed the latte to her the day they met.

"At least I didn't smell this bad."

"That's true, for sure. We'll be even after this."

Grace laughed, "We don't need to worry about even. For now, let's get this girl in the bath because I can't stand one more second of the smell."

"Good plan," but Simone hesitated, frowning. "It does seem like a suspicious coincidence that he's Thai though; right?"

"I was thinking the same thing. Let's give him the benefit of the doubt that he's on the right side of this for now, but . . ."

"Exactly. Let's be cautious."

The tub was mostly full when—Simone's hands under Suda's armpits and Grace's at her feet—they maneuvered her to the bathroom floor and removed her filthy clothing, exposing her bone-thin, bruised body.

"My God," Simone whispered.

"It can't be easy to cross the ocean in a shipping container. Even so, some of these bruises are old."

"What can her life have been like to end up in this situation?"

"I can only imagine," Grace whispered. She supported Suda's back while Simone gently sudsed up her hair. "She seems peaceful for the moment."

"Let's try to keep it that way." Simone paused, thinking, then looked from Suda to meet Grace's eyes. "We have a spare room right now."

"I was thinking the same thing," Grace agreed. "If possible, let's keep her here where she's safe."

"She must be illegal," Simone said, wringing out her hair while trying not to tug too hard on the long black strands.

Grace guffawed. "You think?" she said.

"Oh, shut up and help me get her out of the bath," Simone said, acknowledging the ridiculousness of her statement. *Of course* she was illegal.

They slipped her into Simone's flannel pajamas even though they were way too large for Suda and tucked her into Simone's bed.

"Let's air the place out," Grace swung open the bathroom window.

"For sure." Simone went to the kitchen and cranked that window open as well. She could see the fog rolling in with wispy white tendrils and brisk, damp air refreshed the room, bringing with it the smell of eucalyptus from the grove of trees in nearby Golden Gate Park.

"Ah, better," she said, washing her hands and reaching for a sweater to ward off the chill in the apartment. "I think this situation calls for tea. Want a cup?" she asked Grace while she filled the kettle and lit the gas burner.

They had just sat down with big ceramic mugs of decaf Earl Grey tea when Chai knocked softly on the door. Simone let him in, and he looked around, confused because Suda was **nowhere** in sight.

"She's in my bed," Simone said softly, before he had a chance to ask. "This is Grace," she nodded toward her friend.

"Chai," he put out his hand and shook hers.

"Tea?" Simone asked, gesturing to her mug.

"That would be amazing. Thank you."

"Sit," Simone told him. "I'll bring you some. You look wiped out."

Chai gratefully accepted her offer. He *was* wiped out. After dropping Suda at the Hope House, he'd then returned to the dock, expressing shock and confusion at the empty container. He just hoped he had pulled it off without arousing suspicion.

"So, a smuggling ring?" Grace asked, sitting across from him and leaning her elbows on her knees, teacup in hands.

"Yes. Thai. We got wind of it, and they assigned me to it because I'm half Thai and speak the language. My father is from the same hill tribe as Suda," he nodded to the back bedroom. "She's undocumented. Never had papers, which makes people more vulnerable because, to the government, they don't exist." He paused at their perplexed faces. "It happens all the time, unfortunately."

"I'm confused," Grace said. "What do you mean?"

"It means that they never recorded her birth. She has no birth certificate, no passport—no legal documentation at all."

"Do you think *she* paid to be smuggled here?"

"Absolutely not. She's being trafficked."

"But you got to her."

"I did," Chai smiled for the first time since he'd walked in, and it lit up his face. The lines around his eyes etched deep groves in his otherwise smooth skin.

Simone returned, holding out a gray ceramic mug of tea to him.

"You don't look like a cop," Grace said.

"Sometimes I do. It depends. When I'm all dressed up and shiny, then I do. But usually I'm in plain clothes, and when I'm undercover, I let myself look a little rough around the edges." He ran his empty hand through his unkempt black hair.

"How do you know she's from your father's hill tribe?" Simone asked.

"That I can't tell you, but suffice it to say that I do. So, I felt an extra connection. Not that I wouldn't have tried to get to her either way, but . . ."

"You were extra determined," Simone finished his thought.

"I was," he paused. "Do you mind if I check on her?"

"Of course not. Please do," Simone said. "She's right down the hall." She followed behind him to make sure all was well.

Suda

BOOTSTEPS; HEAVY that made no attempt to be quiet.

She was suddenly, jarringly awake and heard a man approaching the room. She froze, paralyzed for an instant and then leapt up with the realization that her only chance to escape might be now. Her eyes flitted around the room, attempting to quickly get her bearings. She had no recollection of how she had gotten there. It was dark, but the plentiful ambient light made seeing her surroundings fairly easy. Her bare feet stealthily crept to the window and slid the sash up as quickly and quietly as possible. She thrust her head out, looked down, and . . . Her stomach dropped with the realization that she was on the third floor; a cement sidewalk ran directly below and there was nothing to break the fall.

Her terrorized mind thought she should jump anyway, and she threw one of her legs over the sash.

"Stop!" Chai—panicked—yelled in Thai. "We're not going to hurt you."

Suda turned back to look at him, her features frozen in fear. Her eyes were not just terrified but they were also deeply sad. Her expression betrayed her. She didn't want her life to end, but staying a slave was more unbearable than the unknown finality that comes with death.

"It's okay," he spoke more softly this time. "This is a safe house. You're safe here. I got you out of the container before they could get to you."

Suda looked back and forth between Simone and Chai, not sure whether to believe him. Simone nodded encouragement, although she hadn't understood a word of what was being said.

"I'm police," Chai explained in Thai, but he knew that for trafficked women that didn't always mean safety. "You're in San Francisco—the United States—and you're safe now," he said, using the word *safe* again, trying to talk her back into the room. "Come inside," he encouraged her to stop straddling the window. "It's too far to jump."

Suda glanced down, again taking in the cement walkway below and quickly calculating what hitting it from the distance she was above would do to her already compromised body. At least it would be over.

"I'm glad to see that you're awake," he said, keeping his voice calm. "Are you hungry?" He kept up a stream of soothing conversation in an attempt to assuage her fears.

She was starving. She looked out the window once more and then brought her leg back inside.

"Do you have anything that resembles Thai food?" Chai, switching to English, turned and asked Simone.

"I think I have some rice and vegetables."

"How about some rice and tea?" Chai asked Suda, switching back to Thai.

"No rice," Suda responded. She was starved, but she knew the scent of Thai food would bring back the nausea and pain of the brothel.

"Eggs?" Chai suggested.

Suda hesitated and then slowly nodded.

"How about some eggs?" he asked Simone, switching back to English.

"Sure. How should I make them? Scrambled?"

"Fried, please. Sunny-side up, medium," he said.

"Done," she said, letting out the breath she had been holding while Suda straddled the window.

Suda's teeth began to chatter, and Simone realized how cold her apartment had become. She crossed the room and closed the window. Then, grabbing a throw off of her bed, she gently wrapped Suda in it and led her toward the living room.

The room was small and a bit spare, with waxed wooden floors that appeared to have seen a century of wear, a shelf of books and pieces of celadon pottery, and an airy gray linen-covered couch that looked like it was the most comfortable thing Suda had ever set eyes upon. Adjoining the living room was a kitchen that appeared to fit only one person at a time but beckoned intriguingly. A pitcher of flowers and a bowl of green apples caught her eye, and she could see mugs—some white and some light gray—with saucers. The thought of a warm, milky tea or, even better, more chicken stock made her salivate.

"Come on," Simone saw Suda eye the couch with longing and steered her in that direction. She spoke soothingly in English and smiled at her to show her that she was friendly. She took her hand and led her to the couch with the blanket still wrapped around her and left her with Grace and Chai while she stepped into the kitchen to fry some eggs.

"Can you tell me what happened to you?" Chai coaxed in Thai, but Suda only shook her head.

"It's all right," he assured her. "You don't have to talk about it."

"Tell her that this is a safe house and that other women live here who have also been sex trafficked." Grace paused. "Including me." She gestured to herself.

Grace was an anomaly among women who had experienced sexual trauma. Most retreated into themselves, talking about it to only a few trusted people, if anyone. But not Grace. For her, talking about what had happened to her was a gift she gave to others who had gone through the same. She hoped it helped them not feel isolated and ashamed.

Chai looked over at Simone, who nodded her head, and then he began explaining in Thai.

Suda's eyes found Grace's eyes.

Simone brought the plate of eggs and handed them along with tea to Suda. Then she turned to Chai, "Tell her we'll introduce her to the other girls when she's ready, but for now she should just rest and eat." Simone paused and considered. "And either you're going to have to spend a lot of time here, or we're going to need someone trusted who can come here and translate."

Chai turned back to Suda and explained the situation.

"I'll figure it out," he told them. "I'll see if my sister can come back with me tomorrow to help with the language issue. If not, we can find someone."

Simone raised an eyebrow. Hours ago she didn't even know this guy, and now she was supposed to trust not only him but some other person as well? She didn't feel comfortable with the thought and turned to Grace whose face looked as skeptical as Simone felt.

"What can you tell us about your sister?" Simone asked.

"She's safe. I promise. She can be trusted. I'll bring her in the morning, and you can decide for yourself whether you're comfortable."

Grace and Simone looked at each other again, and then they both nodded after a fleeting nonverbal conversation.

Chai exhaled and stood up to leave. He was exhausted, and it was late. He guessed that, all adrenalin from the situation aside, Grace and Simone were probably exhausted, too.

"Good," he nodded. "In the meantime, don't touch her unless she touches you first and never touch her head. To Thai people, the head is sacred and not to be touched by others."

Simone put her hand to her mouth, "I washed her hair," she said with panic in her voice.

"Don't worry about it. There were extenuating circumstances. Oh, and don't sit with the soles of your shoes showing and don't sit with your legs crossed for now because you'll probably accidentally point the toe of your shoe toward her and that's extremely rude in the Thai culture."

"Got it: watch the feet, watch the head."

"Exactly," he smiled. "See you in the morning."

Claire

"HOT PLATE," SIMONE SAID, HER BACK TO CLAIRE, hands covered in hot mitts to her elbows. She slid the steaming loaves off the tray onto the butcher-block countertop.

Claire was convinced Simone had a third eye or something, because otherwise there was no accounting for how she knew exactly where everyone was at any given moment. Claire was groggy and thankful that she didn't have the early shift in the bakery for once.

Grace was standing at the stove, pouring pancake batter onto a skillet.

"What was going on last night? You were so noisy," Claire asked.

"We have a new resident," was all the explanation Grace gave her. As a rule, they never told the other residents about what situation each had been in. Their experiences were their own to tell or not.

"Yeah, well I saw a hot guy going up and down Simone's staircase at all hours last night, so I figured it was either a new resident or Simone was finally getting some action."

Grace snickered. "I can tell you for sure that she wasn't getting any action."

"Too bad," Claire said in her wry monotone.

"Our new resident doesn't speak English, though, so it's going to be a bit tricky."

"Interesting story there no doubt," Claire gave Grace the side eye.

"She's fragile and young. Hopefully older than eighteen, or it's really going to complicate things."

"The plot thickens," Claire said. "I'll try to care."

She grabbed a pancake off of the stack Grace was making.

"It's good to support each other."

"What is it my therapist said I have again? Traumatic narcissism? That says it all; doesn't it?"

"You don't have to live into it, Claire. You can become anyone you want to be. It's called healing."

"Yeah, yeah," she gestured toward the stack of pancakes with her fork.

"What's the magic word?" Grace asked only half kidding.

"It's 'give me a pancake.'"

"I'm pretty sure it's not that." Grace moved the plate of pancakes further away from Claire but smiled at her all the same.

"Fine. *P l e a s e*," she intoned with saccharine sweetness.

"Now you're talking, sister," Grace passed two pancakes over to her plate.

"Whatever."

"Group therapy this morning," Grace reminded her.

"I hate group," she said. "We all just lie about our pasts anyway."

"Well, here's a crazy idea: don't lie about your past. Your past is what happened. It doesn't make you a bad person. It just makes you someone who was in a bad situation. Don't judge them; they won't judge you."

Grace sat down across from Claire but didn't look at her. Instead she focused on companionably eating pancakes for a few minutes before she then said, "You know, there's nothing you've done that's so terrible that it makes you a lost cause."

"Come on, Grace. Isn't being preachy Simone's department?" Claire got up, set her plate on the counter, and then walked away, thinking: *If she only knew.* But those were secrets she'd never tell.

Simone

STREAKY SUNLIGHT FILTERED THROUGH GLASS PANES. The tops of the verdant leafy trees, in view from Simone's window, moved gently first in one direction and then another as the breeze blew against the branches. In Simone's opinion, one of the best things about being on the third floor was looking out at the ever-changing sky. This morning, the fog that had crept over the hills the previous night was still in, although it was thinning now to allow in a few touches of sun. Yet, in spite of the stray beams, it still hung heavily enough to give the city a hushed, misty aspect.

Simone awoke early, stiff from sleeping on the couch. She tiptoed down the hall to peek into her room and smiled, relieved to see Suda still asleep—nestled deep under the down duvet in her bed. She jumped in for a quick shower, dressed, and was down in the bakery kneading dough to Mumford and Sons before it was full light. A restless sleep had left her tired, so she put an extra espresso shot in her morning coffee. As she took a large sip of the milky latte, she fretted. Was she nuts to trust Chai? After all, he was from the very country where Suda had been trafficked. What if he was in some way involved and only posing as a police officer to gain her trust? On the other hand, she sighed, why would he bring Suda to a safe house if he had some sort of nefarious intent? Yes, he showed up out of the blue, but to rescue her, right? She wished she could be sure.

She picked up her phone and dialed.

"I've already checked in on her, and she's fine." Grace started talking before Simone had a chance to get a word in. "Don't be such a worrier. She's still completely zonked. And probably will be for a while, I would think."

"Good to hear it, but that's not why I called actually."

"Oh, what's up?"

"Do you think we're nuts to trust this cop? What if he's in on it?"

"I've been thinking about that, too, but if he was in on it, why would he bring her here? Wouldn't he bring her to some brothel or somewhere to fatten her up before putting her back on the street?"

"That's the direction my thoughts were taking me as well, but I needed to hear it from you. I was afraid I was being an idiot."

Grace snickered. "You're a lot of things, Simone, but an idiot isn't one of them."

"Thanks, I think," she paused, brows furrowed wondering what "things" Grace was thinking about.

She hung up and went back to work, relieved to have gotten a second opinion about Chai. She hoped he would come by soon because she realized in all the chaos of the night before, she'd forgotten to get his cell number.

By the time she turned the sign on the bakery door to "open," she had finished baking the requisite loaves of bread as well as the croissants, muffins, and pastries that would shortly be gobbled up. She pulled a large metal bowl from a lower shelf and started on the scones, knowing her early customers loved the fact that they were still warm. While she methodically cut butter into flour, she intently listened for any sounds from the floor above. She wondered whether Suda was awake or still fitfully sleeping. While her mind fretted, her hands continued by rote, no recipe needed. Simone hoped Chai would cross the threshold soon so Suda would have someone with her who spoke her language. Waking in a strange place would be terrifying enough without the added difficulty of being unable to communicate.

Her relief arrived in the form of not only Chai himself, but also a beautiful female version of him, who turned out to be his sister, Nittha. The siblings' eyes were mirror images: both upturned and angular in shape and a light golden brown instead of the classic dark chocolate eyes of most Thai people. Their skin was smooth and light, and their hair fell dark and wavy.

"I hear you could use an interpreter," Nittha said after introductions.

"Yes, that would be great," Simone nodded. "Why don't I get you each a coffee and pastry, and then Grace can meet you and bring you up to my apartment? I left Suda sleeping, but I'm guessing she'll wake up soon, and I think it would be a relief to her to be able to communicate with someone when she does. I don't want her to be scared."

Simone handed each of them a coffee and current scone.

"Before we go up, can I ask you a question or two?" Chai asked.

"Of course," Simone gestured to an empty table. "Grab a seat. I'll be there in a minute," She turned her attention to a customer who had just entered. A couple of minutes turned into a few more, and by the time she was able to sit down at the table, Chai was cleaning the last few crumbs off his plate with his index finger after having demolished his scone.

"I love those," he told her.

"So good. Thanks," Nittha agreed.

"Thanks," Simone smiled. "We make them right here. It's part of our learning skills preparation to help the women enter the workforce."

"I'm glad you mentioned that," Chai looked serious. "I realized in my, uh, hasty decision to bring Suda here that I failed to get a few requisite details about your program."

"Just thinking about that now, huh?" Simone good-naturedly chided him. "Fortunately for you—and Suda—

you're in luck because Hope House is a fully accredited facility for trafficked people who have been traumatized."

"Wow." Nittha looked at her brother. "I've gotta believe that's no coincidence."

Simone thought that was an interesting thing to say and wondered if Nittha was spiritual and about to quote the universe knowing that Suda should be there, or something like that. Instead she surprised her further with her next question. "Are you a Christian?" Nittha asked, taking Simone off guard. It wasn't often that people in San Francisco asked others questions about their religious beliefs.

"Um, yes, actually," Simone answered, cautiously, not knowing where the situation was leading. "I generally don't mention it, though, because I want the people I'm around to feel comfortable saying whatever they need to say, and I think sometimes some Christians give off a vibe that can discourage that. Besides, I've been known to drop an F-bomb here and there, and I am *far* from perfect."

Chai guffawed. "You and I are two peas in a pod on that one."

"Same," Nittha agreed, "I like to think of it as being accessible."

Simone laughed, liking them both right away.

"So," she pivoted back to the subject at hand, "about Hope House: we're full service in that we provide room, board, counseling, and job training. Suda will be our first non-English speaker, though, so that'll be an added challenge."

"I just have to gather enough evidence to nail these guys and then . . ."

"We'll cross that bridge when we come to it," Simone held up her hand. "For now, let's just get her what she needs."

"I have a discretionary budget when I'm undercover, so I can get some money to you for her."

"If you can do that on the up and up, great. Otherwise don't worry about it for now; we've been fortunate to have some amazing private donors, so we'll be fine for a while."

"Thank you. I can't begin to express how grateful I am."

"You're welcome," Simone waved her hand dismissively and got up from the table to head back behind the counter, another customer having just walked in. "Oh," she turned back to them, "please feel free to make her breakfast if Grace hasn't had a chance yet, ok? Just make yourself at home, open the cabinets at will."

Chai and Nittha found Grace waiting at Simone's open apartment door as they walked up the stairs.

"Hi!" she called to them even before they reached the landing. Her eyes warmed at the sight of them, relief spreading through her nervous system. Her animated face was warm and inviting in spite of the slightly dark circles under her eyes from getting to bed so late the night before. She wiped her nervously damp hands on her soft, faded jeans and reached out to meet Nittha's. "I'm so glad you're here. Suda just woke up, and she's understandably freaked out. I keep telling her that she's safe in a soothing voice, but she doesn't understand. Hearing it in her own language will be so much better."

They followed Grace through the door and found Suda standing in the kitchen, rumpled, in too-large pajamas. Her eyes looked wild and frightened, reminding Chai of a cornered animal.

"*Sawadee khrup.*" Chai said "hello" calmly, trying to give her a sense of safety.

"*Sawadee kha,*" Nittha touched her pressed-together palms to her forehead, giving the feminine form of the same greeting, and smiled at Suda.

"This is my sister," Chai told Suda in Thai, pointing to Nittha. "She's here to help."

Nittha smiled at Suda. "You're safe here," she told her, speaking calmly in Thai. "This is a safe house," she explained in case Suda hadn't understood the previous night.

Suda eyes moved between Chai and Nittha, but she didn't speak.

"Tell her she doesn't have to worry. No one is going to hurt her or force her to be with men," Grace said, and Nittha translated.

"Come on," Nittha gently held out her hand, touched the top of Suda's arm, and then led her toward Simone's room. "I brought you some clothes."

Grace followed them and helped unpack the bag of clothes Nittha had brought with her. The jeans looked practically child sized. Chai had obviously done a good job of explaining how emaciated Suda was because Grace thought the pants actually had a chance of fitting her. She brought out a few long-sleeved cotton tee-shirts, a hoodie, and two cotton crewneck sweaters—one turquoise, the other a soft pink. She pulled undies and a bra out of a bag as well as some thick, snuggly socks and slippers.

"Once we know what shoe size you are, I'll pick up some shoes for you, too."

"*Kop khun kha*," Suda said to Nittha and bowed her head.

"We'll leave you to get dressed," Grace said, and Nittha translated.

Chai, meanwhile explored the kitchen, feeling surprisingly at home in Simone's space.

"Ask her what she wants for breakfast," Chai yelled, and Nittha relayed the question in Thai.

"I have a hard time eating," Suda explained, eyes cast down.

She told them in the briefest terms about being kept above a restaurant and how the smell of food now made her nauseated, and then Nittha relayed the information to Grace.

"Hmmm," Grace mused and then had the perfect idea. "I've got it: I'll just pop downstairs and grab a croissant, a muffin, and a scone. Hopefully she'll like at least one of them, and they definitely don't smell like Thai food."

"Perfect," Nittha said. "Let's try it," and yelled the plan back to Chai.

"I'll go," he offered and was back a few moments later with the pastries on a plate and a cup of Thai tea to go with them. He brought it to the coffee table in front of the couch where the three women were sitting.

He gave them space to talk while pretending to keep busy in Simone's kitchen, but after about a half hour, he decided it was time to leave them on their own. He didn't want to disturb any progress they were making, so he nodded to Nittha, and quietly slipped out. He peeked into the window of the bakery as he walked by, seeing Simone inside, amiably chatting up a customer while she made coffee.

He couldn't help but be intrigued by her. She was beautiful inside and out. Not a striking beauty that would make a person pause when he saw her, but she had some sort of sparkling loveliness that he'd noticed when he'd been in the bakery before. Kind of a vibrancy, he thought, trying to put his thumb on it. It wasn't the combination of her brown hair, fair skin with a smattering of freckles, or green eyes, because any of those features on their own wasn't necessarily beautiful, but it was the combination of them and . . . what?

He paused thinking and then opened his car door, realizing what he was doing and correcting his direction of thought. *This is no time for complications,* he told himself and drove toward work.

Claire

"WELL, ISN'T THIS AN INTERESTING CONFABULATION?" Claire said with a snarky tone as she walked into Simone's apartment and saw Suda, Grace, and Nittha sitting together.

"Hey, Claire," Grace said and waved her in to join them. "You know, for someone who dropped out of school in ninth grade, you have an awfully sophisticated vocabulary."

"And do you know why?" Claire asked, as she brazenly opened one of Simone's cupboards, helped herself to a tea bag, and then continued what she was saying before Grace had a chance to answer. "It's because drug dealers and johns don't think to look in the library for young girls—especially ones who sit at a table right in front of the librarian's desk and keep their noses in books."

"Genius!" Grace closed her eyes visualizing a young, vulnerable Claire there, "If only I'd thought of that, I would have been a corporate mogul by now."

"Ha!" Claire smirked. "It's never too damn late. Isn't that the mantra you all are always pushing?"

"Language, darling. Would you talk to a librarian that way?"

"Depends on which one. The head librarian at the main branch is pretty saucy."

Grace snorted and shook her head. She couldn't help loving the secretly tenderhearted girl who kept such a hard shell around herself.

Claire hadn't been joking about the library as a safe haven. It had been and still was the place she felt safest in the world. The dusty smell of the stacks, the reverent hushed speaking tones, and all those words. How many pages of words were in any given library? When she entered a library and smelled that unique combination of paper, glue, and dust, she felt safe and at ease.

One of the things she had loved most about her mom was that she had enjoyed a good book. The woman had nary a maternal bone in her body, but damn it if she didn't love to read. In her case it was thrillers. She was a voracious but broke reader, and because she didn't have two dimes to rub together, purchasing a book was rare indeed, so it was the library for her. She would dump little Claire in the massive children's section of the San Francisco main branch and then meander through the stacks looking for the perfect escape read until the librarian—who by then knew her well and had a soft spot for the young mother—tracked her down with Claire in arms and explained, once again, that she couldn't leave her toddler to fend for herself.

By the time Claire was in kindergarten, she was walking to the hallowed halls of her safe haven alone after school because home had become a scary place. Their apartment was filthy and devoid of food, and her mother "napped" on the couch all day and had "friends" over at night.

When her mom was awake, she was either overly jovial—laughing at the slightest provocation—or sullen and zoned out. Little Claire couldn't make heads or tails of it and even at five years old knew to stay away as much as possible.

The fact that librarians usually had snacks behind the counter and were willing to share with plainly hungry little girls was an additional enticement.

By the time Claire was in third grade, she had become a thoroughly self-sufficient ragamuffin. Her long, blonde hair was unkempt, and her blue, waifish eyes were overly large in her thin, intelligent face. Her clothes were generally grubby and mismatched, but that somehow added to her scruffy appeal. She poured over the well-worn Boxcar Children books and fancied herself as street savvy as the four fictitious orphans who had to navigate life on their own. Later, when she discovered *From the Mixed-Up Files of Mrs. Basil E. Frankweiler*, featuring the brother and sister who lived in the Metropolitan Museum in New York, she dreamed endlessly about moving herself into the library's glorious and elegant main branch with its glass dome ceiling, beautiful woodwork, and many secret nooks in which to read. The book's great trick about collecting coins from fountains was a helpful tip as well. She was able to buy many a taco-truck meal from the quarters she fished out of the fountains she scoured throughout the city.

Then things looked up when Nick moved in. She actually allowed herself to become hopeful—which she later regretted dearly. *Trust*, she discovered, is much more of a "four-letter word" than the F-bomb she now loved to drop.

It started when she was thirteen, at her most awkward and vulnerable. Although her favorite clothes were still a tomboyish combination of a soft, faded blue hoodie and dirt-smudged jeans, by then the Huck Finn fantasy her younger self clung to had crumbled, and she wanted, more than anything, to be like other kids with a stable family life. Her school friends grumbled endlessly about their parents, but they had no idea what they were talking about as far as Claire was concerned.

Too strict? *Please*, she longed for strict. It showed parents cared. Woes about her friends having to eat all their food, whether they liked it or not, made her salivate. *Carnitas*? Yes, please! Glass noodles? She dreamed of the delicious, saucy dish. One of her friends moaned endlessly when her mother made chicken *again* even though she knew she was sick of it. Claire pretended to have similar problems but instead *fantasized* about having chicken so frequently that she became sick of it—which she believed would be never. The neighborhood where they lived, which bordered the Tenderloin, was home to people of all ethnicities, and the variety of spices and food she smelled while she walked from school to home every afternoon was at once dreamy and torturous.

By then, Claire and her friends were starting to get curvy, and the other girls constantly told Claire how much they wanted her flat stomach and jutting hip bones instead of their suddenly fleshed out selves. Claire never admitted that it was lack of food that kept her so thin and that she was hungry all the time. She would have traded places with them in a heartbeat.

And then one day, Claire arrived home after school to find the apartment in some semblance of order and her mother, not only tidy as well, but laughing at an unseen visitor's joke while throwing some pasta into a pot of boiling water.

Claire's cautious, "Hello?" was met with the appearance of a man wearing decent clothes, which was a far cry from any of her mother's previous "friends." He actually looked fairly normal.

"Is this the lovely and studious Claire I've been hearing so much about?" the guy asked.

"Indeed it is," her mother responded having produced a smile replete with a twinkle in her eye. Her hair was clean and her face was made up nicely.

"*Indeed?*" thought Claire. What was happening?

"I'm Nick," he said and shook her hand as if she were an adult.

Claire looked warily between the two.

"Dinner in about a half hour, sweetie," her mom said, pouring herself a glass of red wine. *When had she gotten actual wine glasses—let alone wine?* Her mom's go to was usually Coke and the cheapest brand of rum available, but Claire wasn't about to let the opportunity of a good meal go to waste by blowing her mother's cover.

"Sounds good," Claire responded. "I'll just hang in my room until then."

Her mind was reeling, but dinner turned out to be weirdly wonderful. Her mom and Nick explained how they'd met while they were each waiting for a BART train during the wee hours and had hit it off.

"Gross," Claire thought and looked away, horrified, when she heard the words "hit it off" because now that she knew a thing or two, she couldn't help but visualize something seedy in the corner of the station.

"I gave him my number," her mom said coyly, as if it had needed to be coaxed out of her.

"I texted her while we were still on the train," Nick said as if they were being interviewed on *The Bachelor* and were recounting their charming first meeting.

"Which was amazing because I looked like a wreck," she said, putting her hand to her now-fresh and styled wavy blonde hair.

"You were beautiful. I couldn't take my eyes off of you."

Claire simultaneously wanted to vomit and felt a spark of pride for her mother who was lovely when she cleaned up.

"You look so much like her," Nick turned to Claire.

"She's the spitting image of me when I was young," her mom said.

"Really?" Claire asked. "You've never said so."

"Well, I've thought it many times," she told her, scooping more penne onto Claire's plate as if they ate that way every night.

Claire tried to keep up her reserve, but instead she drank in the attention as thirstily as her mother sipped her delightfully robust cabernet.

Suda

SUDA HAD LONG AGO STOPPED FEELING. It was easier that way. Instead she had become an observer. She watched herself from afar. She watched others. She existed—nothing more.

But still, after Grace and Nittha left, Suda felt a terrifying, miniscule sense of hope. A crack in her wall, a pea-sized crevasse that oozed blood of yearning; she put her hand to her heart to stop it. Was safety a possibility? The concept was so unbearably desirable that she hardly allowed herself to consider it.

Although Nittha had brought the bag of clothes, Suda hadn't wanted to change out of Simone's pajamas. There were two pieces: a long-sleeved shirt that had buttons and a collar and long pants with an elastic waste that helped them stay up in spite of Suda's tiny frame. Navy blue with thin white stripes, they were made of the softest material Suda had ever felt—somehow both smooth and fuzzy. How could that be? She rubbed her cheek along one of the sleeves, and it felt warm to the touch. Almost like a blanket.

She was thirsty but was afraid to help herself to a glass of water. It would be horrifying if Simone walked in and found her with the cupboards open. And even though Chai had brought her breakfast earlier, her stomach was gnawing at her again. She didn't want them to think she was stealing or being sneaky and send her away, so she put aside her thirst and hunger and decided to climb back into bed. They had told her she could rest all she wanted and that mattress and the thick white comforter were calling to her, so she decided she would nestle back in.

On the way, she tiptoed into the bathroom, her feet cold on the tile floor. She looked in the mirror and was absolutely shocked when she saw the shape she was in. Her wrists looked like a small child's and the pajamas she wore looked as if they were hanging off of a skeleton. Her hair was clean but still uncombed from sleep. Her brown eyes, sunken. Still, she thought, none of it mattered as long as she wasn't going back.

She was in a strange country where she didn't speak the language, but for now she wouldn't worry about that. She would focus on getting better, and then she would decide what to do. And if needed, she would plan her escape as soon as she was strong enough.

She wondered if her aunt knew she was no longer in Thailand. Would the money she was making for her end? She supposed so. What else could possibly happen? She both hated and loved her aunt. Hated her for selling her into the karaoke, but she loved her, too. She looked a little bit like her mother, which pulled at her heart. If only she hadn't died, Suda thought, and tears burned her eyes even though it had happened years ago. Suda knew her auntie had only done what she had because she needed the money for the family. It was the way it worked in her village, plain and simple. The girls provided. The family had to eat, and Suda was what allowed them to do so. Sacrifice one for the good of all. That was the way. She wondered what would happen to them now. Her cheeks burned at the thought of letting them down, and she hoped they weren't hungry at this very moment.

She tried to put that out of her mind, though, as she snuggled back in bed. Ignoring her own hunger pangs, she fell into an exhausted sleep only to startle awake sometime later, drenched in terrified sweat, dreaming of the moment the storage container door clanged shut and she found herself in complete darkness. It was now night, but she could see a light coming from the kitchen. She listened intently but couldn't hear any sounds. Was there someone there waiting for her? Had Gan sent someone to get her? They must be looking for her. What would they do to her when they found her?

She threw the blankets off and tentatively got out of bed. She crept down the hall to peek into the living room and stopped short, terrified when she saw the man who had brought her here standing with his back to her. He had a gun tucked into a holster at his side. Her heart raced. Had he been lying to her? Was he going to kill her?

He said he was going to help her, but now here he was, waiting for her with a gun.

She flattened herself against the wall, trying to become invisible. Was this it? Had they *all* lied? Were they working with Aanwat? She walked silently backward, formulating a plan of escape, but unwittingly brushed against a picture on the wall, and it came crashing down. The man turned, startled, and saw the terror on her face.

She gasped, gulped down a shriek and pointed to his gun.

"Why do you have that?" she asked, keeping her eyes locked on the weapon.

"Oh!" he realized what had frightened her. "I'm sorry. I should have put it away. I sometimes forget it's on me when I'm on duty. Police; remember?" He gestured to himself and put his hand on his chest.

He explained it to her in Thai. "You're safe. We're not going to hurt you."

"Where are the others?" she asked suspiciously, wondering why it was only him in the apartment.

"Simone's been here all afternoon while you've been sleeping, but she just stepped out to check on something. She'll be right back. She left me here so I could talk to you if you woke up."

Suda looked at him, cautious relief showing on her face, but she continued to keep her distance as well as one eye on Chai's gun.

"I made you some *tom yum goong*," he said gently, as if trying to lure a frightened kitten toward a saucer of milk. He gestured to a pan of spicy shrimp soup warming on the stove, but Suda shook her head and backed away.

"All right, no soup. How about *gang kiew wan*?" he asked, knowing he could quickly order some of his favorite green curry chicken and rice from a nearby Thai restaurant.

She shook her head again.

"Bread?" she asked, remembering the sweet muffin she'd eaten for breakfast, but forgetting the name for it.

"Sure," he said, opening cupboards, trying to find a loaf of bread and striking it lucky in the second cabinet he searched. He took out a couple of slices and put them on a plate. "Do you want butter?" he asked. He then opened the refrigerator and took out Simone's butter dish. He slid the dish with a full cube toward her and then backed away so she wouldn't be afraid.

Suda tentatively walked over, picked up the plate of bread, and lowered herself onto the floor with it, knees folded under her. She knew how to sit at a table perfectly well, but sitting on the floor is how she had always eaten growing up, and it still felt the most natural to her. What he had given her wasn't the muffin she had in mind, but in her stage of extreme hunger, simple slices of bread would do just fine. She had no idea what the cube of yellow stuff was, so she left it untouched.

"Do you mind if I eat the soup?" Chai asked, and Suda shook her head to indicate that it was fine.

He poured a generous helping for himself, sat on the floor a comfortable distance away, and began eating. It was into this scene that Simone entered, holding a bag and looking at them each, cautiously.

"Everything good?" she asked Chai, keeping her face neutral.

"Yep, we're good. Suda doesn't like my soup, but she's eating some bread, so I thought I'd join her. Want some soup?"

"Sounds great." Simone put the bag down, helped herself to a bowl, and then sat down on the floor with them, carefully tucking her feet under her as Suda had. She smiled at Suda, who gave her a surprisingly warm smile back.

"We have a bedroom available for her," Simone told Chai. "Will you ask her if she'd like to have her own room? It's on the level below me, but it's right next to Claire's room. Grace told me she and Claire have already met."

Chai turned to Suda and explained, but she looked terrified and mutely stared at the floor. He explained that it was safe, but she still wouldn't meet his eye.

"Hmm," he looked over at Simone.

"She doesn't seem enthusiastic."

"She's probably afraid she'll be kept in the room against her will."

"Yes," Simone thought for a moment. "Would she be more comfortable if she stayed here with me?"

"I'm guessing so, but that's a lot to ask of you. As it is, I showed up in the night and foisted a half-starved, semiconscious young woman on you. Having her move into your space would be above and beyond."

"Don't worry about it. You should have seen how crowded my apartment was before we got a grant and moved in here. It's the least I can do. And after all, what's the alternative?"

Chai rubbed his hands over his face. The truth was that the situation was getting more and more complicated, and to say he was skirting the law was an understatement. He was compromising Simone as well now and wasn't even sure how much he could tell her.

For now, though, all he said was, "Are you sure?"

"Yes," she told him, gently taking Suda's empty plate from her, putting two more slices of bread on it, and then handing it back. She took Chai's soup bowl and refilled it for him as well while he explained to Suda the option of staying with Simone.

Suda looked up, relieved.

"I'll take that as a 'yes,'" Simone smiled.

"I would say so."

"We can bring a bed up from downstairs," she pointed to the far end of the living room, "and put it there."

"How long do you think this case will take? Are you close to getting evidence against the men who did this to her?"

"The best evidence is Suda herself, but I would like to get something more as well, to really nail them because if I have to bring Suda in, she'll end up in immigration hell, and she's already been through enough. I have plenty on the minor players; don't get me wrong. But it's the higher-ups that are more difficult to nail down."

"Is it legal, what we're doing?"

Chai looked at her impassively but didn't answer.

"I'll take that as a definitive "no" but luckily for you, I'm not above skirting the law here and there where someone's safety comes into play."

"Thank you," he exhaled. "I can't express my appreciation. You hardly know me, and yet you've . . ."

Simone waved her hand dismissively, which Chai noticed seemed a common expression of hers. "In case you haven't noticed, this is a safe house; we're used to keeping a low profile."

"In this case, it's going to have to be even lower profile than usual because if these guys even get a glimpse of her, it's serious trouble."

"Good to know. Have you told her she has to stay inside for now?"

"I had Nittha explain it to her. It seemed like it would be better coming from a woman."

"You're probably right. So, that's it. We're settled. We'll let her rest, try to fatten her up a bit, and start therapy with her as soon as we can get our hands on a therapist who speaks Thai," Simone said matter-of-factly.

"Um . . ."

"Is there something you're not telling me?" Simone asked when she saw him hesitate.

"Well, kind of. The reality is that young women are a dime a dozen to these traffickers. They would usually just try to find her for a while and then replace her with another young woman."

"But?" Simone prompted.

"But," Chai continued, "this is the first girl this particular guy sent over. He's new to the organization. He was trying to make his mark, and because it didn't go according to plan, it doesn't look good for him."

"So, now what? He's trying to make it right, so to speak?"

"Exactly. He's worried he'll be out." Chai paused. "Or worse if you know what I mean because he's now considered unreliable. And my guess is that he's freaked out. I heard he's sending one of his guys over. And from what I gather, it's the guy who put her in the container in the first place. He'll be motivated to get *himself* cleared, and he knows exactly what she looks like."

Simone exhaled loudly.

"Yeah, I know."

"Ok, well, we'll double down on keeping her out of sight while he's here and then you can let us know when the coast is clear."

Chai smiled at Simone, loving her efficiency and attitude.

"I brought her to the right place," he said. "I knew it without even giving it a moment's thought. It's strange."

"Not strange." Simone pointed up toward heaven.

Aanwat

AANWAT PAUSED AND LEANED against the warm stone of a high-rise office building, allowing the sun to warm his face for a moment as cars and pedestrians passed him in a stream of foreign humanity. He closed his eyes against the glare and reflected on how he had gotten into this strange situation. When he'd left home and gone to Chiang Rai to get away from his family and all the drugs, he thought everything would be better. And it had been once he'd met Gan and gotten the job cleaning the karaoke. He finally had somewhere off the street to sleep. He no longer had to curl up in doorways to sleep at night—as out of sight as possible but still at hand if anyone with ill intentions had come across him.

A feeling of nostalgia washed over him when he thought back to the gangly boy he was then. But life at the karaoke had gradually sucked him in, and before he knew it, he liked the power and was taking money for girls. He hadn't actually given it a second thought until Suda had arrived. She had been the youngest girl there by far. He had found himself worrying about her and didn't like the thought of her having to go with the men who frequented the services of their business. But he had no control over the situation. Gan was the boss, and Aanwat reminded himself that people with no documents were easy to replace. So, he didn't make waves. He did his job and after a while, he became resigned. He did what he could to steer the worst customers away from Suda, but even that didn't always work.

Now he was in San Francisco, walking down the street in a neighborhood worse than theirs in Chiang Rai. He passed glaring traffic lights and a raucous group of drunken men pouring out of a corner bar. He had to step over vomit on the sidewalk as he made his way back to his hotel.

The Tenderloin hotel, where Aanwat was staying, was run down, faded, and gritty compared to some of the luxurious interiors he'd seen through hotel windows as he'd walked around San Francisco, tourist map in hand. But at least the hotel was warm. The fog and wind were killing him, and he hated both with a passion he didn't know he could feel toward *weather*. He didn't have warm clothes and out of desperation had bought a ridiculous, touristy sweatshirt that proclaimed he loved San Francisco off of a street vendor to ward off the chill.

He rubbed his eyes, trying to erase the memory of what got him here in the first place. He wished he could make the whole thing disappear. If he could have rewound the last months, he would have done it in a second. He no longer wanted the extra money he had dreamed of. It was tainted now. He sighed, weary.

But time didn't rewind, and he was in it now, so he began searching for Suda at Thai massage parlors and nail shops that employed young women from Thailand. He told them his sister had run away, and he was worried for her safety. He'd shown them all a photo of her, but so far had gotten nowhere.

San Francisco wasn't the largest city in the world, but trying to find Suda here was like trying to find a particular seashell on an overcrowded beach, and Gan wanted results. He'd already been blamed for one mistake and needed to fix it to show that he could be in the game with the organization here. Gan had sold Suda for fifty thousand American dollars, and it was either come up with her or return the money. And he didn't have the money to return. So, it was up to Aanwat to find her.

Gan was supposed to have had seven girls delivered to the shipping container to be sent over, but most of the group had been grabbed the day before by some human rights organization. He had no idea how they'd gotten wind of the plan, but they had. And now, even though he had nothing to do with the mishap, Aanwat had been blamed for not sending enough girls; a mistake that was costing the organization both money and their reputa-tion to deliver.

The whole operation had been cursed from the be-ginning. The one girl who *did* get delivered being Suda was just the worst of it for Aanwat. He hadn't planned to know any of them. He could have lived with it if they had been strangers, but he looked up when he heard his name spoken with a tone of shock and horror and saw her.

He shook his head and closed his eyes for a moment. He never meant to hurt *her*.

He imagined he saw her several times a day, but when he chased down the various petite young women with silky black hair, they invariably were someone else. He even went so far as to grab the arm of one passing woman, but when she whirled around, fear and confusion on her face, it wasn't Suda, with her dramatic cheekbones and particular hill tribe beauty, but a stranger instead.

Days and then weeks passed, the search continued, and Aanwat was becoming increasingly afraid. The pre-vious day, the local boss had taken him out for a meal, and Aanwat couldn't help but notice the gun slipped into the back of his jeans. His heart had raced at the sight, but he tried to keep his face impassive, correctly assum-ing that portraying confidence in his ability to find Suda would at least temporarily prevent him from ending up on the recipient end of a bullet.

They didn't care about one girl; they'd made that clear. It was the fact that she had disappeared out of a locked container that had their attention. They needed to know who had let her out, because *that* information would tell them if someone was working against them from the inside. Learning that was important enough to the local boss to keep Aanwat searching until he found her.

With every passing day, he worried that she was further away. Maybe she wasn't even in the city anymore. He almost hoped so. If he failed, maybe he could simply go back to Chiang Rai and gradually regain Gan's trust. He just didn't want to be killed.

Then again, another idea materialized. If he could find her, they could disappear *together*. He began to turn the idea over in his mind. There had always been something special about her. He'd felt it from the first moment he had seen her dragged into the karaoke when she was just a girl—frightened but not resigned. Besides, he might need to vanish himself soon if he wasn't able to come up with Suda, so why not plan to disappear *with* her, if he could? She would be the best link to his past. Someone who understood where they had come from.

He had missed his chance back in Thailand where she had been accessibly tucked into her room at the karaoke. It would have been easier to run away with her there. They could have gone to Bangkok and lived on a boat in one of the floating markets. He could fish, and she could sell trinkets. He'd never been there, but he'd heard about it and had wanted to go ever since. But instead he'd been a coward and shoved her into the shipping container. He had no idea what to do.

Or maybe he could stay and gain the trust of the organization in San Francisco. A few of the men on the inside had been born in the United States to Thai parents. They hardly gave him the time of day, but perhaps he could do some small jobs for them to show them he could be helpful. Some of them spoke Thai with an American accent, which he found odd. But he'd understood well enough when he'd heard them joke that they could fill Suda's missing spot with him. He'd laughed with them at the moment, pretending they were messing around, but he was deeply afraid they actually meant it.

Claire

CLAIRE'S HOME LIFE HAD BECOME what she'd always dreamed of: the pleasant anticipation of a cooked meal; a refrigerator filled with actual nutritious food instead of a single expired carton of yogurt; music from her mother's youth emanating from a music app; humming—actual bona fide humming.

Her mother was around more, alert, and keeping herself looking fresh and pretty. She actually cooked food. Nick seemed to be at their apartment more and more often until it felt almost normal to come home to dinner cooking and the two of them in the kitchen, drinking wine and whispering.

That night, Nick—who seemed to actually work during the day—had his jacket thrown over the nearest chair.

"Hey, beautiful girl," Nick called from the kitchen when they heard her clatter in, backpack slung over her shoulder.

"How was your day?" followed up her mom's voice.

"Good, thanks," Claire said, heading to her room to drop her stuff. On the way, she spied a stack of brand new novels.

"What's with the books?" she asked her mom.

"Nick knows how much I love to read, so he set up an account at my favorite bookstore. Now I can pop in and buy novels whenever I want to. Can you believe it?" Her mom beamed. She actually beamed, Claire noticed. Her eagerness and excitement was almost embarrassing for Claire to witness. Could she be bought so easily?

"I put you on the account, too." Nick told her. "I've noticed you have your nose in a book more often than not."

"Wow," Claire almost beamed as well but checked herself in time to prevent her own self-contempt. "Thank you," she said, her good manners kicking in, in spite of her wariness about anything that seemed too good to be true. Still, she decided to buy a few books soon so she could sell or trade them if things went south again. Already she'd started hiding nonperishable food in her room, too. You just never knew, she reminded herself before she tucked a can of tuna under her socks in a drawer.

Months sailed by before the first crack in the foundation of her newfound security appeared. She arrived home after school to find Nick there earlier than usual and her mother looking angry. They were arguing in the kitchen rather than cooking dinner, and neither said a word to her when she walked in the door.

She snuck into her bedroom and ate one of the granola bars from the box she'd hidden in her closet for dinner. Anxiety churned in her stomach that night as she occasionally heard angry words through the walls of her room. She was simultaneously irritated with her mother for potentially blowing their good deal and protective of her because, based on Nick's smooth cajoling voice, it seemed he was trying to bully her mom into doing something she didn't want to do. Ear pressed to her bedroom door, Claire tried to hear exactly what was being said, but couldn't make out the words. Finally, she gave up, climbed into bed, and pulled the covers over her head to tune out the sounds of discord.

The next morning, she found her mother asleep on the couch and no sign of Nick. She quietly gathered her homework, slipped into the bathroom to get ready for school, and tiptoed out.

She tried to forget her fears while she was at school, but anxiety stole into her mind whenever she didn't purposefully keep it at bay with an algebraic equation or the recitation of the elements in the periodic table.

That afternoon when Claire warily opened the front door and peeked inside, she found no sign of Nick and, more worrisome to Claire, no sign of dinner.

"Mom?" she called out tentatively into the quiet apartment.

"In here," she received a reply.

Claire sucked in her breath, her heart seizing at the slur she could hear in her mother's words. Claire dropped her backpack in her bedroom and then cautiously looked into her mother's—afraid of what she would find. Claire stood perfectly still in the doorway, allowing no worry to show on her face while inside she cried out. Her mom was sitting on the bed; hand clutching a tall drinking glass full of what Claire surmised was her old go-to, rum and Coke. There was no Nick, no dinner cooking, and no wine glass being sipped over banter. Her mother wore the same clothes she had had on the night before, clearly having not changed since she awoke. Claire was afraid to approach her—not wanting to confirm the drunken state she already knew from the familiar tableau.

That night she didn't dare dip into her stash of squirreled away food. She would keep everything for now in case she had to sustain herself on the secret cache for a while.

By day three, when there was still no sign of either Nick or food, and her mother looked downright unkempt, Claire felt both fear and contemptuous pity for her. Why couldn't she just hold it together? Was that too much to ask? Claire wondered. Finally, she gathered her courage and asked what had happened.

"He wanted me to entertain one of his friends," her mother said bitterly, using air quotes around the word *entertain*.

"Entertain?" asked Claire. That didn't sound bad. "Like as in having someone over to dinner?" She wasn't sure why that would be something to be angry about. Her friends' parents had people over to dinner all the time.

Her mother snorted. "No, not as in 'having someone over to dinner.' He wanted me to help him close a deal another way." Claire understood from the tone that she was definitely not open to further discussion about it.

"Um, speaking of dinner, is there something I can make for us to eat?" Claire asked, hoping that offering to cook would not only allow her to get fed but also make her mom feel better.

"Food? Nope. Who do you think was bringing the groceries every night?"

"Nick was bringing the groceries every night?"

"Ding, ding, ding!" her mother said, and Claire felt like an idiot for not realizing it before.

On day four, her mother had clearly acquiesced. When Claire came home, food was cooking, Nick was in the kitchen with her mother, but somehow the tone had shifted. The flushed happy look on her mother's face was gone even though Nick kept hugging her and calling her "his darling."

Claire had no idea exactly what was going on, but she wasn't sure she was happy to have Nick back.

Her mother's wardrobe began to subtly shift from jeans and T-shirts—thin from having been washed many times—to low-cut dresses that allowed her breasts to bulge revealingly. She went out with Nick on week-nights more and more often. There was still food in the apartment, but in the form of frozen boxes stacked on the freezer shelves. Her mom—doused in perfume—seemed more liquid lately, not quite like when she used to be glazed during the day, but somehow not herself. Claire wanted to hug her and beg her to stay home, like she had when she was little, but Claire couldn't figure out why she had her hackles up. After all, it wasn't as if she had been an ideal, caring mother before. But this new lipsticked version of her mother made Claire uncomfortable in a different way.

Alone again that night, Claire defrosted prepackaged macaroni and cheese from Trader Joe's for dinner. When the microwave dinged, she brought the food to the table and ate while she read her history chapter. The apartment was too quiet, with only the hum of the refrigerator and the sound of traffic to keep her company. Even when her mother had been passed out on the couch, Claire thought, at least she had been at home.

And then one night, she didn't come home at all.

Claire had always had a difficult time sleeping when her mother was out, and this particular night she had lain awake, tensing with every creak of shifting floorboards and every sound of raised voices from the street outside. At last she heard the familiar key in the lock, and the door clicked open. The sound of gentle footsteps heading to her mother's room lulled her into an easy sleep. But morning told another story.

Claire slipped out of her room, ready to grab breakfast before school, but instead of her mother sitting at the table in her familiar, threadbare bathrobe, Nick was there alone, looking rumpled in a wrinkled suit. Seeming testy, he stared at his phone and scowled while he ate a bowl of cereal.

"Where's Mom?" Claire asked when she emerged from her room.

"No, 'Good morning'?" Nick asked without looking away from the screen. His shirt collar was open, and Claire could see a pulse at his throat. She had never noticed it before and found it repulsive for no clear reason. She looked away.

"Sorry, and good morning. Where's Mom?"

"She slept over at a friend's house last night. I told her I would come take care of you and that she shouldn't worry. She deserves a night off after all; don't you think?" He said it in an offhand way, meant to cajole Claire into agreeing, but Claire looked at him warily.

"Don't sweat it, beautiful girl," he said in a lighter tone this time, but the nickname he'd taken to using for her only served to make her anxious.

"When will she be back?"

"I'm sure she'll get home while you're at school, so off you go," he waved his hand dismissively as if to shoo her out the door. She gathered her homework and books and then took off like a shot, but her mind was spinning.

"What *friend* was he talking about? Her mother had hardly any friends and absolutely no one whom she'd want to spend the night with. Something weird was going on, and Claire didn't like it.

Simone and Hailey

SIMONE EFFICIENTLY USED ONE HAND to crack egg after egg into a steel bowl, while with the other, she whisked them into a froth. She was a fanatic about using only free-range eggs, with silky yokes that were more orange than yellow. Simone wore her "concentration face" as Claire had come to think of it. She could tell Simone's mind was far away, and she wondered where she was and whom she was worrying about now. Or, maybe she wasn't thinking about the bakery or any of the residents. Maybe she was thinking about a guy, Claire mused. She'd noticed Chai had been hanging around an awful lot recently.

They all loved to chide Simone about her love life—or lack thereof—because she consistently seemed to find one or another reason to stop seeing men after a few dates. It wasn't for lack of interest on the man's part. Claire had heard her getting hit on or flirted with more times than she could count when Simone worked the register.

"Simone!" Claire heard Grace nag her. "What about him? You know, when he brought up that movie and said maybe you two should go together, he wasn't just making conversation to pass the time until his coffee was ready."

"What? Who?"

"That cute dark-haired guy who comes in all the time and casually maneuvers it so that you're the one who takes his order."

"Marco? I don't think so," Simone waved her off. "He's just friendly."

"You're so oblivious sometimes," Grace gave Simone an exasperated look.

"Why are you always pushing guys on Simone anyway?" Claire pressed Grace. "All men are just out to get laid."

"I totally get why you think that, Claire. Actually though, there are plenty of good guys. You just have to get to know them."

Simone jumped in. "Grace is right. Some men are caring, smart, and nonabusive, and women can start or stop dating any of them at any time."

"Thanks for the pep talk about men," Claire rolled her eyes. "But I know what I know."

Truth be told, part of the reason Simone went out with guys was to show the girls that she could stop dating them without fear that they would hurt her. She wanted them to understand that a woman could spend time with a man simply because she enjoyed his company. That's what she told them at least.

The reality of it, though, was that for Simone, breaking up with men was less about whether she liked them and more about the fact that getting up at 4:00 a.m. most mornings left her thoroughly exhausted by 9:00 p.m., which made getting through a movie, a Giants baseball game, or some other fun evening event a bit difficult no matter how charming her date was.

But for now, Simone didn't worry about her love life anyway; she would let "later" take care of itself. Helping these beautiful wounded women held her focus for now. Her thoughts turned to them. At the moment, they were housing three women: Claire, Suda, and Hailey.

Her mind fixed on Hailey as her hand continued to furiously whisk the eggs she had cracked into the bowl. Hailey was a difficult case. She had been a regular, well-adjusted suburban teenager, who had the bad fortune to encounter a handsome young man when she was shopping at a mall. She had confided in Simone with the exact story, and the knowledge that Hailey's story was like so many other girls' chilled her to the bone.

The young man's vivid blue eyes and chiseled cheeks were what had caught Hailey's eye first. He was older, lean, and lanky in a way she liked—which was a refreshing change from the jock-types she usually hung out with at school.

"What do you think of this shirt?" He'd approached her, holding up a flannel shirt in a soft teal and light blue plaid. She had already noticed him across the store but was surprised to have him not only suddenly beside her but also talking to her. She furtively looked over her shoulder to make sure he was directing his question to her.

"Um . . . I like it." She said, immediately feeling young and inarticulate for not having something more witty at the ready.

"It would look good on you, too." He held it up, just under her chin and looked into her eyes. "Gorgeous eyes," he said, which was true. Hailey's eyes were large and chocolate brown below striking slashes of very dark eyebrows that matched her equally deep brown hair. She was suddenly aware that she hadn't washed it this morning because she hadn't been up to anything special that Saturday afternoon. She now regretted it, thinking her long hair probably looked lank but hoping fervently that he found it tousled and sexy instead.

"Thanks," she faltered and looked down at the shirt so she didn't have to keep up the strong eye contact.

He smiled and moved away, continuing his shopping, but she noticed him surreptitiously keeping tabs on where she was in the store, while she did the same with him. When she walked outside, he was once again beside her.

"I'm about to go for a latte," he said. "Want to join me?"

She bit her lip, took out her phone, and checked the time. "Sure," she said with nervous relief, seeing that she had a half hour before she had to head home anyway.

"Thank God," he said, as if he'd been holding his breath. "C'mon." He pointed to the mall's Starbucks with his chin. "I've been dying to talk to you since I saw you, and I couldn't stand the thought of you leaving before I had my chance." He gave her a shy smile. "What's your name anyway?"

"Hailey," she said, her stomach lurching. She had always been second-tier popular, but somehow that had never seemed like enough to catch the attention of a guy like this.

"What's your name?" she asked, trying to appear casual, as if she went for coffee with older guys all the time.

"Dante," he told her and steered her toward the line to order.

"Is that Italian?" she took in his appearance, which didn't make sense based on what she visualized when she thought of Italian coloring.

"Yes, but northern Italian. Hence the piercing blue eyes and blond curls," he said in a joking, self-effacing tone as if he was making fun of himself.

"Hey, have you seen a French film? I saw an amazing one when I was in the city recently," he paused. "Called *Lolo*."

Hailey looked up from her coffee. Her cheeks flushed.

"Um . . . I'm embarrassed to say I've never seen a foreign film. None of my friends want to watch anything with subtitles."

Later she'd told Simone, "At the time, I thought he was so sophisticated." She remembered the exact feeling she'd had when he'd asked her about the French film. Even the recollection that he called it a "film" instead of a "movie" had made him seem like someone she wanted to be with. That day, she'd bitten her lip, sure he would think she was a loser. But if he had, he'd covered it well, and she had fallen right for it.

"We'll have to watch one sometime," he raised his eyebrows at her.

Her heart lurched, and she nodded. "That would be great."

By the time they sat with their lattes, they had already entered their phone numbers into each other's phones. He put her at ease, which none of the guys she'd dated from school had ever managed to do.

"I was desperate to be as cool as he was," she confided to Simone later, admitting how easily she had been lured.

Before they parted ways that day, when he suggested they keep their relationship quiet, just something for the two of them, it seemed right. An exciting secret. They began to see each other, ignoring the fact that she was seventeen and he was twenty-five.

She was nervous the first time he took her to his apartment, but when she walked in and saw it, she immediately relaxed. The furniture was spare—brown leather couch, tatty coffee table with an empty used coffee mug sitting on it. It had a tidy-but-lived-in feel that she liked. It fit her vision of him: neat but still a guy's guy.

The window in the living room was large and had wooden panes that were in need of a fresh coat of white paint, but their tattered appearance didn't matter because it looked onto the tree-lined street, which drew the eye away from the battered trim to the outdoors. It was raining lightly but did not dim the trees' brightly-colored orange autumn leaves. Their color created a golden light that streamed in the window. She loved it. She felt as if they were playing house. It had been easy for him to convince Hailey that he loved her. A few weeks passed, and she felt a sense of euphoria. Love was exactly what she thought it would be like. She was happy, giddy, elated. She felt like half of the perfect couple. They spent long afternoons sitting on his couch, her feet up on his lap, drinking craft beer out of glasses instead of Coors Light out of cans, talking for hours about their hopes for their futures instead of which football team would be winning the big game. The boys at her school seemed stupid to her now.

The day he talked her into trying a little blue pill, she thought it would be fine. They had been cocooned inside while wind and sheeting rain howled outdoors.

"It's nothing scary, babe," he'd said. "Nothing to worry about. Just some extra fun." She loved the sense of well-being that flooded her system after she took the pill. No worries about tests, homework, whether it would be ridiculous to ask him to come with her to homecoming, or whether he would want to finally meet her friends.

"Mmmmm," she said after a while. She felt such a sense of contentment. And having sex with him seemed right. They loved each other, she was sure of it.

One afternoon not long before Thanksgiving, he gave her a different-colored pill, but she trusted him. She assumed they'd spend time together in their bubble of happiness as usual. Instead she woke up hours later in a strange room, in a strange bed, with a camera focused on her.

"What's going on?" She sat up in bed, naked and gingerly placed her pounding head into her hands.

"We had a little extra fun," he said, unclicked the camera from the tripod, and began to rewind the recording. He showed her what had happened, and she was horrified. She hadn't been with only him; there'd been another man, too. But she had absolutely no memory of it.

"Why?" she cried. "Oh, my God, Dante, why did you do that? What happened?" She immediately burst into tears, humiliated and horrified.

She suddenly felt dirty and disgusting.

He laughed.

"Babe, you loved it," he'd told her. "Look at yourself." He began to replay one section of the video. "You were so into it."

"I had no idea what I was doing!" She screamed and then had a realization. "The pill," tears and mascara were streaming down her face. "What did you give me?"

"Nothing you didn't want. Remember? You took it willingly."

"I trusted you. I thought it would be like the other pill you gave me."

"It was even better, babe."

"Stop calling me 'babe'!" she cried. "I'm calling the police," she looked frantically around for her clothes. She remembered her cell phone had been in her jeans pocket.

He laughed again, as if she were hilarious. "Your clothes are in the other room, but calling the police isn't an option. Don't you get it? You did everything willingly. You took drugs. You begged for it. Are you going to show them the video?"

"I wasn't in my right mind. You *drugged* me!"

"You think they care about little girls who pick up men at malls? Girls who pop pills? Think again," he told her.

Her hands shook, and she felt nauseated. The thought of having her parents or strangers see the video was the worst thing she could imagine and that's exactly what she knew would happen if the police got involved. She pictured her father's beaming face at every flute concert she had ever played in. She would never be able to look him in the face again.

She grabbed for the camera, intending to smash it to pieces, but he beat her to it.

"Not so fast." He held the camera above his head, his lanky arm kept it out of her reach. "I love this video. You're never going to get it from me. Besides," he paused, "this is my insurance policy. You and I are going to be a team now."

"What are you talking about? We're not a team. I don't ever want to see you again." Another wave of sobbing overtook her.

"We're going to make some money."

"Money? We're not making any money. I'm getting out of here," she said frantically pulling on the clothes she finally located in the adjacent room. Maybe she wouldn't tell her parents or the police, but she suddenly knew with certainty that she had to get as far away from him as she could and as quickly as possible.

"Look," his tone was sweet, consoling. "I'm sorry if you were confused. I thought you'd like it. But now that you've done it, we're going to keep on doing it. We made good money already. See?" he peeled off two hundred dollars in twenties and handed them to her. "This is your cut."

She slapped the money away. "I'm not a prostitute!"

"I think you're mistaken there," he said, calmly, with a tone of condescension. He tried to tuck a strand of hair behind her ears, but she slapped his hand away. "You are now." He reached forward and shoved the money in her pocket.

"Take me home. I never want to see you again," she hissed, digging the money back out of her pocket and throwing it on the floor.

"Have it your way then." He bent, picked up the bills, and then held the door open for her.

What Hailey thought was the end of her humiliating nightmare was just the beginning. Her hope of never seeing him again and pretending the entire horrifying thing hadn't happened was dashed when he texted her later that night.

"Leave me alone," she texted back from the dinner table before her mother set her plate in front of her.

"No texting at the table, sweetie," her dad reminded her, and she clicked off her phone and slapped it, face down, on the table.

"Gentle," her mom said, sitting across from her.

"Sorry," Hailey picked up her fork and began rearranging sautéed green beans on her plate, putting one in her mouth just frequently enough to keep her parents from noticing she wasn't eating much.

"Is everything all right?" her dad asked, looking between Hailey and her mom. "How was your day? Didn't you have that big trigonometry test today?" he asked, missing the sweet chatter from when his daughter was younger.

"It was fine," she said tightly, an image of waking up earlier and learning she had been with a strange man skidded across her vision. She couldn't even look at her parents. She had slipped in the back door, raced up the stairs, and gone straight into the shower, where she'd scrubbed herself until her skin was tender to the touch.

Her mom looked at Hailey and took in the red eyes and blotched skin.

"Have you been crying?" she asked, concerned.

"No, Mom," Hailey tried to brush her off. "I worked out with some friends after school and just got overly hot. I'm fine. I showered. It's nothing," she said, stuffed some of the pork chop her mom had made into her mouth, grabbed her phone, and escaped back upstairs to her bedroom as soon as humanly possible.

Her fury and hurt were profound, but her fear of being exposed was even more compelling. He threatened to send portions of the video, edited for maximum effect, to her parents and attached one example to make sure she realized how graphic it would be.

She bowed her head and cradled it in her hands, eyes closed. Helpless. He had her. She sat on her bed, rocking back and forth, panic gripping her chest. How had this happened? And how could she get out of it?

"Once more and then I'm out," she texted back. "Then you have to promise to leave me alone."

His empty promise turned into one more, then one more, then one more—over and over again.

Hailey thought back and shuddered at the memory of the day she opened her front door, and it all fell apart.

When she swung the door open that day, she saw not just her mother but also her father home and waiting for her in the middle of the afternoon. Her eyes darted to the pill bottle sitting between them on the coffee table, and her heart squeezed in her chest. She was addicted to the pills he'd been giving her, and now her parents had found them. The white pill gave her a sense of contentment, and the blue pill made her forget. She had sex with whomever he wanted in exchange for his silence.

"How did you know about the pills?" was all she asked, not even trying to deny that they were hers.

"How could we not know?" Her mother's voice was full of concern rather than anger, which might have been easier for Hailey to bear. Hailey burst into tears.

"I need help," she whispered, the relief of her parents knowing temporarily outweighing the horror of her situation.

"Talk to us, sweetheart," her dad urged her. "What's happening?" He looked at his daughter who no longer smiled, had greasy hair, and was edgy all the time and implored her to tell them the truth.

The story poured out of her. She tried to hold back some of the most sordid details, but they understood the gist of what had been happening once she was finished talking. Seeing her parents' faces almost killed her but also brought freedom from being alone with the dark secret.

Her father closed his eyes, his face temporarily ashen, and then he got up from his chair and began to pace. He stopped, clenching his jaw, and Hailey watched— pained—as she saw the internal struggle play out on his face. She could tell her usually calm father wanted nothing more than to kill Dante.

She looked at her usually lighthearted mother's face as she too processed what could be done to punish her daughter's tormentor. She sat next to Hailey on the couch, holding her hand. She might be angry with her daughter later, when she had more time to contemplate how secretive she'd been, but for now she was strictly in protection mode.

They contacted the police.

"Don't think you're getting away from me," came a text from an unknown number and then he posted a clip of her on social media. Nothing too horrifying, but it was enough for her to know that he was going to make good on his threat if she didn't come back.

They shut down all of Hailey's social media.

"You're mine, babe," came another one.

They changed her phone number, but he always managed to find her.

"You can't go to school," her mother wrapped her protectively in a hug—the thought of that man getting a hold of her daughter chilled her to her core.

"I know," Hailey pressed her face into her mom's shoulder. "I'm so . . ." she paused. "I'm just so . . ." she searched her mind for words. "I wish I could die."

"Don't say that," her mother whispered. "I know it doesn't feel like it, but this will end. We will get past this."

"It's not over, though. He won't let me go."

"The police are on it, sweetheart."

"Mom," Hailey said. "There's nothing they can do. He's going to humiliate me in front of everyone. He's going to post a video of me. I know it. It's just a matter of time."

"As long as you're safe here with us. That's what counts."

"To you maybe, but you don't understand," she sobbed. "My life is ruined. When I think about everyone seeing. It's horrifying! And," she paused and looked down, whispering, "I can't see a way out. When I think about my life, I just can't see a future anymore."

For days, she alternately laid in her bed sobbing in frustration and paced back and forth, chest tight with anxiety. She couldn't stop visualizing the video he would send. She knew it was coming and felt powerless to stop it.

The police weren't able to track him, and Hailey found herself waiting, waiting, waiting until she felt as if she would burst with anxiety.

Every hour felt like a century. Every day an eternity.

Until the waiting was over.

He sent the video of her to a few key students who spread it around until almost everyone she knew had seen it. It was taken down, of course, but the damage was done.

She couldn't eat. She couldn't sleep. She could hardly look at her mother, and meeting her father's eyes was out of the realm of possibility. She spent her time lying in her bed in the dim light.

—

It was months before her parents felt it would be safe for her to leave the house even for the closest of errands. Hailey wasn't convinced it was clear, but she hadn't heard from him in weeks and had gradually allowed herself to hope he had given up. That he had punished her by showing the video and **now it** was actually over.

She started by going to an In-N-Out Burger drive through. She got behind the wheel, started the car, and rolled the window down on the way there. She allowed the breeze to blow against her face and reveled in the feeling of freedom. She turned up the radio and even allowed herself to tentatively sing along. Placing the order was uneventful—even though she had a slight feeling of being trapped when she was hemmed in by the other cars on either end of hers in the order line. But, she came home with burgers and shakes for herself and her parents. True when she was back in her own driveway, she had dashed out of the car, slammed the car door shut, and—heart racing—bolted to the front door as quickly as she could. But still, she had gone out. And returned home. It had felt like a victory.

Another few days passed before she wanted to go out again. She thought going to the grocery store with her mother would be a good second outing. It was just the local market. A quick errand, and her mom would be there the whole time.

"Stay with me," her mom told her while she dug through her purse for her grocery list.

"Do you think he is going to grab me by the cucumbers?" She tried to laugh lightly, but in reality the thought of it made her sick.

"I don't know," her mom looked levelly at her daughter, "but I'm not willing to take that risk."

Hailey smiled and took over pushing the cart.

"I'm scared, too. I just don't want to let him have that control anymore; you know?"

"I do know," her mom ran her hand down the back of her daughter's hair.

"Cucumbers," Hailey said with bravado, looking at the list, then steered the cart toward the vegetable section all by herself—deciding to be brave.

Her mother still didn't know exactly when or how he had grabbed her. They had finished shopping and loaded the car with the bags of groceries; she turned her back for just a moment while Hailey steered the cart off to the side of the car. And then she was gone. Just like that. Every parent's worst nightmare.

It took the police months to recover her, and by then she was hardly recognizable: skin and bones, track marks up her arms. Her parents wept with relief and horror when they got her back. "It could have been worse," they said to themselves and each other, over and over again. They told themselves they were the lucky ones.

They never brought her home from the hospital. Instead they whisked her away. They moved cities, changed their phone numbers, got new credit cards, and erased themselves as thoroughly as they could, but still they were terrified he would find her again. She was traumatized—they all were—and she clearly needed more help than they knew how to give her, which was when Hope House was recommended to them. That had been almost two years ago, yet she was still fragile and quiet. Nothing like the vibrant girl she'd been. Still, she was safe.

But healing slowly, Simone thought. She'd observed progress: an occasional genuine smile and a bit of light in those brown eyes. She would get there, Simone believed. Hailey had been going to church with Simone and seemed to be opening up to the idea of forgiving herself for getting involved with Dante. Everyone said it wasn't her fault; that she was the victim, but it didn't feel that way. Not at all. But the idea that she could give away the guilt? That was a start.

When Claire arrived at Hope House months later, she and Hailey found that they'd shared a similar experience. They learned that being caught in someone's snare happens—even to intelligent girls—and that it just maybe wasn't their fault.

Even so, Hailey couldn't let herself off the hook just yet. She had ruined her family's happiness and their sense of safety as well as her own.

Now, Simone saw her heading toward the stairs, on her way down to help in the bakery.

"Hey," Simone said and walked over to her, enveloping her in her arms for a quick hug. "Shoulders back.

Remember: posture of strength," she lifted Hailey's chin and smiled into her eyes. "You're loved; you're strong."

"Thanks Simone," she smiled meekly—the counterpoint to Claire's brashness.

"Go bake some bread."

"Yes ma'am."

"Don't *ma'am* me, young thing. I'm not an old lady," Simone bantered with her, trying to bring her out of her shell.

"Not yet at least," Hailey smiled mischievously much to Simone's pleasure.

There, Simone smiled inwardly. That's definable progress, right there. Hailey rarely spoke when she first arrived; the thought of saying something playful would never have been considered let alone undertaken.

As Hailey disappeared down the stairs, Simone's mind switched over to Suda and with her, to Chai. She pulled her phone out of her pocket and dialed.

"Hey," she said when Chai picked up.

"Hey, yourself. Is everything all right there?"

"Yeah, fine. Just wondering how the investigation's going. Just thinking about what would happen if the safe house were discovered. Should I put a plan in place in case someone comes after Suda?"

The thought of organized human traffickers being involved made Simone shudder. She wasn't exactly sure how dangerous a situation she had landed in.

Suda

PLAID FLANNEL PAJAMAS, HEAVY BLANKETS, nubby sweaters, and a fresh breeze that came through the window left open a crack, even when it wasn't warm out. The floral scent of shampoo and conditioner and hot shower water. The sound of Cheerios—Simone's favorite—as they hit the ceramic bowl on the way to becoming breakfast. Suda saw her pick up a handful and toss them into her mouth before she poured the milk. She smiled, watching the easy way Simone moved through the world. She was quietly confident and clearly at peace with who she was. Suda hoped she could be like that someday.

Simone saw Suda watching her, raised her eyebrows in question, and held up the box of cereal. "Want some?"

Suda nodded, hopped off the couch, and joined Simone in her apartment kitchen. She believed she could live on cereal. She had been wary of it at first. After a lifetime of steamed rice, the thought of pouring a bunch of milk over the little crunchy things seemed like it would be disgusting. She wasn't used to cow's milk, or any milk for that matter, but once Simone got her to try it with almond milk, she was hooked. Suda found it tasted best while eating it standing at the counter with Simone. Not talking but companionably crunching away. She felt the same about fluffy sourdough bread with butter. The unusual tang didn't exist in Thai food. Croissants, raspberries, apples. Jam. All were new and beloved tastes. Simone kept a shallow cream-colored ceramic bowl of Fuji apples on her kitchen counter, and they were beautiful and delicious.

And Suda was allowed to eat whenever she wanted. She could help herself to anything. It still felt strange— just picking up an apple and eating it. She had never experienced a bounty of food before. When she was young, food was scarce, and they mostly subsisted on rice with— when good fortune was upon them—a bit of scrambled eggs mixed in. When she first arrived at the karaoke, the only good thing about it had been that she'd had more food. But even that had been ruined once the smell of it became associated with being trapped in her room— her body being used. Even thinking about the scent of fish sauce wafting into the tiny, stifling hot space where she was kept, and the smell further entwining with the scent of human bodies, made her involuntarily gag. Here though, food smelled different and new. Meals were a time of everyone coming together. It was unlike the family meals of her childhood, but she was getting used to it and found that she enjoyed mealtime even though she didn't speak to anyone. She simply drank in the babbling voices—incoherent-yet-soothing to her.

At what stage do four walls become a home? Although she couldn't speak English and had arrived in this country against her will and near death, she wanted to stay. She didn't know what it would take, but she wanted to make it happen. Day by day, a feeling of security she hadn't felt since she was a small child was growing inside her. She felt safe with Simone, Grace, and Nittha, and she had begun to trust Chai, even though he was a man. The language barrier made it difficult with Hailey, who seemed to feel as awkward with Suda as she did with her.

Then there was Claire. Suda scrunched her eyebrows together just thinking about her. She found the beautiful young blonde woman confusing. Suda often got the feeling that Claire disliked her, but when she was near, Claire spoke to her almost constantly—as if she were picking up a conversation she had just left off. She knew full well Suda had no idea what she was saying, and yet, she kept it up. Suda usually smiled and nodded to show that she was trying to understand. And sometimes a word or two was now familiar. She guessed she would figure it all out if she were lucky enough to be allowed to stay.

Still, she looked around the room at mealtimes, taking in each person, wondering if any of them would betray her the way both her aunt and Aanwat had. She reminded herself to be wary, to remain on guard. *Be careful*, she thought, standing next to Simone, chewing on her delicious crunchy cereal, looking out the window and watching the treetops bending in the light wind. Yet in spite of her determination to remain on guard day after day, she allowed a ray of optimism in.

The next time Nittha visited, Suda asked her how to say, "What is the word for this?" in English and used that one phrase incessantly while gesturing toward objects whose name she wanted to learn. Her list of nouns was growing exponentially and included things like *shirt*, *pants*, *hairbrush*, *toothbrush*, *bowl*, *spoon*, *almond milk*, and of course her newly beloved, *cereal*. She learned how to say *please*, *thank you*, *hello*, and *good night*.

"Nittha," Suda turned to her one morning when Nittha had come to check in. Suda spoke in a low voice, relieved in this instance to speak a language different from Grace and Simone. She wanted some information but didn't want to see the disappointed look that the others tried to hide from her when she didn't get the answer she hoped for.

"How can I stay here? In San Francisco, I mean. How do people get papers?"

"Do you want to stay?" Nittha paused. "I mean, once this is all over. Would you want to stay here instead of going back to Thailand?"

Suda hesitated and rubbed her chin, as if to show that she was considering Nittha's question, when in fact she already knew the answer. "Yes, I would like to stay."

"Do you have any idea what happened to your Thai identity card when you got to the brothel?"

Suda shook her head, but her answer wasn't what Nittha has expected.

"I'm pretty sure I never had an identity card." She looked at her feet. "I don't think my parents ever registered me. Or my brother. We were born at home. We're from a hill tribe. No papers."

Nittha took a deep breath and then let it out gradually. "It will be tricky."

Getting the necessary papers to remain legally was going to be difficult if not impossible. But Suda was in danger, that was a proven fact, so didn't that make her eligible to stay? Nittha was pretty sure it did, but she would have to check with Chai. He knew more about that than she did.

"I'll work hard. I'll do anything," Suda said, "as long as it doesn't involve sex. I don't want to do that anymore."

Nittha squeezed her hand. "Of course you don't. And we're going to make sure that never happens to you again." She gave Suda a reassuring look. "I've been praying, and I will keep praying!" Nittha said with enthusiasm.

Praying, Suda mused. That word seemed to mean something special to Simone, Nittha, and Chai.

Simone prayed before dinner, so they followed suit. Suda had difficulty grasping this. When she tried to pray, she found herself visualizing a large statue with folded arms, but she saw that Simone, Nittha, and Chai all had a peace about them when they prayed that she found noticeable.

"The pastor at my church says, 'God will make a way when there seems to be no way,'" Nittha told her.

"That makes no sense," Suda frowned.

"Faith is weird," Nittha shrugged and smiled.

Suda had been living at Hope House for almost three weeks when Simone thought she was finally strong enough to help out in the bakery if Suda wanted to.

"Yes, yes, yes!" Suda used her favorite English word when Simone—through Chai—broached the possibility.

She had been down to the bakery before, but on the first day that Suda walked into the large industrial kitchen to actually work there, she felt as if the possibilities for her future life were suddenly viewed through a new lens. She loved everything about it: the warmth of the oven, the smell of yeast, the stretchiness of dough. Simone taught her the skill of meticulous cutting, cutting, and cutting in of chilled butter to make croissants. She felt as if she could be happy for the rest of her life if she was allowed to bake every day. The open space and industrial oven were entirely different from her past frame of reference. At her childhood home, they had cooked over an open flame outside the kitchen door, and in the brothel, well, the kitchen had been off limits.

Simone and Grace had painted the walls a slate blue-gray, but because the windows were huge, it didn't look dark inside. Instead, the walls acted as frames to the outside scene. Aside from Suda's health, the large windows had also deterred Simone from letting Suda try her hand at working in the bakery. Suda's first argument that the windows faced a narrow alley rather than the street didn't sway her. What finally did it was Suda's idea to bleach her hair white and start wearing fake, heavy-rimmed glasses when she was in the industrial kitchen. The 4:30 a.m. start time helped as well. Because, really, how many people were out before dawn?

Suda didn't mind getting up early with Simone. Knowing she was going to the warm kitchen made throwing off the covers and getting out of bed easy. Besides, it was a relief to be free of the nightmares that plagued her sleeping hours.

Simone drank cups of jasmine tea one after another out of the oversized light gray mugs that reflected the steel and chrome surfaces in a way Suda noticed and liked. She stacked loaves as they came out, baked golden brown and still hot to the touch. She couldn't understand many of the words being spoken, but the murmur of the customer's voices from the front of the bakery—although out of her view—was a welcome contrast to the background noise of her old life. In Chiang Rai, her waking hours were filled with the sound of street vendors selling their wares, drinks being ordered at the karaoke, and the sounds of the other women with men through the too-thin walls.

These noises felt safer. Even with her lack of understanding, the cadence of orders being taken, friendly conversation being made, and the wrestle of baked goods being slipped into paper bags was a comfortable cacophony and a welcome change from the years she'd spent in the brothel. She was even beginning to pick up a familiar turn of phrase here and there. She looked forward to the day she could work in the front. She was desperate to learn how to operate the complicated espresso machine. She appreciated the hissing sound it made as it forced steam through the thin pipe and the roar of the milk being frothed. The loud noises pushed her thoughts of her previous life to the back of her mind.

She noticed Claire was the best at making art out of the steamed milk. Intricate layered hearts, vortexes of swirls, tulips. Often when Suda was working in the back and Claire was in front, the lanky, aloof young woman snuck to the bakery's kitchen and headed straight to Suda, arm outreached, holding a cup, the top adorned with one of her elaborate designs.

"Here," Claire said, no preamble.

Claire's tone was dismissive, but Suda could sense a fearful kindness behind it. When Suda's eyes met Claire's, she recognized a wounded soul and gleaned that Claire's life must have been derailed in some horrific way to land her in Simone's care. Before reaching for the cup, Suda pressed her palms together and bowed to Claire, fingertips delicately touching her forehead, so Claire would understand the gesture of kindness was appreciated.

"Thank you," Suda said, pleased with her ability to communicate her pleasure and gratitude. She made a mental note to ask Nittha how to say, "It's delicious," the next time they were together.

One afternoon, as the wee morning hours gave way to afternoon sunshine, Suda's shift in the bakery had come to an end, but she didn't want to leave the haven of the kitchen. She wanted to create something of her own—do something for Simone and Grace—to show appreciation for everything they were doing for her.

She stood, one hand on the open door to the walk-in pantry, fingers tapping her lips as she eyed the boxes and bags of ingredients stacked on the shelves. Her cooking abilities were extremely limited, but when she spied the container of rice, she had an idea.

She picked up a bag of the rice, set it on the counter-top, and stared at it for a moment, trying to visualize how her mother used to make the sticky rice she prepared on special occasions. When Suda inhaled, she could almost smell the sweet scent of the condensed milk and ripe mango. It took just a few simple ingredients, she remembered, so Suda decided to give it a try.

She hummed while she worked, in this new world she was in. She steamed the rice until it was good and soft, then drizzled in the sweetened condensed milk. She sampled a taste and added more of the sweet liquid to the bowl. She stirred again, tasted, and was satisfied with it, so she spooned it into ramekins, set them on a tray, and slipped it into the refrigerator to cool. While the rice set, she took stock of the available fruit. She didn't want to be presumptuous and use too much, and there was no mango to be had among the ingredients Simone had on hand, but her eyes fell upon some beautiful red raspberries, deep crimson strawberries, and purply-dark blueberries. She nodded to herself, imagining the striking colors nestled against the pale rice. She reached a large serving spoon into the fruit containers stacked neatly in the walk-in refrigerator, drew out a heaping portion of each type of berry and poured them into a bowl.

She slipped out of the chilly walk-in, leaned against the door to shut it behind her, and then moved to the closest workstation. She carefully set a white plastic cutting board on top of the stainless-steel countertop and began to slice deep red strawberries. Once sliced, she gathered them in her hands and dropped them back into the bowl with the other berries. Suda used the same spoon to combine the berries into a jewel-toned medley and found she was humming the music from one of the songs Simone often had playing in the background.

She had watched Simone drizzle a squeeze of lemon juice over fruit before, so she did the same and sprinkled on a bit of sugar to create light syrup. Once she was satisfied, Suda spooned the fruit on top of the rice that was cooling in the ramekins. It was then that she remembered the shredded coconut and visualized it lightly scattered on top of the berries. She smiled, walked to the shelf in the dry-goods area of the kitchen, and found a container of shredded coconut. She delicately sprinkled on just enough to look pretty and add a hint of flavor.

She stood back, surveyed her work and smiled—satisfied. She would surprise them after dinner.

As Suda went back upstairs, Aanwat's face, as he shoved her into the shipping container, flashed through her mind unbidden. She had been at Hope House almost a month and was beginning to wonder if the smugglers would have given up on trying to find her. Chai would have told her if he'd arrested anyone, so his silence on the subject made her believe they were still out there.

With the vision of his face came a sense of betrayal. Although they had been far from friends, the tightness in her chest she felt when she thought of him almost matched the feeling of treachery that came with the memory of her aunt selling her to the karaoke in the first place. Because, although he was working for Gan, Aanwat had given her reason to believe she could trust him. She thought he had been secretly on her side. Hadn't he sometimes subtly steered the worst men away from her? She knew he had done his best to keep her away from the man who liked to knock her head against the wall. And there were other little things, too. He tried to get her to eat and sometimes brought her favorite dumplings to her before she had even thought to ask. And she was sure he sometimes gave her a look of empathy. His eyes told her he was sorry she was there and wished he could help, as if he knew that she was a real person with thoughts and feelings—not just something to be used and thrown away. Although he'd hardly interacted with her any more or less than he had with the other girls in the karaoke, she had thought he had cared. Had it been her imagination? Clearly she'd been mistaken.

Aanwat

EXHAUST FUMES OF FISHING BOATS slowly motoring
back to the dock at the San Francisco wharf, the chop of
cold bay water, wooden cases of iced crab smacking hard
on the top of a stack of the same, voices yelling to tourists
and enticing them to buy some local specialties. Aanwat
had tried the clam chowder, which he'd found pleasantly
briny, the salty clams chewy. He came back most days
after that first tasting because it was a hearty meal, even
if the cream seemed to upset his stomach a bit. Cheap
and filling was the most important thing to him.

He needed to find a way out of his situation. What
he couldn't decide was whether to try to disappear in
San Francisco and then stay in the United States illegally
while he continued to look for Suda, or to try to exchange
the return ticket to Chiang Rai for one going to Bangkok
and then disappear there and start life over. Either way,
he knew life as he'd known it was over and his attempt to
make some easy extra money had been his undoing.

He was no closer to finding Suda than he was the first day he'd arrived. How could someone disappear so completely? He had finally concluded she must be either long gone or dead. Or the story about the container being locked but empty was a lie or maybe a cover up for something else, and they were trying to milk Gan for the money they said they had lost. Maybe she was here and already at work. Or perhaps Suda died during the voyage, or they shot her while she was trying to run away. Those were the only explanations that made any sense to him.

His feet became more painful each day as the soles of his shoes became more battered and worn—giving him less support. He wondered whether Suda was out on the streets, too. Were her shoes also stripped of the soles by now? He felt as if he had walked every street in the city; had visited every nail shop, Thai massage parlor, and Thai restaurant; had inquired at every grocery store, cheap motel, and everywhere else he had thought of, and yet he had not even one positive indication to go on.

With each painful step and empty search, he became more convinced she was dead. He could feel the emptiness of the world without her. And he was partially to blame. He wished he had convinced her to eat more and stop fighting; then she wouldn't have been sent away in the first place. Or at least, once he discovered it was Suda he was supposed to shove into the shipping container, he should have grabbed her and run right then. Instead of panicking and going through with it, he should have whispered to her, telling her what was happening, so she would have been ready to run with him. He convinced himself they would have made it. He wished he had told her how he felt about her when they were in Thailand. He hoped she knew from the hints he gave her, but she was difficult to read.

It doesn't matter now, he thought as he sat on the dock at the wharf, eating the last of the crackers that came with the soup. He crumpled the little bag they came in and threw it into the trash can then dropped his head into his hands. He was sure she was dead and he was going to be, too, if he didn't disappear.

He made his decision that afternoon: He would change his ticket and go to Bangkok and then stay there. He'd never be found.

As he made the long walk back to his hotel, he peered absentmindedly into the windows of shops and restaurants. The fog's tendrils had once again wisped in, and the wind had whipped into periodic gusts. He was desperate to be back in a warm climate. He let his mind drift as he turned a corner and then stopped in place when he saw two young women, one of them Asian, run from an alley door to a car parked at the curb. Something about the petite Asian woman felt familiar to him—grabbed his eye. Had Suda just dashed into a waiting car? Could that have been her? He shook his head, disbelieving and convinced he was seeing things.

But still. He paused; furrowed his brow. *Was that Suda's face?* Even with the baseball cap she was wearing, he could see that the girl's hair was white instead of natural black. And she wore glasses. He shook his head. It couldn't be her. He must have imagined it. But something about the way she moved had caught his attention. Her upright posture and the lovely thin neck like Suda's, which he had studied over the years.

Adrenalin coursed through his body. It couldn't be, and yet his mind wouldn't let go of the possibility. The line of her jaw, the distinct cheekbones. He tried to get another look, but the car pulled out and began to drive in the opposite direction. All he could see was the back of the bleached hair as it disappeared down the street.

Heart racing, he turned from the alley and walked around the corner to see the name of the store. He was pretty sure the side door from which she emerged went to a place called Hope Bakery. Why would she be there? If it even was her. He couldn't be sure. He told himself that it probably wasn't Suda.

But if it was Suda?

He hardly dared hope.

His mind inexplicably swung in an ugly direction. If it was her, he could be saved if he wanted to be. He would be the one who came up with the goods, and it would mean money now and probably more money once he got back to Thailand. But could he betray her again when he had just been regretting his past betrayal?

He told himself that he hadn't had a choice when he shoved her into the container, but he had a choice now. Did he care about her enough to keep her whereabouts to himself?

He needed to think. He walked to a nearby bench and sat, first resting his head in his hands and then tilting his head back. He closed his eyes so he could tune out the world around him. He needed to clear his mind. He wondered where the girl was going and how long she would be gone. He needed to get another look at her. After a while, he left the bench and slouched in a doorway, hood of the blue sweatshirt proclaiming his love of San Francisco pulled up so he would be less visible. He leaned his shoulder against the building and settled in to wait.

He rotated various scenarios through his mind while time passed and finally knew what he would do.

He slipped away from the doorway where he was lurking to the front of Hope Bakery to see the address. He pulled out his map and carefully noted where it was. His stomach growled, and he realized it had been hours since he'd eaten the soup. As he wondered how much longer he would have to wait, the car came around the corner. He dashed back to the doorway and crouched down. The Honda came to a stop beside the same alley door. From his vantage point, he had a clear view of the passenger, but she wouldn't notice him unless he called attention to himself. The door swung open, and he sucked in his breath: there she was. He could clearly see her face. Horrible bleached hair but Suda's face. He *had* found her.

He watched as she slunk back into the building with that other woman. He stood, watching the building, and then—yes—a light turned on in one of the third-floor windows, and he watched a silhouette remove a hat. He smiled.

He was still smiling when a half hour later, greasy Fatburger food bag in hand, he opened the door to his motel. He stopped short and inadvertently gasped when he saw the boss sitting on his bed, a gun resting next to him.

Claire

THE LAST FEW MOMENTS of what Claire now thought of as her old life often crept to the forefront of her mind uninvited. The stale smell inside the city bus she took home from school that fateful day; the fact that the sun had broken through in the morning causing unseasonable warmth for some reason entered her remembrances; a lump in her throat she recalled not being able to shake. Her first view of the apartment after she'd opened the door told the story of emptiness. The sun shone on dust motes floating in the air on their way to settling on the worn sofa that, at some point, had been covered in beautiful taupe linen but now just looked dingy. She remembered it had been the first day she'd tried to write a poem—hoping to empty herself of her worry. She'd scrawled the phrase "beautiful relentlessness" on her napkin at lunch—having no idea where the phrase had come from, but once the words had entered her mind, she'd not been able to shake them. They turned over and swirled around each other. Perhaps it had started as "relentless beauty," but with the mental churning, had reversed into the opposite order, which she preferred, liking the cadence of the sounds.

Claire had immediately recognized the particular feeling of entering an unchanged apartment. Her mother's favorite sweater—still thrown across the couch exactly where it had been left—signified the fact that she had not come home.

She avoided her friends after school and had hidden in the safe haven of the library to do her homework, knowing she would be unable to fake caring about which of her friends liked which boy in her class and which teacher was a jerk, because her mother was *gone* and Claire had a *very bad* feeling about it.

Her goal had been to be away from the house as long as possible to ensure enough time had passed for her mother to get back before she returned home, but her plan hadn't worked. When she'd arrived, Nick was still conspicuously present in their apartment.

"Hi, beautiful girl," his voice was jovial with a forced undertone. "I'm making your favorite dinner."

"Thanks," she swallowed hard, pausing for a moment to moor herself before asking the question. She dropped her backpack in her room. The smell of Bolognese sauce bubbling on the stove was a hopeful sign. "Is my mom back?" She tried to keep her hopefulness tamped down.

"I texted a bunch of times and tried and tried to call her, but it keeps going straight to voicemail."

"Not quite yet," he smiled warmly. "She was feeling under the weather, so she decided to stay put, but I promised her I'd take good care of you."

"Under the weather?" Claire questioned dubiously.

"You know. She must be getting the flu or something."

"Stay put where? She doesn't have any friends. She would want to spend the night here, especially if she's sick. She should come home."

"Look, Claire," Nick began in a soothing tone. "I didn't want to have to tell you this, but your mom is sick. Really sick. And she doesn't have good health insurance, so she decided to stay put for now with my friends," he paused. "My friends, um, Amy and Frank are looking after her."

"Really sick, like pneumonia?"

"Kind of like pneumonia, yes."

"I want to go see her."

"No, kiddo, she just needs to rest. I'm sure she'll be fine. Let's just eat dinner. Come on; it'll be fun," he said, dishing spaghetti noodles onto two plates and spooning deliciously aromatic sauce on top. He handed her a wedge of Parmesan cheese and a grater. "You can grate the cheese."

He smiled and topped off his glass of red wine. He even held up a wine glass to her and raised his eyebrows, making her understand that he was asking if she wanted some.

"Um, no thanks," she said and moved past him to get a glass of water from the tap.

"Suit yourself," he said and placed the two plates of spaghetti on the table across from each other.

She twirled too many noodles onto her spoon, which made the first bite a struggle to get down. She picked up her water and took a large gulp to help.

"So," he searched for a topic of interest. "How was your day?"

"Weird," she said, not looking up, concentrating on twirling a smaller amount this time.

"Weird why?"

"Weird because my mother is missing apparently." Claire looked at Nick with an accusatory expression.

Nick raised his hands, "I haven't done anything."

"And yet," she paused, looking again at her food, not sure how far to push it.

"And yet what exactly?"

"Where's Mom? I'm not buying the whole 'she's sick' thing."

"Fine, I didn't want to have to tell you this, but I think your mom needs to go to rehab." He paused dramatically. "She's been doing drugs."

"Drugs?" Claire asked incredulously dropping her fork and spoon, which clattered onto her plate like a couple of unruly thugs. "No kidding? Really?" the sarcasm dripping. "I'm pretty sure she's been 'doing drugs,'" she made air quotes around the words, "since before I could walk."

Still speaking in the soothing tone that was bugging her, Nick said, "You don't have to use air quotes around the words 'doing drugs' and stop acting like a brat. I wanted to shield you from this bit of nasty information, but since you're pushing, I guess I'll just come out with it and tell you that your mother overdosed."

"What?" She felt the blood drain from her face.

"I'm trying to protect you, here. I'm not the enemy."

"Mom *overdosed*? What happened? What did she take?" Claire's heart raced, and her mind was suddenly on hyper focus. Was it heroin? She kept hearing that there was practically an epidemic of it these days. But she didn't think her mom went in for that. Was it pills? She seemed to always be taking something, but what was it? She had no idea. "Is she in the hospital? Which hospital?" She leapt up from the table and ran to her room to grab her backpack.

"Claire," Nick got up from the table and came around to her. "I'm so sorry to tell you this, but your mom . . ." he paused. "She didn't make it."

"What are you saying?"

"I'm saying she died."

"What the fuck!" Claire screamed. She had never sworn around a grown-up before, but it seemed to come out of her mouth of its own accord. "You're lying to me. You've been lying all along. *Where's my mother?*"

She heard the hysteria in her voice and tried to check it. It felt like her world was fracturing—every one of her worst fears happening at once.

She had always tried to be good. Always tried to do things right. She'd studied, been polite, didn't eat too much of the scant food they had so her mom could eat, too. She'd tried and tried to make sure nothing bad happened but now . . . She couldn't bear to finish the thought. She was at once furious with her mother for putting them in this situation and desperate to have her back.

Nick began to pace and then stopped in front of her.

"Okay, yes. I did lie to you, but only because I didn't know how to tell you."

"So you just made up something about her being sick? Are you saying she has been dead *all day?*"

She went to the bookshelf and ran her hands across the spines of her mom's books—wanting a connection. A sob escaped before she bit down hard on the knuckle of her index finger to stop herself. She paused to compose herself.

"Even when I got up this morning you *knew*, and you just let me go to school without saying a word?"

"Look, kiddo," Nick was seemingly unruffled. "We did everything we could."

"Who's we? Did you call an ambulance? Did she go to the hospital?"

"We . . . me . . . what difference does it make?"

"It makes a *big* difference. Did you call an ambulance?"

"Yes, an ambulance was called, but she was unresponsive." Nick ran fingers through his hair, and Claire suddenly noticed that he looked ashen, as if maybe he hadn't slept since the day before.

"Where is she now?"

Nick hesitated, and she could tell he didn't want to answer her.

"She's at the morgue." He sat down, leaned back in the chair he'd pulled away from the dinner table—defeated.

"Let's go. I want to see her."

"No," Nick said definitively. "I'm *not* taking you. Listen, Claire: we have to stay away from the police, the morgue, the whole thing." He tried to take her hand, but she shook him off.

"Claire," he said her name again, trying to get her to look at him. "Your mom was doing something illegal. I'm not sure what, but . . ."

"*What?* I don't understand. What do you mean, *illegal*? Besides doing drugs?" The emptiness Claire felt was like a chasm. She wanted to disbelieve, but knowing her mother's history, she couldn't deny the possibility.

"Listen, I don't think you should tell any of your friends about what happened. We should keep it just between us."

"Why? She died. *Death* is not a crime."

"She was involved in illegal stuff, Claire, so, yeah, there would be problems. But you don't have to worry," he looked at her with stoic, tired eyes. "I'll take care of you as if you were my own." He smiled wanly, as if it were just the two of them together against the world. "Trust me," he said and put his hand on her shoulder. Against her better judgment, she let it stay there.

She had never in her life been at a complete loss as to what to do. She took a few steps toward the door, her instinct telling her to go to the police for help. But then what if they took her away? What if she ended up with strangers? Wasn't being with Nick better than that? She stood, hand on the knob, unsure, hesitating, and then she turned and walked to her bedroom.

It was a moment she would relive over and over as the years passed. If only she had walked out then. Her life would have been . . . what? She wondered. But she would never know because she hadn't gone to the police to find out exactly what had happened. She had been too afraid.

"I'm going in my room now," she whispered instead, voice almost inaudible.

She walked in and closed the door behind her, wishing the cheap metal knob had a lock. She leaned her back against the door for a long moment and then slid against it, down to the floor, arms wrapped protectively around her knees.

The dark night seeped through her thin, ragged curtains and entered her fragile torn heart. Her arms were limp by her side as she lay in bed that night. Her eyes, wide open, felt as heavy as the world.

Chai

CHAI'S LIFE WAS CURRENTLY ONE OF CONTRASTS. Hope House was the allure. The thought of Simone's green flecked eyes and quick smile, her loose curls pulled back into a hasty ponytail; the smell of fresh, strong coffee; seeing Suda safe and slowly putting on weight brought him a sense of contentment. It was a feeling he hadn't had in a long time. The haunted look in Suda's eyes was gradually abating, and he felt honored to have been allowed into the small circle of women. The trust they had given him was a privilege not to be taken lightly.

These thoughts contrasted with the feeling of the weight of his gun resting at his back, hidden from plain sight; the fact that he hadn't made more progress on gathering hard evidence to arrest the real players of the smuggling operation; his hunger for a more normal existence. He was weary of it. Especially of being under-cover. He had become a cop because he wanted to help people, but too often he now felt he served simply as a spoke in a damaged, rickety wheel wobbling over a rutted, cobbled road.

In the five weeks since Chai dropped Suda off at Simone's apartment he and Nittha had quickly become fixtures at Hope House. He often found himself smiling at his sister—proud of her for jumping in wholeheartedly when he had needed her. The two had always been close but watching her in action with Suda and acting as a go-between with Grace and Simone had made him appreciate her more. They all become a part of each other's new reality that was surprisingly easy and comfortable.

Yet one evening when Chai showed up at the apartment near dinnertime, his lips were pressed, and his eyes showed tension. They knew immediately that something had gone wrong.

Chai pulled a chair up to the table where Suda was chopping vegetables under Grace's tutelage.

"What is it?" Simone asked while turning from the counter. She set down the head of lettuce she was about to clean.

Before explaining, he began with a question in Thai to Suda.

"Do you know a guy named Aanwat?" he asked, knowing it was time to tell her about his arrival.

"Yes," she hesitated, not sure how much or what information he was looking for. "He works at the karaoke back in Thailand," she told him, unable to meet his eyes. She stared at her hands, color in her cheeks as she remembered her life there, standing in line, waiting to get chosen. The humiliation of it. "Why?"

"He's here."

"What?" she looked up. "How can that be?"

"Gan sent him to find you." He told her as gently as possible, but he saw the fear immediately jump to her eyes.

Simone and Grace saw the expression on Suda's face and exchanged a look of concern between them.

"What is it?" Simone asked.

"Remember the guy I told you was being sent here to look for Suda?"

"Yeah." Simone tilted her head to one side.

"He's here now. I wanted Suda to know." He paused. "I didn't want to frighten her by telling her before, but I know how easy it is to start thinking that because nothing *has* happened, nothing will. And with the weeks passing, I realized she could start building a false sense of being secure. We need to make sure she stays cautious and out of sight."

He tapped his fingers on the table and furrowed his brow. "There's something more going on than the regular drugs and trafficking. Usually there wouldn't be this much effort put into finding one girl. It wouldn't be worth the time. But Gan, the guy who runs Suda's brothel, has something to prove. He wants in, in a bigger way, and things have gone wrong. I think he's trying to regain trust."

"So now what?" Grace asked.

"Unfortunately, there's nothing different to do. You keep Suda hidden. I keep working from the inside. That's about all there is to it for now."

For his part, Chai watched Aanwat's every move and had redoubled his efforts to make sure not to inadvertently lead him to the safe house. He spent more time at his undercover apartment and less at his real home. He backtracked obsessively when he moved from one place to another to ensure that he wasn't being tailed. Staying on top of Aanwat's progress gave him a sense of assurance. Aanwat was on the hook with his boss in Thailand and was genuinely afraid of repercussions. But there was something else, too, and Chai wanted to understand what it was.

The bakery was empty the next time Chai stopped in. Simone looked up as the door chimed, and Chai, arms laden, walked in and stopped in front of her at the counter.

"These are for Suda," Chai said, foregoing the usual greeting. Simone came from behind the counter as he held out a large shopping bag of clothes his sister had picked up for Suda. He allowed himself to say her name aloud only when they were alone in the bakery. He was cautious when it came to protecting people. "And these are for you." He took a small shoebox-size wooden crate from under his arm and passed it to her.

His shirtsleeves were rolled up, and she noticed the lower part of an intricate tattoo on his muscular forearm as he handed it over. She had noticed that tattoo previously and wondered what it was that he felt strongly enough about to have permanently marked on his body. Although she didn't see herself ever getting a tattoo, they did fascinate her. It was the permanence of them that gave her pause. Her practical side couldn't help but wonder how the tattooed would feel about having the mark on his or her body twenty years down the line. She didn't want to ask about his, though. It seemed simultaneously an invasion of his privacy and like a pickup line, which was not her intent. She did wonder though.

She lifted the lid from the box, and inside were three rows of perfectly ripe white peaches.

"For me?" Simone bent forward and deeply inhaled the heady scent of the fruit. She pulled one out and cut into it, freeing the sweet scent. She sliced it up and handed two wedges back to him, which he took, popping one into his mouth.

"I'm a sucker for a farmers market," he said after he swallowed, "but don't let the word get out or it will ruin my reputation," he jokingly mocked himself. "I saw these and thought you might like them."

"I do! Thank you."

They each put wedges into their mouths. Chai closed his eyes for a moment as if he were seeing rows of peach trees in the sun.

"Mmmmm, so good. I love white peaches." She chewed for a moment. "And, I hate to be the bearer of bad news, but I think your "bad guy" cover is already blown with me."

"Yeah, well," he wiped his juice-streaked fingers across the leg of his jeans. "How is our charge?"

"Doing really well, actually. I started her in the kitchen, and she's in love with it. I don't blame her; I am, too. And, she's looking a little bit less gaunt, which makes me happy. It's been a relief to see her transformation from emaciated to just plain skinny. I'll admit, her sustenance is pretty much composed of bread, so I feel like I've been a little bit of a bad influence, but still, she's eating." Simone paused for a moment. "I need to get a bit more variety into her body, though. Some protein and veggies wouldn't hurt. Maybe these will entice her." Simone pulled another peach out of the box and felt the weight of it in the palm of her hand. "They're gorgeous. Thank you."

"My pleasure," he looked at her and hesitated as if he wanted to say something further.

"Is everything okay?"

"Yes . . . yes. Everything's fine. Sorry. I didn't mean to worry you."

"You're sure?"

"Nothing new. I would tell you if I had any news."

"All right," she breathed, realizing she'd been holding her free hand over her heart. She moved it back to rest on the counter and decided not to press him. She would do her job and let him do his. She had to believe that he would be able to make an arrest soon.

In the meantime, she was determined to make sure Suda wasn't seen, prayed that Chai wouldn't be discovered, and did everything in her power *not* to freak out about the legal ramifications of harboring someone undocumented who was a victim of a crime—assuming it was illegal, which she believed it must be.

"I trust you," Simone said. And it was true. She did trust him, although she ruminated constantly about *why exactly* she did. He was, after all, connected to the very region of Thailand where Suda came from and could easily be playing her. He could be in the trafficking ring itself and posing as an undercover cop. So, what was it about him that she trusted? She wasn't sure and prayed she wasn't being taken in. Could she be that foolish? Could her instincts be that wrong? She knew it was a possibility but didn't think so. There was just something she trusted about him. And Nittha, too.

She focused on the fact that he wouldn't have brought Suda to a safe house if he had a nefarious intent. That didn't make sense. So, it must be that he was trying to save her. Right?

Simone picked up another wedge of peach and popped it in her mouth, savoring the flavor.

"Oh, hey, I have something you might like," Simone told him, visualizing the bowl of sticky rice she had in the walk-in fridge. "Be right back."

She spooned a portion of sticky rice into a to-go container and dashed back to the front.

"Suda made it," she told him as she handed it over. "It's delicious, and I couldn't help but add it to our menu. I think it made her happy." Simone smiled at the recollection of the look on Suda's face when she told her how good the dessert was.

He tried to pay her, but she waved him away.

"We're past that now."

Chai smiled. "I guess we are. And thank you for this." He lifted the to-go cup of coffee she'd poured for him to take along with the sticky rice in a salute.

"Keep me posted," she said as he turned for the door.

"You'll be the first to know anything," he said and raised his cup of coffee in farewell.

"Well, well," Grace said appearing beside her.

"Well, well, yourself," Simone intoned. "What's on the docket today?"

"I just got back from taking Hailey to her therapist's office," Grace told her.

"You have that look on your face that tells me you got some surprising news."

"What gave it away?"

"You raise your eyebrows, and your face looks extra animated."

"Those are my tells?"

"There could be worse ones," Simone smiled at her friend. It still amazed her on occasion to realize that the young girl who had been her first success story had become not just a co-worker but also a close confidant and friend. She thought of it as a miracle.

"Anyway, what's the news?"

"Her therapist thinks she's ready to move to a less-restrictive environment. She thinks she's gotten to a healthy emotional level and that she can move to transitional housing. Still work here, but live there while she tests the waters."

"Really?" Simone asked. "I'm surprised. It seems to me that Hailey's been making progress, but ready to leave? I'm not so sure. Did you talk with Hailey about what she thinks?"

"We talked about it the entire ride home. I can tell she's still processing, but she seemed enthusiastic. Nervous but excited at the possibility."

"I don't want to move her out of here if we're not absolutely sure." She paused, closed her eyes and thought for a moment. "I worry."

"I know you do, Mama Bear." She wrapped her arm around Simone. "That's part of what I love about you."

At the sound Hailey's name being spoken, Claire, working in the kitchen, stopped kneading the bread she was elbow deep in and lifted her head, suddenly tuned in and alert. If she stood still and held her breath, she could just make out what they were saying. She silently inched toward the door to hear better. Was Hailey's therapist nuts? Her ears tried to catch every word over the hum of the convection oven.

Claire closed her eyes and dropped her head when she heard they were thinking of letting Hailey move out. Was Hailey *ready*? Claire knew the answer was an emphatic "No," but she had never told Grace and Simone what she had seen. And not just once.

At least two months ago, Claire had spotted Hailey acting a bit strangely when a certain guy came into the bakery. Claire couldn't tell whether he was going for the grungy hipster look or if he was just plain old grungy, but she did notice Hailey noticing him. At first, she thought Hailey had a crush on the guy. After all, in spite of the greasy-looking dishwater blond hair and a skinny phy-sique, the twenty-something guy was pretty cute. But then, one afternoon while she was steaming milk for a cappuccino, it caught her eye when he passed a small white envelope to Hailey who was at the register. Claire managed to turn a gasp into a deep intake of breath, so she didn't call attention to herself, and surreptitiously peeked out of the corner of her eye, watching as Hailey slid the packet into the front pocket of her jeans. When she made change for his scone, she saw her palm an extra twenty-dollar bill or two, folded into a small square, and slide it into his hand. It was subtle, Claire had to give her that, and she wondered how long that little exchange had been going on.

That afternoon, Claire's mind replayed the exchange nonstop while she methodically made coffee drinks, brewed gourmet tea, and seethed.

~~~~~

"What's eating you this afternoon?" Hailey had asked, when Claire slammed the small pitcher of steamed milk too hard against the counter once again before pouring it over the espresso waiting at the bottom of the cardboard to-go cup.

"What do you care?" Claire had retorted. She jutted her chin out and pulled her Giants baseball cap lower on her forehead.

"Um, I guess I don't." Hailey stammered her response, surprised and hurt at Claire's tone. She thought the two had become friends.

Hailey picked up a small white towel and began wiping the counter while she gave Claire the side eye and wondered if she'd done something to make her angry.

"Did I do something wrong?" she finally asked, after a few minutes of stilted silence.

"I don't know," Claire said snidely, realizing she sounded like a petulant elementary school child, but unable to stop herself. "Did you?"

Claire wanted Hailey to know she saw her get the drugs from the skanky hipster but couldn't bring herself to just come out with it. It wasn't just that, Claire realized. Now that she knew, she realized she had seen the same vacant look in Hailey's eyes that her mother had sometimes had.

"How could I have not noticed?" she mumbled out loud. She stood still, facing the counter, saying nothing else for a moment as she allowed that realization to sink in.

Hailey looked at her, confused.

"And don't give me the big innocent eyes, either." Claire turned her back to her and then practically threw a gallon of milk into the under-the-counter refrigerator and slammed the cooler door.

Hailey looked around wondering what had gotten Claire so riled up. It didn't occur to her for a moment that she would have noticed the exchange when her connection dropped off the pills, and Claire's hostility just made her that much more eager to get alone and take one.

And now, Claire, still lurking as close to the front and trying to catch every word spoken, heard Grace talking about Hailey being ready to *leave*? Claire closed her eyes remembering the day she saw Hailey buying pills. Since then, she had observed Hailey's pupils being a little bit too large and her demeanor being a little too calm. She shook her head, lips pursed, furious that Hailey was blowing it but not willing to be a snitch.

She walked back to the counter where she had been working before she began eavesdropping, grabbed the bread dough, and pounded it against the kneading board. She reminded herself that this scenario was exactly why she shouldn't get involved in other people's lives. *Don't care about them, and it all works out.* She sighed, her mind switching to Suda.

"Ugh!" escaped her mouth involuntarily as the fact that she was ignoring her own advice occurred to her. She couldn't help herself; she liked that waif. Suda was kind and smart. Claire could tell she was by the look in her eyes when Claire talked to her. And she was pretty sure Suda was starting to understand. She could tell. Against her better judgment, she was not just letting her in but seeking her out. "What's wrong with me?" she murmured under her breath. "I never learn."

Claire began rolling out the baguettes, knowing she'd beaten the dough so much they'd be ruined. *But, hey, that was how life was; right?*

She heard Grace and Simone change the subject and tried to get on with her work. She could understand why Simone would miss what was going on with Hailey because she'd never lived the life, but Grace? *Come on.*

Simone was about to close for the day when the door chimed and a slight young Asian man tentatively stepped in.

Simone turned to him with a smile. "Hi," she said. "What can I get for you?"

He didn't say anything, but his eyes darted around, and something about him made her uneasy.

"Coffee?" she asked cautiously, but he shook his head.

"We have a few croissants left, but I'm afraid it's slim pickings at this hour because we are about to close."

His confused look bespoke the fact that he wasn't a native English speaker. That itself wasn't terribly uncommon in San Francisco, given the number of tourists who passed through the city, but because of his features, she couldn't help wondering if he was Thai. The thought made her overly cautious, given the circumstances, and she touched her phone, which was tucked in her pocket, to make sure it was available in case she needed to call 911, Chai, or both.

The young man seemed slightly agitated, and she noticed a sheen of sweat on his forehead although the day was cool and mild. He looked around the space again and caught sight of the door to the kitchen.

His eyes turned back to her, and she met and held them. Something about him was off, and she wanted him to know that she wouldn't be easy to get past. She was someone to contend with.

"Tea?" she asked, keeping her voice purposefully calm, and he nodded.

"Yes," he hesitated, adding "please," and fumbled in his pocket. For a split second, she thought—terrifyingly—that he was going to pull out a gun. Instead he took out some money and furrowed his brows at it; the uniformity of the size and color of the bills made it diffi-cult to immediately determine the value of each.

She wondered if she was being unduly worried. Per-haps he was simply feeling out of his element in a strange country or sweaty because he had a fever.

He nodded his thanks when she handed him the tea and gave the place one last look before walking back out to the street. *Was he the guy Chai had warned them about? Had he found them? If so, how?*

She shook her head, not sure whether she was see-ing something that wasn't there. He was probably just a guy who stopped in for tea. Still, trusting instincts that hadn't led her wrong in the past, she decided to heed this frisson of concern. She made a note of what he looked like and planned to tell Chai about him the next time he was in.

Suda

THE SMELL OF YEASTY BREAD AND WARM BUTTER; the back drop hum of American voices; the constant hiss of the coffee steamer; another bouquet of flowers brought in from the farmers market.

Suda had learned many English words in the weeks since she had been at Hope House, but the two words Suda heard often were *love* and *healing*, frequently in the same sentence. *Breathe* was another of her favorites. Simone rubbed circles onto her back and reminded her to inhale and exhale. Suda liked the sound of the word. The gentle *ee* sound matched the calm breaths she was supposed to take in and let out.

The women at Hope House seemed to form a family of sorts—Simone being mother to all—even though the others were not much younger than she was. She had a certain strength and joyfulness in her being that Suda found mesmerizing. Like bubbly water, she thought, enjoying the image.

Once she had stopped being terrified every waking moment, Suda had noticed that when you can't speak the language others are speaking, it's easier to observe people's body language, emotions, and hidden intentions. Even those aspects that they don't realize they're expressing.

For example, Suda noticed that Chai seemed to be in love with Simone. Suda saw it even though Simone herself didn't seem to realize. Maybe Chai didn't know it yet either. She observed him finding excuses to be around even when it was unnecessary. And she witnessed the fact that Chai liked to touch Simone casually on the arm or gently on her back when he scooted around her, as if it was coincidental. He was definitely more American than Thai in his mannerisms, she thought, because a Thai man would never so be so bold. And Suda could see that it was purposeful from the subtle yearning on his face. He also brought baskets of produce and bunches of flowers from the farmers market, ostensibly for everyone, but Suda noticed he always looked at Simone's face to see her reaction and whether she was pleased with them.

Suda sometimes smiled at how obvious it seemed to her, although he believed he was giving nothing away. She liked him, though, and, more importantly, she trusted him. She hoped he succeeded with Simone, who seemed unaware as far as Suda could tell. When Chai looked at Simone, he reminded Suda of the way her father looked at her mother before they died and she was forced to go with her aunt, who sold her to the karaoke as soon as she could. Suda shoved that memory to the back of her mind and turned to observe the others in the group.

Hailey was more difficult to read. She kept to herself mostly. She was polite when she was in the group but rarely joined in the conversation. Instead she observed shyly from the outside. Suda wondered what had happened to Hailey to bring her to the safe house, but she had no way of knowing.

Suda had made several observations about Claire, though, who seemed to want people to believe she didn't care about anything or anyone. Her tone was dismissive when she spoke to people, but she saw that Claire hung around Grace and Simone at every opportunity. She brought Suda coffee each morning but pretended it happened accidentally, as if she had suddenly found herself with an extra cup of coffee in hand—elaborate foam art included—that she needed to offload on someone. Suda tried not to show that she saw Claire's kindness because she observed that Claire didn't like to be noticed. She also saw that Claire followed them all with her eyes, as if she were afraid of having people out of her sight and therefore out of her life. She wondered whom Claire had unexpectedly lost. Suda sometimes found herself wanting to hold Claire's hand but had noticed that whenever Simone or Grace touched her, she shied away, awkwardly.

Another observation Suda had made about Claire was that she often wrote on scraps of paper. She couldn't make out what it was, but she sometimes later found the papers, forgotten, with a line or two of words scrawled on it. She was curious about it, but something told her not to ask, that Claire wouldn't want her to have noticed her habit of staring into space, often with her fingers tapping her lips, and then searching for a pen or pencil and scratching words out on whatever paper she could find close to her. Sometimes it was even the baking paper Simone had them place scones on before putting them in the oven. Suda wondered what it meant. She had never seen anyone write anything before. Why just a few words? And then why did she leave them behind? When she came across a scrap that had been abandoned, Suda would take it and slip it into her pocket. She tucked them away for someday when she could read.

Mostly, though, while everyone else communicated over dinner in a language she couldn't understand, Suda passed the time thinking about her own future. Even before Chai had given her the warning about Aanwat, she had felt deep in her core that he and Gan were still searching for her as much as she wished they had simply given up.

"I think there was some sort of mix-up," she had confided to Nittha one afternoon when she was visiting.

"What makes you say that?"

"I heard them say there were supposed to be more girls," Suda had closed her eyes, seeing inside of the container for that fleeting moment before she was closed into darkness. "I'm grateful for it, though."

"Why?"

"I arrived half-starved. If there had been others, some of us would have died before we got here, I think."

Suda ran her hands over her stomach and across her hips. She was definitely fleshing out, and she liked it. She had been so skinny and weak before, and now she felt stronger. She thought back to her emaciated arms trying to throw a bucket of her own waste on Chai. She actually felt herself smile at the memory. It was a good thing she had been weak, otherwise he would have been covered, and she would have run to who knows where. She might have died from starvation by now. Or worse, she might have been caught.

Instead she was in this house in San Francisco, surrounded by kind people. It still amazed her.

Claire looked over at her, wondering about Suda's small, amused smile. "Hey," she nudged Chai, who had joined them for dinner. "Ask Suda what's so funny."

When Suda told him what she had been thinking about, he burst out laughing and recounted his first encounter with Suda, skinny arms wielding the bucket. He was a good storyteller and made the entire situation seem humorous instead of tragic, which kept the mood light. The vision of the slight-framed Suda taking on Chai had them all laughing.

"It sounds as if you did a 'shitty' job of protecting yourself," Claire said, using air quotes in hopes of not getting busted by Simone for language. It worked; they all rolled their eyes while Chai translated Claire's joke.

Suda drank in the feeling of close-knit comaraderie—the kind of family she'd wished for since being torn from hers so long ago. Even though she couldn't understand what they were saying, she could clearly see that they were laughing with her and not at her. She felt their pride in her for trying to save herself and could tell that Chai was probably embellishing the story for laughs, which she appreciated.

At that moment, her decision crystallized. Suda was determined to stay, not just in San Francisco, but at Hope House, working in the bakery. She felt content—which was a new emotion for her.

Grace had found a therapist for Suda who spoke both Thai and English and smuggled her—hat on head, large, dark sunglasses on her face—twice a week to an office on the other side of San Francisco. It was part of the program, she had Nittha explain. All the young women at Hope House did therapy. Nittha had started by explaining what a therapist was, but Suda still found the concept odd. She was supposed to tell someone she didn't know about her feelings of humiliation and describe the pain she had gone through. Why would she do that?

Her therapist told her that she would need to deal with the losses she'd encountered in life in order to heal, but for now, Suda preferred to simply live in the present. She did like the car ride both ways, though. It was interesting to see a little bit of the city where she had landed. The buildings were so tall, and people of all different colors walked the sidewalks. She could see businesses and trees. The buildings looked different from the buildings in Chiang Rai. They were taller, bigger, imposing.

Suda's therapist told her that a transition from fear, real fear as she had experienced, took a long time. The woman added that it made sense that it would take time for Suda to trust her, so, for now, they would just spend time together. That seemed odd to Suda. Drive to see a stranger and spend time together to build trust so that someday, if she wanted to, she could talk to her? Americans were confusing sometimes, but she did like them.

Instead of talking about her trauma, Suda asked her how to say different words in English. At least that was helping her, she thought, even if it wasn't in the way Grace and Simone expected it to. Learning English was difficult, and it was slow going, but she was determined. The linguistic sounds were very different from what she was used to, but she was curious about the name for things and that was a starting point.

She had a vision of a possible future, and she wanted to do it right. She would study English. She would become a baker so she could serve others the warm bread and muffins she had come to love. She would stay right where she was.

She was excited to learn to read. Suda noticed Claire always had a book in her hands. When Claire read, her face softened and relaxed. It made her look different, even prettier than she already was. Claire often absentmindedly twirled a strand of hair around her finger when she was lost in a book. She looked as if she didn't have a care in the world. It seemed very American to her: baking bread and reading books—perhaps because at Hope House they didn't watch television, so she had nothing to compare her sense of American culture to. But for whatever the reason, instead of longing for an expensive car or trendy clothing, Suda longed for the ability to immerse herself in a book.

Grace, Suda noticed as she continued looking around at the others seated at the table, seemed like an open book herself. She knew a bit about her story because Nittha had told her, and Grace herself had told Nittha so she could translate for her. Grace was the exact opposite of Suda, who would prefer to keep everything that had happened to her hidden. But Grace said sharing what had happened to her with others who had similar trauma was her calling. Suda had no idea what that meant, but the fact that Grace told her she'd been forced to become a prostitute did make Suda feel less alone. Less ashamed. Because Suda could see that Grace had come through it. In fact, she seemed to gain power when she talked about it, not from having been a prostitute but from the fact that she'd overcome her past. Her face became more animated, more intense, when she spoke about her time on the streets. Grace stood tall and was confident and comfortable with herself in a way Suda had never encountered.

At first Suda had difficulty getting a handle on Grace. Her messy blue hair, brash tone, and expansive hand gestures when she spoke reminded Suda of the Thai street hawkers who tried to lure her to buy their wares on market day. She even saw her throw back her head and laugh without covering her mouth once when Claire said something to her, which Suda found intriguing and strange. It was not only that she would be so exuberant but that she seemed actually happy. Joyful. But how could that have happened? It made Suda a little bit uncomfortable.

Yet in spite of that, Grace's unwavering kindness had shown Suda that she had good intentions. She wanted Suda to be safe and to heal. Suda felt her protectiveness and appreciated the way she somehow included her even with no shared language.

Suda had been shyly hiding in Simone's apartment for the better part of a week when Grace first lured her out to the shared part of the house.

"Come," Grace had said, waving her hand in a gesture Suda understood to mean that she should follow her. She led her to the kitchen, pulled out a chair, and brought Suda a cup of tea. She made Suda feel a part of the house, invited into the rhythms of the day.

Grace even laughed at herself easily if things went awry when she tried to do something new and joked with all of them about the horrors of the experiences they'd had in a way that made them seem less like victimized girls and more like humans who had gone through something difficult and survived. Grace often threw her fist into the air to show her power. Suda had tried it when she was alone but felt foolish. She was determined to keep trying though, so she could someday show her power, too.

Aanwat

A REEL OF SUDA HOPPING INTO THAT CAR replayed in Aanwat's mind as he walked back to his hotel. Had she been staying at a bakery the whole time he'd been looking for her? How did she get there, and why was she there? He wondered if she had been moved from one place to another for some reason, or whether she'd been there since she'd arrived in San Francisco. He couldn't imagine how it had happened. It was all too strange. *And who was the woman she was with? Was she in the business? Was the bakery really a brothel? Maybe it was a front.*

But his thoughts had immediately frozen when he'd opened the hotel door to find Chakrii sitting on the bed with a gun resting menacingly by his side. Aanwat's mind immediately began to spin in a new direction.

The man wasn't someone low down in the organization; he was the boss. Aanwat hadn't actually spoken to him aside from an initial introduction upon his arrival. Since then, he had seen him at the warehouse by the dock plenty of times, though he'd never dared make eye contact.

And yet here he was, sitting on the bed in Aanwat's hotel room, and he couldn't imagine that there could possibly be any positive reason for it. The man terrified Aanwat. Even Chakrii's expensive tailored suit did little to curb the man's thug look. His face was broad and flat with a long, jagged scar running down the left side. The remnant of the ragged wound made Aanwat wonder what had happened to the other guy, because surviving a gash like that could only mean that his adversary had ended up dead. He hoped the same thing wasn't about to happen to him.

He believed Chakrii didn't actually care about finding Suda, but was in his hotel room, intending to do harm to send a message to Gan. No doubt Chakrii would want to make sure Gan understood that he had to make things right for the sake of honor and the ability to do future business together.

Aanwat's chest contracted at the realization, but he didn't want to show how afraid he was. He tried to force his features into a deferential look rather than one that bespoke his fear.

"*Sawadee khrup*," Aanwat said, bowing, hands clasped, sweat immediately formed under his arms, and he felt his body tense with stifled fear.

The timing has to be a coincidence, and yet, he could hardly force himself to swallow normally, his fear somehow concentrating in the back of his throat. *He can't possibly know I saw Suda today*, Aanwat tried to assure himself. *Right?*

His palms became clammy, and he desperately wanted to wipe them on his pants but didn't dare.

He couldn't help thinking: How could it be a coincidence that Chakrii paid him a visit the very day he had found Suda? Confusion swirled through his mind. Had he been followed? Did they already know where she was and were simply toying with him to determine whether he would give them the information? Or had they stashed her there themselves, and the entire story about the storage container being empty was a lie? His thoughts began to dart to all sorts of scenarios while he worked hard to keep his face looking neutral.

Were they playing some sort of cat-and mouse-game? If so, Aanwat wasn't at all sure he was going to get out of the situation without giving Suda away.

He felt sweat soaking the underarms of his shirt and was glad his dark blue sweatshirt would hide that fact.

He doesn't know, he told himself again and looked directly into the boss's impenetrable, almost black eyes with an air of being on the same side. His sharp face was menacing, and Aanwat's breathing shallowed as he tried to hide his nervousness. After all, why would they follow him when he was supposed to be the one giving them information?

If he could stay calm, he knew his chances of getting out of the situation were better, so he forced himself to inhale deeply and smile as if he were in complete agreement with the boss. Yes, he said, the situation was ridiculous and, yes, something weird was going on. He threw out the idea of a traitor in the organization working against them because it was the first thing that came to his mind but was surprised when his boss concurred with the possibility.

"You better not be on the wrong side of this," he said, his eyes icily looking at Aanwat.

"Me? How could I be? I wasn't here when she went missing."

Aanwat's heartbeat raced, and he felt nauseated with fear.

"Humm," he responded, but Aanwat could tell that his absence from the point of Suda's disappearance didn't get him off the hook as a potential traitor.

"Are you police?" he yelled, shocking Aanwat with the abrupt change from the initial soft conversational tone he was taking.

Aanwat's face paled. "Police? No. How could I be police?"

"Undercover," he said tightly through thin lips, forcing his tone back down, giving the impression that he was barely keeping himself in check. That violence was a whisper away. Aanwat gasped when the man reached his hand into his pocket, but in place of the knife Aanwat expected, he brought out a business card. He used the edge to clean his thumbnail.

"Thai police you mean?" Aanwat asked. "No," he stammered. This had gone in an unexpected direction. Was it possible that Thai police and American police were somehow working together to catch them? His mind reeled. "No," Aanwat said again and raised his hands in surrender. He raised his eyebrows in disbelief and shook his head.

The realization came to him that telling where Suda was at this point would only make him look guilty. As if he had been holding out until he was pressured. How had this all gotten so out of control?

Abruptly the boss heaved himself off of the bed and walked to the door. He stood there for a moment, his back to Aanwat. "You better make sure you don't have anything to hide," he said then reached for the doorknob.

"I don't," Aanwat's stammered reply assured him. "You know all there is to know."

When the door closed behind him, Aanwat heaved a sigh of relief and almost fell onto the bed, his legs devoid of strength.

He hadn't cracked. And he hadn't given up Suda's location. The boss thought he was incompetent and that helped. Aanwat *felt* incompetent. Certainly he was in way over his head, and he'd found Suda only by happenstance. But, it was clear that Chakrii had no confidence in Aanwat's ability to come through, which bought him some time.

But the questions had thrown him. He'd blurted out the idea of a traitor only because it had been the first thing that had come to mind in the moment. Maybe there was something amiss, though. It would make a lot of sense. If there was a traitor, who was it? And did he also know where Suda was?

He hoped it would come to light before he was killed by either Chakrii or his next in line: a thug who always seemed to be at the warehouse when Aanwat had occasion to be there. The guy was big and looked as if he might be only half Thai. He spoke Thai with an American accent. Everyone called him Tea. He didn't know why, and there was no way he was going to ask him about his nickname. Aanwat couldn't bring himself to speak to the man directly, and he tried to avoid him entirely whenever possible. He had an American-born arrogance about him, and he deeply chilled Aanwat. He had caught a glimpse of a tattoo under his shirtsleeve one day and couldn't stop wondering what it was. A list of people he'd already killed or some symbol of it? Aanwat was sure it was something menacing and, when they had occasion to be in the same room, he found it difficult to stop staring at that little hint of what he was sure was something ominous at the base of his sleeve. The man had caught him looking at it once and given him a stare that turned him into a frozen block of fear.

What Aanwat didn't know was how much time he had left before they shot him, sent him back to Thailand, or, worse, dragged him deeper into something he wanted no part of. No matter which way it went, he understood that he was involved in an organization that was doing much more than human trafficking. He'd seen caches of packages that he believed were heroin and overheard them laughing about removing a few fingers from an "associate who was uncooperative."

Aanwat sat down on the bed and slowly unwrapped the hamburger he had bought for his dinner. It had gotten cold, and as he swallowed, each bite sat like a lump in his esophagus, barely going down with repeated swallowing, but he couldn't afford to waste money on uneaten food, so he kept chewing until he was finished and then sat on the bed thinking about how he was going to get his hands on Suda.

Claire

When darkness and loneliness are bedfellows in the night.
When the only arms we feel around us
are not to assuage our pain and fear,
but are a caress purchased and required.

Unaided and abandoned,
vulnerability is our daily nourishment.

CLAIRE TOSSED HER PEN BESIDE HER onto the bed. Writing poetry was not easy. Snippets of words—some lines coming together—were all she had. When she tried to compose full verses, the lines became fragmented and faulty. She crumpled her attempts.

Claire tucked her pen into her notebook and closed the cover. She laid on her bed, staring at the ceiling and listening to the sounds of Hope House. Things were a little more quiet than usual now that it was just Claire and

Suda, Grace and Simone living in Hope House. Hailey had moved to a less-restrictive placement the week before; in the end, Claire hadn't said a word about her discovery of the secreted pills. Now she closed her eyes and leaned her head back against the wall, the anxiety brought about by her silence weighed her down.

She opened up her notebook again and scrawled, "minimal involvement" on a line. Maybe she would try to write a poem about how to keep your sanity by not caring about other people. Claire wondered how long before some other depressed, thrashed girl showed up. It was inevitable. But for now, she kind of liked it being just the four of them. She heard the hiss of the coffee maker and the sound of Grace sliding a baking sheet into the oven and closing the door. She wondered what Grace was making for breakfast and sat up. She scrawled a few more lines of poetry before being called in to eat.

She picked up the latest novel she was reading. It was *Possession* by A. S. Byatt. *That chick can write poetry,* Claire thought. She only had thirty-eight pages to go and would soon need to check out a new stack of books from the library to quench her voracious thirst for the written word. Every other Tuesday, after her crack-of-dawn bakery shift ended, Claire gathered her stack of old reads and made the trek to the library for a new batch of novels. But for now, she was desperate to know how this one ended. The book was infused with poetry, and Claire loved the way the way the words entwined and created a miniature story within the larger story.

She realized now that the teachers she'd had who had tried to teach poetry had done a miserable job. The poems they'd used as examples had been either too obvious or too boring. Not long after she arrived at Hope House, though, she found herself doodling interesting words and phrases that came to mind on scraps of paper that she found laying around here and there, but they were hopeless and stupid. She wanted to ask Frances, her favorite librarian, to suggest a book of poetry. But Frances was off limits because Claire wasn't allowed to go to the main branch in case Nick was lurking nearby, still looking for her.

If she could be anyone, it would be Frances. She had an old-fashioned name, but she also had purple hair and an unexpectedly edgy look. No one would ever guess she was a librarian because she was vivacious and outgoing instead of the reserved stereotype people still expected. As far as Claire could tell, Frances knew more about everything under the sun than anyone else in the world. And what she didn't know, she could find. There was also the matter of the Samuel Beckett poem tattooed on her forearm:

Ever tried, ever failed.
No matter.
Try again. Fail again.
Fail better.

Claire sighed deeply. She missed the San Francisco main branch library desperately, but one of the rules of the safe house was that the women were to stay away from places they had been known to frequent in their past, which ruled out the regal building she so loved. She still sought out the stacks, but was forced to go out of the city, just to be extra safe. Or sometimes, in a pinch, she would furtively slip into the library at the Mechanics Institute, but that was smack dab in the middle of downtown, which always brought back bad memories.

Truth be told, she checked over her shoulder constantly whenever she was away from Hope House because the fear of running into Nick made her blood run cold. Whenever she did have occasion to leave the safe haven of the bakery, she—unbeknownst to Simone and Grace—slipped a switchblade she'd procured with some tip jar funds into her pocket. She had decided that if she ever was grabbed, she sure wasn't going to allow herself to be taken again. She'd rather die fighting than end up under his thumb again. When it happened the first time, she didn't have the wherewithal to fight back, but she did now.

The days after Claire learned of her mom's death had passed in a blur of grief and disbelief. Her friends and the school had been told she was sick with a bad flu and would be out for a few days.

Nick constantly hovered: making her breakfast, assuring her that everything would be okay. She was wary and watchful. Nick didn't go to work those first days, and she was left alone only when he went to the store to get all of her favorite food. He cooked and cleaned while she existed in an almost fugue state: her eyes turned inward to her sense of loss to a point of feeling cut off from her surroundings. It wasn't that she was surprised that this had happened. Hadn't she always kind of known it would? But it was the finality of it. It was the loss of hope. It was fear at a new level. Now it wasn't just wondering whether there would be enough food, or whether her mother would be passed out on the couch, but the fear of the absolute unknown. What was going to happen now?

She wanted to go back to school. She craved normalcy. Nick agreed that it was all right for her to go, but she was forbidden from telling anyone what had happened. It wouldn't be difficult to deceive her friends about it, even though her heart cried out to confide everything. After all, they had never met her mom because Claire always had been afraid of letting them see how they were living. To a certain extent, they had never truly known her because of it. She was embarrassed and always had been. Her life was not like life was in books. It was not like life was supposed to be. She had never been loved the way her friends had.

She put on her favorite clothes for her first day back to school. Her jeans were soft with pre-purchased holes and her designer tee-shirt had been found at a secondhand shop.

"Hey," her friend Kate found her at her locker. "Are you feeling better?"

"Yeah," she slipped into an easy lie. She tucked a long strand of hair behind her ear, feigning preoccupation so she didn't have to meet Kate's eyes.

"God, it's so unfair. You're skinnier than ever! I wish I had gotten the flu instead of you."

"Trust me," Claire felt her eyes threaten to well up and immediately swallowed her emotion. "You wouldn't have wanted this. It . . . it sucked. Really bad."

"Still, look at you. More beautiful than ever. Ugh!"

"Shut up, Kate," she said more harshly than intended. "Stuff like that doesn't matter." Then to soften the effect of her tone, she closed her locker, linked arms with her friend, and walked with her to their algebra class. "Sorry."

"You're such a bitch sometimes," Kate said.

"I know. I don't mean to be." She bumped her hip against Kate's to show that she regretted her harsh tone and even pretended to be interested in the school dish that had happened while she'd been at home.

Every day it was the same: go to school and then the library for homework and escape; feign happiness; pretend to have a normal life; go home to Nick, who had taken over her mom's room at the apartment. At home, he cooked dinner and continued to offer her wine every night, but she continued to eschew the offer with a vague and ongoing sense of heightened wariness. They would make awkward conversation until she could escape to her room. Then she would do it all again the next day.

Her teachers thought she was a superstar. She was getting straight As. The kids at school envied her because she was beautiful and had an aloofness that made them want her attention but was in fact a profound need for self-preservation. Yet, because of both her surprising beauty and her fierce intellect, there was a piqued sense of intrigue around her no matter how much she tried to imitate normalcy.

She said "Yes" to every sleepover or dinner invitation possible, grabbing any excuse to stay out of the apartment. Nick seemed increasingly off. Agitated. Nervous. His hair was occasionally greasy, and he was getting too thin. There was something not right, but she was too afraid to tell a soul about it. If she was sent away, she would lose even the last memories of her mom and her former life because they felt contained within the apartment, which they'd had her entire life. It was home, even though it was a messed-up version of it.

"How old are you these days, Claire?" Nick asked her one evening over dinner.

She looked up from the piece of chicken she was cutting. "Fourteen. Why?"

"When's your birthday?"

"Not for months." She answered, for some weird reason not wanting him to know the actual date.

"You're really becoming the spitting image of your mother."

"Yeah, you've told me that."

"I loved her very much, you know."

She didn't know what to say, so she just looked at her plate.

"She helped me out sometimes."

She looked up at him. Put a bite in her mouth so there was no need to respond.

"She was great. You could be, too." His tone was off-hand. Like it would be something nice for her.

Then her natural curiosity got the better of her. She had wondered many nights what the two of them were up to when they were out.

"How did she help you?"

"She entertained clients. Important clients. Helped me close deals with her charm," he said, leaning back in his chair. He pointed his fork at her. "You could do the same."

"I'm too young."

"Not at all. Besides, you look older than you are."

"Yeah, well. I have to go to school, so I can't be staying out late like the two of you did. And," she paused, "I don't want to."

"You seem a bit unappreciative, Claire. I'm here supporting you. Looking after you. Paying the rent. And what are you doing in return?"

Claire's heart had begun to beat rapidly. She had no idea how to respond.

"Just think about it, beautiful girl." Nick said. "That's all I ask."

Claire let out a sigh of relief when he got up and took his dish to the kitchen.

"I can help out more around the apartment," she called to him. "I'll clean the kitchen tonight."

"That'll be a start," he said curtly, then sat down with his computer and began rapidly typing.

She quickly finished her dinner, cleared the dishes, and then scrubbed the kitchen until even the old, cracked tile looked better than it had in years. But she knew. Deep in her heart, she understood that cleaning wasn't going to be the end of it.

Aanwat

TO GET SUDA, AANWAT NEEDED A GUN, which he didn't have because there had been no way to get one through airport security, and he hadn't wanted to admit to Chakrii that he didn't have one when he'd arrived. But his plan depended on it. The question was where to get one. His best guess was that he could get one through Tea, but he was too afraid to approach the guy because he seemed like the kind of guy who would like to kill him just for sport. He would try one of the others and hope for the best.

He had spent the better part of a week trying to see Suda, and while he never got a good look at her through the window, he could see someone her size with long bleached hair, and he believed it had to be her.

Once he decided where they should end up, he would make a plan to get them there, but that was a problem he would worry about once he had her. He wanted it to be somewhere warm, though. He was tired of the cold wind. But, first things first: he had to get her to the motel. He'd need a car as well as a gun. That meant he would have to steal one.

When he'd first started working at the karaoke, he'd felt a small internal thrill at the fact that there had been a gun tucked out of sight behind the bar. It gave him a sense of power, and he sometimes liked to hold it when everyone had gone for the night. But he had never had to use it. Now he felt he was becoming an entirely different person. He not only had to buy a gun of his own, but he also had to steal a car somehow—like some degenerate. His life had taken more of a turn than he had imagined when Gan had approached him with a proposition to make a bit of extra money.

He sat on the bed and put his head in his hands, palms pressed against his eyes. His tormented thoughts were tearing him in two. He wanted out, not further in. But sometimes the temptation was there. If he wanted to get in good with Chakrii, he could now. He could tell him he'd just found Suda, and he could stay here and become part of the organization instead of going home. He could have more money than he ever dreamed of. And some *other* girl. He told himself that he could forget about Suda if he had to. But he knew that wasn't true because her face was permanently stuck inside his mind.

He took out his wallet as well as the money he had stashed under a corner of the rug he'd pulled up in the closet and counted out the bills he had. It totaled almost $2,000. Surely that would last them long enough if he was careful. He'd have Suda. They would make do. He paused, thinking. He hesitated to contemplate it, but it came to him unbidden: if worst came to worst, he could arrange for Suda to make a little side money for them. He shoved that thought away. No, he wouldn't do that. Still, they had to eat, and she was used to it. He hated to think of her with other men, but . . . He sighed. It was a backup plan.

"Stop being weak," he almost growled, yet he stared out the window and chewed on his bottom lip.

Chai

THE FACT THAT HIS TRUE APARTMENT—rather than his current undercover hovel—was in the same neighborhood as Simone and the Hope House was one of his favorite coincidences. It was a quick, easy walk along the park from his apartment on Fulton Street to the bakery. He liked the neighborhood because to him it felt almost suburban with kids walking hand-in-hand with their parents on the way to school, no high-rises, more houses instead of apartments. It was almost quaint. And with Golden Gate Park across the street, he felt connected to green spaces when he needed a break from city life.

So stopping into Hope Bakery in the morning had become the best part of his day. If Simone had time to join him for a quick coffee, it was even better. He loved the normalcy of it before he had to head back to his hated undercover apartment where he worked out and had associates stop by for one reason or another to keep up appearances. It was all part of his immersion into his work.

"You look tired," Simone said, when she brought coffee and a fresh scone and grabbed a chair at his table for a few minutes.

"I am. It was a late night. You don't want to know." Elbow on the table, head in hand.

"It must be hard." She had been wondering how he could stand being among those men every day at all hours.

"It's the job."

"Is it hard going to church on Sunday then pretending to pimp girls on Monday?"

"I don't know whether it's any more difficult than for anyone with a strong moral compass, but I can tell you that what I personally find the most difficult is the normalizing of what happens. At first the language, the topics of conversation, the actions of the people on the inside was so shocking. Seriously sordid."

"And now?"

"When business decisions are made about people in the organization or about moving drugs to evade the police, I sometimes shrug my shoulders and think, 'Smart move.' Like we're just playing chess or something. I'm part of it even though it's to try to stop it."

"Do you ever feel as if it's breaking you?"

Chai snorted and looked out the window for a moment. "Absolutely," he sighed. "I've done stuff I never thought I would," he told her. "But not in the way you're thinking, based on the look you have on your face."

"Sorry. I would never want you to think I'm judging you."

"No, it's fine. What I mean is that it's easy not to compromise myself sexually, because there's no desire there. When I think about how these young women, girls, boys, are used, I see them only as desperate, terrified people. Certainly not people I would want to have sex with. No, the compromise is in the violence, the anger, and the words that come out of my mouth."

Simone reached across the table and rested her hand on his arm, trying to comfort him.

"I cut a man's fingers off once." He looked her in the eye, to assess how disgusted she would be by the admission.

"Did he deserve it?" She surprised him with the question.

"He was a scum and a drug-dealing pimp, but never in a million years would I have imagined I would cut off a person's fingers."

"You had to do it to keep your cover?"

"I'm ruthless, and most of my associates are terrified of me."

"Will it help in the long run?"

"God, I hope so."

"Then you did what you had to do." He looked at her, surprised at her frank attitude about it. He felt the tension in his body relax at her words. He had expected her to be repulsed by him after the admission, but he had decided he wanted to be real with her. He wanted her to know him, the entire him, not the "good guy" facade because if he'd learned one thing it was that there's both bad and good in everyone.

"When I went undercover, I decided the best way to live through it was to be someone nobody would consider messing with. So I went in hard. I rarely spoke, leered at everyone, pumped a lot of iron, and tried to be as intimidating as possible. And it worked. I seem to scare the shit out of people, even the other guys on the inside."

Simone smiled at her visualization of him. "Do you ever think of getting back out?"

"All the time." Chai paused and sighed. "Lately even more than I used to." He smiled at her.

"It's been great having you around so much. For the girls, it's a chance to see what a normal man is like."

He smiled again. "Normal man? I don't know about that anymore." He put his hands on his thighs and made a move to get up from the table. "I just want you to know who I am."

"Like I said, it's nice to have a good man around. And that's what you are."

He lifted one of her hands to his face. "Thank you for that."

She smiled at him. "You're welcome. We're all flawed. We all fall short. You can't be in the situation you're in and not have it affect you." It was strange to think of him as ruthless to those he worked with now that she'd gotten to know him.

"The normalizing I was talking about? That's what I hate. What I hear has seeped into my brain, and I don't want to be surrounded by it anymore. But then I think about getting out and that means I wouldn't be able to stop it. I wouldn't be able to help people like Suda."

"Maybe you could still help them. Just from the other side. There's never only one way. You just have to figure out what the other way is."

"Yeah, I guess so. That's something to think about," he said, crumpling up his bag and tossing it into the recycling bin. "But for now, I have to wade back in."

"I wish you didn't have to. Are you getting any closer?"

"I think I am. There are some rumblings. Something's going to happen soon. I can feel it."

"Cop's intuition?"

"You could say that."

"Will I see you tomorrow morning?"

"Absolutely. At the latest. I might even find myself free around dinnertime. If so, can I crash your dinner table?"

"Yes," Simone told him. "I've been having a hankering for pot roast, so I'll make a lot just in case."

"Say no more," he said, waved, and was out the door.

Simone

AFTER CHAI LEFT, SIMONE COULDN'T STOP thinking about him having to cut the fingers off of some guy. The thing she couldn't shake was not the horror of it but, rather, the realization that if she were in the same position, she might do it without any qualms at all. Heck, with no provocation, she might happily cut every one of Nick's fingers off if she ever encountered him after what he had done to Claire. His fingers and thumbs, too, just for good measure.

She sighed and tidied up the sugar and creamer area of the bakery before another wave of customers came in. She knew she should pray for the predators, but it was hard to have compassion for them. And frankly, she wanted them to be punished. No matter how hard she tried to pray for Nick or Hailey's "boyfriend" Dante, or other of the men who had hurt the women she had worked so hard to help, she just couldn't do it. When she tried, she usually ended up praying that God would kill them in some terrible way, and she was pretty sure that wasn't God's intention for prayer.

"Hey," Grace walked in from the back, catching Simone staring out the window at the passersby instead of her usual full-speed-ahead *modus operandi*. "You look deep in thought."

"I was thinking about cutting the fingers off of some of the dirtbags who hurt women."

"So, nice light pondering on a lazy afternoon?" Grace smiled at her fierce friend.

"Exactly," Simone concurred. "Actually, that's where I started, but then I found myself debating whether I should pray for them instead, which I often think about, but I just can't do it. When I try, it feels forced and disingenuous."

"I get it," Grace rubbed her shoulder. "Believe me."

"Sorry. I know it must be much harder for you."

"Yeah, well, I've devised a work around," Grace told her.

"Of course you have."

"I just pray that someone *else* will pray for them."

"I love that. You're a genius," Simone hugged Grace.

"Glad to be of service. Hey," she said, changing the subject, "Have you tried actually talking to Suda lately? She's learned so many English words. I'm pretty impressed. She clearly has some serious smarts to pick it up so quickly."

"Yes!" Simone laughed with delight. "I actually heard her say, 'Shut up, Claire!' this morning, with her heavy Thai accent. It was hilarious. You should have seen Claire's face. She was so surprised. And I think a little bit impressed, too. There's a sweet bond happening between them."

"Which you're surmising from Suda telling Claire to shut up?"

"I don't think Suda realized it was rude. She was just saying what Claire says to everyone."

"I think Suda's innate good nature is rubbing off on Claire a bit. She realizes that Suda went through something horrific, even if she doesn't know the exact details, and sees that if someone can go through what Suda did and still come out with a positive view of life maybe she can, too."

"I think you're right," Simone concurred.

"Healing is creeping up on her."

"I think it is. Have you noticed that Claire has been dropping fewer F-bombs and smiling more?"

"Yes!"

"This is why we do what we do."

"You know it, Sista."

"Well, I've got to run to the grocery store. I'm going to make pot roast for dinner. It's feeling like fall, and that always triggers my taste buds to crave pot roast. Chai might join us."

"I've noticed he's been doing that a lot."

"Yeah, I think he likes being here. It's a good counter-balance to his day job, so to speak."

"You think that's it?" Grace asked, one eyebrow raised.

"Yeah, I think that's it. Or as our articulate young ladies have taken to saying: 'Shut up, Grace.'"

Simone, head down and list in hand, went through the front door and almost ran into the same man she had helped a few days before. The slight, suspicious one, whom she suspected was Thai. She internally yelled at herself because she had meant to tell Chai about him, but somehow always found herself distracted when he was around.

"Sorry," she said, quickly sidestepping him so they wouldn't collide.

Still, he was a customer, so she smiled at him and held the door open so he could go inside. Instead of leaving as she had intended to do, she turned back around and followed him into the bakery. She sat at a small table, got out her shopping list, and pretended to add something she'd forgotten—feigning complete absorption in her task. She then got out her phone and casually took a photo of him while he stood at the counter. It wasn't a good shot. It didn't get his full face, but at least she had a record of him now.

At the counter, Claire was already feeling that this guy was taking too much time. She preferred customers to come in, order, and get out. But this guy was in no hurry and continued to look around as if to memorize his surroundings.

"Can I help you?" Claire tried to keep her voice upbeat as Grace had instructed her.

"Yes," he said with a heavy accent she now recognized. "Tea," he said pointing to the medium-size paper cup.

"Coming right up," Claire said grabbing the wooden box filled with little cubbies of tea bags. "Breakfast tea, herbal tea, Thai tea?"

"Thai tea."

"Are you here on vacation?" she asked, attempting to be gracious.

He shook his head.

"Visiting?" palms up, she moved her hand and arm in a gesture to indicate the area around them.

"Yes," he said.

While the tea steeped, Claire caught Simone's eye and raised her eyebrows. Simone had an intent look on her face. Did she think something was up? The guy continued to look around until Claire handed him the cup. He passed her a few bills, gave one more look over his shoulder, and then left.

Claire

WHEN THE BAKERY SLOWED DOWN later that day, Claire's mind drifted to the past, as happened all too often when she didn't keep her thoughts occupied with a book.

Nick had waited until she was in high school, acting the chivalrous gentleman instead of the disgusting pimp he turned out to be. By then, she'd finally begun to trust him. He'd been good on his word for more than six months and her fifteenth birthday had come and gone. He had stayed at the apartment, cooked her dinner, provided. Yes, he'd ask her to help him out with clients more than once, but had always accepted her answer of "No."

She'd begun to believe that diligently cleaning the apartment and doing the dishes after dinner was earning her keep. Now, she snorted with self-derision at the thought. No, her keep had cost her much more than chores. She wearily rubbed her eyes and allowed her thoughts to come.

Her cheeks still burned with humiliation when she remembered. She had woken up, completely naked in a hotel room with a man. She saw one of her mother's favorite dresses strewn across a chair. *Was she there?* She jumped out of bed, ran into the bathroom—woozily— and vomited into the toilet.

"Mom?" She shakily called. Had Nick been deceiving her this entire time? Was her mother alive? Was she in the hotel?

"Mom?" she called again.

"Shut up!" a deep voice called from the bedroom.

She crouched, terrified, behind the bathroom door.

Whose voice was that? Was it a friend of her mother's? Her head hurt and swam with nausea. Was she alive? What was happening?

She had no idea how she had gotten there. Her last memory was of eating street tacos with Nick at the dinner table. He'd brought them home from her favorite taco shop in the Mission. He knew she loved them, and she'd been excited when she'd seen the bag in his hand. Carnitas! They had both dove in with relish.

Thinking back, she should have known he was up to something. He had been in such a good mood. They'd even laughed together at some joke or another.

She started crying in earnest. She reached her arm out and slid a towel off the rack and wrapped herself in it. It was white and starchy and smelled like hotel.

She was frozen in place and shivering behind the door, but she couldn't bring herself to move. She didn't know how long she'd been crying in the hotel's bathroom before Nick arrived.

"Sweetheart, sweetheart," he'd soothingly intoned through the door. "There's no reason to be scared. You were having fun; remember?"

"What are you talking about? Where am I? Where's Mom?" Claire threw open the door and stood there in a towel, tear streaked and smelling of vomit.

"Your mom? What do you mean? She's not here. She's dead; remember?"

"I saw her dress. She's here. I know she is."

"That's not her dress anymore. It's yours. You put it on last night. It looks great on you by the way. Even better than it did on her."

"What are you talking about? I don't know what's happening. I woke up here. Where are *my* clothes? What happened?"

"How could you *not* remember? We had a party. You, me, and my boy Ian over there. He nodded to the man sprawled on the bed snoring obliviously.

"I'm calling the police!" she moved toward the phone.

Nick grabbed her arm. "No, you're not," he said. His mouth was smiling, but his eyes were hard. "Because nothing happened here that you didn't want. Remember? We started with tacos, moved on to margaritas, and then finally you begged me for a roofie. Just a little fun, beautiful girl. You said you wanted to forget."

"No, that's not what happened. I wouldn't drink and do drugs. I would never do that."

"Never say *never*, because clearly you *did*, and no one would believe otherwise."

"Of course people would believe me. Why wouldn't they?"

"Oh, you're wrong there, sweetheart. A picture's worth a thousand words. I will humiliate you. I will tell all the little girls you hang out with at that precious school of yours. You think you're their friend? How quickly do you think they'll drop you once they know what you've been up to?"

Claire suddenly had a vision of herself dancing around their living room laughing and Nick holding her up when she stumbled. But when was that? Had he drugged her first? Had he put something in the tacos or in the diet Coke he brought her? That's the only explanation she could think of.

"Did you *drug* me?" she asked, her voice small, stunned, and hurt. The betrayal pierced deeply.

Her mind flashed on the way he'd been looking at her recently.

"You disgusting creep!" Claire hissed.

Nick laughed. "That's all you've got? Wow, Claire, I'm scared."

The violation of her very core made her feel like screaming, but something in his eyes stopped her.

"Did you *drug* me?" Nick repeated her question in a falsetto singsong voice, imitating her. He looked her square in the face. "I gave you what you wanted. And believe me, you wanted it."

"But I didn't."

"Clearly you did, or we wouldn't be here right now."

"Did you put something in my food?" Her tone slipped from confused to accusatory.

"Claire. Sweetheart. Stop saying I drugged you. I didn't. We had tacos. I was drinking a margarita, and you asked for a sip. You loved it. You wanted your own, remember?"

A flash of asking for a drink raced through her mind. Had that happened? Was he right?

"I want to go home." She started crying in earnest. "I . . . what time is it? I have school today. I have a biology test."

"Always studious," Nick laughed. "Fine. I'll get you home, but it's already almost 11:00, so you've probably missed it."

"You said you'd take care of me. Not . . . not . . ."

She looked around the room. It smelled, and there was a disgusting passed out naked man in the bed. Nick looked wrecked and her body was sore in all the wrong places. The situation really sunk in and another sob escaped.

"Nothing happened to you that you didn't want. Come on, Claire. Don't be a child. You knew what was going on. And I have taken care of you, just like I always said I would. And you helped. You charmed a client, just like I knew you would."

Claire shakily put her mother's dress back on. It hung loosely on her thin frame. She had no idea where her underwear was. She just wanted out. She wanted to be home. Immediately. Now.

Nick grabbed his phone and called for a Lyft. He smiled at her as if there was no problem in the world they couldn't handle together.

Claire wrapped her arms protectively around herself. She walked out of the hotel room, and into the elevator without looking back. When they reached the outside, the cold fog whipped through the thin dress, and the fact that she had no coat made her teeth immediately begin to chatter.

"Hey, there. Are you okay?" the doorman asked her.

"She's fine." Nick answered for her as he followed her out into the morning. Then he opened the door to the waiting car, and she slid inside averting her eyes.

They rode home in silence. All Claire wanted was a shower, and the second she walked into the apartment, she went straight into the bathroom, locked the door, and started running hot water. The sound drowned out the crying that she didn't even attempt to contain.

She made it to the sanctuary of school just as the bell rang to signal the end of lunch, and students began filing back into the halls for afternoon classes. She walked into the attendance office, wan looking, wet hair thrown into a bun on top of her head.

"Overslept," was all she managed to say to the secretary, not able to meet her eye.

She smiled and winked at Claire. "Any other student, and I'd be sure it was a cut, but for you, one of our star pupils, I'll just give you a hall pass, no questions asked."

Claire wanted to scream. "Do ask. Please ask." But what came out was a mumbled, "Thanks."

All she could see was herself, naked in a hotel room, and that man. She shook her head in attempt to clear the vision, but it wouldn't leave.

"Hey!" Kate spied Claire getting her books out of her locker. "Where have you been? You look like a drowned rat!"

"Overslept," Claire said and then turned to her friend and hugged her tightly, trying to control her emotions.

"Um," Kate pulled back. "You all right?" She furrowed her brow taking in her friend.

"I'm fine," Claire said, realizing she would never be able to bring herself to tell Kate what had happened. She would sooner jump off a cliff than speak the words aloud. She slammed her locker and turned away.

"Wait!" Kate called after her, grabbing her books and trying to catch up, but Claire rounded the corner and practically sprinted all the way to Biology, leaving Kate standing confused in the school's hallway.

The door to Hope Bakery chimed, and a customer interrupted Claire's memory.

"Hi." She forced her face into a smile. "Can I get you a coffee?"

Suda

GRACE PULLED HER BATTERED OLD blue Honda Accord up to the side street by Hope Bakery's back door, and Suda—San Francisco Giants baseball cap pulled low on her forehead—dashed for the passenger door, although she was convinced she'd never be recognized. Not with the bleached hair and glasses. Still, the thought of being caught sent shivers through her body. She would try to kill herself, she had decided, if they ever got to her, because she didn't want to live through being trafficked again. She had been made to do things she hated to even think about and had been beaten so many times she shuddered at the memory.

Grace told her to crouch low in the seat, but Suda was already slumped so low only her eyes and baseball cap were visible through the window. Still, she was able to watch the city go by as they made their way to her therapist's office.

She wished she could tell Grace how much she liked looking at the buildings. It was incredibly different from the Thailand she knew, having never been to a big city. She liked the brightly painted homes with all their fancy shingles and intricate colors. And the hills were so steep. Her village had steep hills. She tried to visualize them covered in buildings like these and couldn't manage it.

She sometimes held her breath as the car zoomed up the hills and crested the tops. There was that brief moment where the street below was no longer visible, and it always turned her stomach for a second or two. The buses were loud and huge! It was difficult to understand how they were able to move on the electricity that ran through the wires rather than on regular engines.

It seemed to her that they could use some *songthaews* and *tuk tuks* here to get around more easily, though. And more scooters. Here it was cars, cars, cars.

She wondered if she could become a new person here. If maybe someday she could forget her past. Forget the pain, forget the humiliation, forget the sadness and longing. She sighed visualizing her mother and baby sister's faces. She wondered if forgetting her past even with its pain would be worth losing the rest. She would never know, she reminded herself, because she could never forget anyway.

And where were the brothels in this city? She didn't see signs of any, but there were always brothels.

Once they arrived, Grace pulled out her phone to check texts and pass time in the waiting room while Suda ventured into her therapist's office and sat on the smooth brown leather couch. The couch was deep, so she had to scoot back and tuck up her legs beneath her, otherwise her feet wouldn't touch the floor, which made her feel like a small child. The walls were painted a creamy white and were decorated with photographs of Thailand's lush mountains, which helped put Suda at ease. She breathed in the sight, feeling homesick for her childhood village and aching to be there, and at the same time relieved and deeply grateful to be safely away from so much hurt.

Suda guessed that her therapist was in her thirties, but her age didn't matter. It was the fact that she had been born and raised in Thailand and then came to the United States for college and never went back that Suda found interesting. Although the therapist was from Bangkok rather than the hill country, Suda liked the fact that she understood Thai culture and spoke her language. She understood, on a different level than Simone and Grace could, all the cultural subtleties Suda didn't even think about that defined her worldview. At the same time, her therapist created a bridge to her life here in San Francisco, where so much was different and strange.

During Suda's visits, the therapist was gradually trying to draw Suda out of her shell. She asked her to describe her childhood in Thailand. Immediately visions of it swam before Suda's closed eyes. For her, there were two distinct parts of her life: *before* and *after*.

Before was when her parents were alive and she was allowed to roam free as long as she remained in her village. The hills were covered with abundant green vegetation and dirt the color of redwood. She could almost feel the hot, humid air filling her lungs and the moist ground under her feet as her mind wandered back.

When she was small, they often still wore traditional dress. She loved the brightly colored clothing. Even the headdress that sometimes felt scratchy in the heat gave her a feeling of belonging. She was part of her people. Her parents loved each other, which at the time seemed normal, but as she grew, she learned that they had been an exception rather than the rule.

It was true that her brother was favored, but to her that was of no consequence because he was good to her. He usually looked out for her. Once they were old enough, they helped harvest the coffee beans together.

There had always been enough rice and eggs to fill her tummy. The corrugated steel roof seemed sturdy enough and kept them dry. When the rain fell, it made melodious pitter-patterings against the steel like a song.

She loved to listen to it as she drifted off to sleep on rainy nights with her mother's arm tucked tightly around her. Eyes closed, she breathed in deeply, remembering. She couldn't imagine ever feeling that kind of safety and contentment again.

She shivered, connecting the memory of rain to her lowest moment in the shipping container during a storm at sea: she had wept bitterly as the rain fell because the sound of the drops against her steel prison was almost the same as the rain sound of her childhood that was so completely lost. The storm had been a beautiful reminder, a haunting memory, and the sound of loss.

But that was not what she contemplated as she recounted her early life.

When she and her brother, Asnee, had reached school age, there was little money for shoes and a uniform, so they went barefoot, which was fine with her until she reached the school room and discovered the other students wore shoes. It was up to each family to equip the student with school supplies, but coming up with paper and a pencil had been difficult. What they had on hand became a point of competition between Suda and her brother, with her brother more often than not winning out. She used the cast-off pencil nubs when she could and begged or borrowed them when there were none to be found because being caught without a pencil at school meant a smack on the forearm or the backs of the legs from a ruler at the teacher's hand. She loved learning, though, and an occasional welt was worth it to her to be there with the other kids.

Suda paused in recounting her tale, and the therapist gently nudged her forward with a simple, "And then what?"

"When I was about to start school, my mother became pregnant. She was surprised and seemed happy. There was a beautiful lightness about her that I will always remember." Suda's face held a melancholy softness as she thought about her mother then. Her lovely wide cheekbones and smiling eyes.

"They drowned when I was about ten years old," she said softly. "My parents. As well as my little sister, Ploy."

"What happened? Can you tell me?"

"There's water at the bottom of our village. It looks like a small lake, winding between jutting mountains. It's beautiful. We loved to play in it during the dry season when it's safe."

Suda looked out the window, as if she could see the water just beyond.

"We had to be careful because the rains sometimes come on suddenly."

"Yes, they do."

"They were in the valley, at a low point, harvesting coffee berries. It started pouring rain. The storm caught us all off guard. It came earlier than expected that year."

Suda's voice was expressionless in the quiet.

"The water made a muddy river. The hill washed out, and they tried to climb up a steep slope to get back up, but my sister slipped and started to be washed away in the torrent. My parents both jumped down after her—they tried to save her—but none of them came home. That's all I know. They drowned on a regular, nothing-special Thursday while my brother and I were at school."

Suda looked back at her therapist and then went on.

"My aunt took us in, but it was difficult. She already had three small boys and our uncle, my mother's brother, had died a couple of years earlier. She did her best for a few years. We helped in the fields, but once I got older, she realized that she could make some money from me." She shrugged. "Sometimes we had to skip a day of eating when there was nothing. So, feeding two more . . . after a while that was just too much for her, I think."

"Mmmm," the therapist nodded and made a noise that could be either soothing or prompting.

"I don't really blame my aunt. It's hard to be hungry. To watch your children getting skinnier and then try to stretch the meager amount you have across two more people. So, instead of a burden, I became an asset."

"You speak about it in such a detached way. What she did to you was not okay. What happened to you is wrong. You are a worthy person with a right to safety and to have your basic human needs met." Her therapist looked into her eyes with a tender expression.

"I appreciate you saying that. But, *my* life made it so that my brother didn't starve. My aunt and cousins didn't go hungry. Now I have no idea what's happening to them. Aren't they worthy, too?" An image of her brother's face with his lopsided grin and chipped front tooth appeared unbidden in her mind. She wondered what he looked like now.

"Of course. Everybody is, but not at the expense of another. Do you understand?"

"Maybe. I'm not sure. Family is important. They got money for me."

"Yes, but you are *not* an *asset*. People are not *things*, Suda; you were treated like one, but you are not one."

It's nice to think so, Suda sighed, but she was undecided about what was true. Her body had come to feel like just a *thing* while she was in the karaoke. She had detached it from her mind as much as possible. After a while, she hadn't felt like a full human anymore anyway. She had hated her life, but at least she knew she was keeping her brother alive. Now she wasn't sure what would happen to him.

Chai

CHAI FELT SURE THAT LITTLE SHIT AANWAT was up to
something. He had been acting extra nervous and eva-
sive lately. The guy had been looking for Suda since his
arrival, but Chai had noticed a change in his demeanor
over the last few days, which worried him more than a
little bit. What was he up to?

Chai knew Aanwat had checked all the massage parlors and nail salons posing as a concerned relative looking for Suda. Seeing him strike out day after day while
Chai knew Suda's exact location was gratifying.

Chai had caught a lucky break the day Aanwat
walked into the warehouse with one of the thugs he was
working for. He was introduced as the man looking for
Suda, and it took everything in Chai's power to stifle his

smile. His job was much easier once he was officially acquainted with Suda's stalker. As the days had turned to weeks and the weeks into months, he'd watched Aanwat become desperate.

He enjoyed occasionally turning the screws on Aanwat by questioning him about where he had been and how he was going to go about finding her, while simultaneously glaring at him and cleaning his fingernails with the tip of a switchblade to instill an extra dose of fear deep in his mind. Chai knew Aanwat was terrified of him, and that was how he wanted it.

Oddly, Aanwat sometimes spoke of her in a tone that appeared truly concerned rather than simply annoyed that he had to track her down. The guy seemed to worry about Suda beyond wanting to find her to save his own hide, which was of interest to Chai. Did they have a relationship beyond what he knew? He made a note to ask Suda about him again. Was there a weakness there? Maybe he could exploit that to get more information.

Aanwat's boss, Gan, was on the hook and had to come up with Suda to make good on his promised delivery, but Aanwat, although he tried to hide it, sometimes seemed genuinely worried, which made Chai clench his jaw at the hypocrisy. After all, he was the one who had put her in the shipping container in the first place. And, as he understood it, it was Aanwat who had also been pimping her out every night back in Thailand. But now he was worried? Chai seethed at the thought. As if being cold and alone outside in the night could possibly be worse than being forced to have sex with strangers and getting beaten up on a regular basis. He was constantly amazed by people's capacity for contradiction. Like when killers begged for their own lives. He shook his head and fumed.

He would have the opportunity to observe him more closely and possibly question him because they would both be at a meeting at the storage facility by the docks, where they kept the drugs smuggled in and out of the area.

When he walked in, he saw most of the guys were already there, sorting and weighing the most recent shipment. He saw Aanwat right away, sitting alone at a table, looking nervous. He had finally gotten himself a jacket, Chai noted, after shivering in the cold for weeks. It was shabby but warm looking; probably something he'd picked up at the Goodwill or Salvation Army. Chai couldn't get a good read on the guy. He seemed both shifty and earnest, which was a weird combination.

"Hey, man," Chai said to him in Thai and sat down in the chair next to him. "How's it going?"

"It's like she disappeared into thin air," Aanwat said, looking at the table between them rather at Chai's face.

"She's got to be somewhere."

"Or dead."

"Yeah, maybe she's dead." Chai agreed.

"Hey," Aanwat leaned close to Chai. "I need a gun. Can you get a gun for me?"

Chai kept his face impassive and gave him a hard stare until Aanwat started shifting in his chair. "Why do you want a gun?"

"I'm staying in a dangerous area. It makes me nervous."

"Hmmm," Chai made a noncommittal sound while he took a moment to think.

"So?"

"So what?" he stalled.

"Can you get a gun for me?"

"Yeah, man. I can. It'll take some time though. To get something that can't be traced. Give me a few days."

He saw Aanwat visibly relax into his chair.

"Great. Thanks."

"You'll just have to keep dodging the thugs in your neighborhood until then," he said, deadpan.

Aanwat looked at him, confused as to whether he was joking. "Yes," he finally said.

When Chakrii came in, everyone abruptly stopped talking. Chai had to look down for a moment to compose his face. It was difficult to hide his hatred of this guy. He was scum, and he could have arrested him ten times over by now, he was so sloppy with his business. But he wasn't who Chai really wanted. He still hadn't met the guy the police force was desperate to nail. He didn't even know his actual name. Everyone referred to him as "Clean" because the police could never pin anything on him, and he was notorious for immaculately clean crime scenes from his earlier days, when he was an enforcer working his way up.

He had been casually asking about him for months, but no one was giving out even the smallest detail. It was driving Chai crazy. If he could get some strong evidence on *that* guy, he could get out of his undercover duty, but until then, he was determined to keep poking away, trying to keep the trust of the guys while not compromising himself too much. It was a thin, high tightrope.

Chai's mind was spinning during the meeting. He couldn't stop wondering why Aanwat wanted a gun. He also couldn't decide whether to mention the fact that he was trying to get his hands on one to Chakrii. He didn't want to get the guy killed. He was a shifty little weasel, but he didn't want him dead. As usual Chai kept mostly quiet during the meeting. He sat with his arms crossed and a stony expression on his face and listened to the plans to move the product all the while trying not to think about Simone and the pot roast she would be cooking.

He barely made dinner that night, but he had been determined to get there on time while still meticulously covering his tracks. It had been difficult to break away, and he went by the apartment he had as a cover directly from the meeting. The thought of any of them getting hurt because of his sloppiness was something he couldn't even allow himself to contemplate. He believed his cover was intact, but undercover cops could never be entirely sure. He opened a beer in front of the window, to insure anyone who was looking would get a clear view of him settling in for the night. It was all he could do not to chug it down and head to Hope House, but instead he calmly and deliberately stood and sipped his beer, then closed his blinds as it became dark, then slipped out the back door.

The smell of pot roast hit him as soon as he walked in, and the homey smell alone seemed to help relieve the tension in his neck.

Simone

SIMONE NOTICED THAT CHAI SEEMED less boisterous
than usual during dinner—although he still managed to
devour a surprising amount of pot roast. He was usually
the first one to crack jokes and entertain the group with
anecdotes about growing up with a dad who was Thai
and an American mom and the funny cultural misunder-
standings that happened along the way. Simone noticed
that he had a way of turning everyday occurrences into
humorous stories. It kept them all laughing, and it was
a nice change for the girls, helping them get out of their
own heads for a while. She smiled, thinking of the story
he told them all last Sunday. It was about his father trying to make spaghetti for the kids when his mom was

out one night and using glass noodles instead of pasta. Simone was intrigued by his ability to tell a story that by any standard wouldn't be amusing, yet somehow he had them all in stitches. It was just a story about using the wrong noodles for a dish, yet the way he told it, they could see the sauce sliding off of the glass noodles and puddling on the plates and Chai and Nittha trying to politely choke it down so their dad didn't know he'd made a mistake.

After dinner, Simone and Claire were on dish duty, so Chai grabbed a dish towel and started drying the larger pots and pans they'd sudsed by hand rather than putting them in the dishwasher.

Simone's petite frame contrasted with Claire's tall, lanky one. Simone's hair was down for a change instead of gathered into her standard utilitarian ponytail. He noticed her brown hair was shot through with streaks of gold. He spent a lot of time thinking about the spray of freckles across her nose and her light green eyes that were intelligent and always lively. She looked pretty even in jeans, a sweatshirt, and flip-flops—which she wore in spite of the fact that the fog had come in.

Claire, on the other hand, was classically beautiful; she looked as if she could have been a model with her perfect nose, light blonde hair, and big blue eyes. But to Chai's eye, she wasn't as pretty as Simone. Her face had taken on a mask of wariness that made her seem unapproachable—which was probably exactly the way she wanted it, he imagined, after whatever she'd been through to end up in Hope House. Claire's face was always bare of make-up. She usually wore a baseball cap pulled low. Chai couldn't help but assume she was trying to hide her looks in an attempt to keep herself invisible. Someday she'd feel safe enough to emerge, he hoped.

He had mentioned his observation to Simone one morning over coffee, and she had looked up at him, startled. "Do you always see the layers beneath the face people present to the world?" Simone asked.

"I don't know." Chai had shrugged. "I guess. Seeing what's underneath people's exteriors is part of the training." His tone was offhand, as if truly seeing people was a common skill among undercover agents, but Simone wondered if that was true. It seemed like a unique quality in Chai, and she both liked it and felt vulnerable because of it. What was he seeing in *her* face? She wondered.

He was careful not to look at or make eye contact with any of the women in Hope House for more than a fleeting moment because he never wanted them to feel uncomfortable with his presence, think he was checking them out, or, God forbid, hitting on them. So, as usual he was just joining in on their conversation while he dried and put away the pots and pans.

As they were finishing, he asked Simone if he could grab Suda for a quick chat.

"Of course. Is anything up?"

"I don't think so. I just want to ask her about that guy she used to work with in Thailand who's here. Aanwat. I mentioned him a while ago."

"Oh, my God!" Simone almost yelled and then put out her hands as if to stop herself short. She set down the sponge and turned off the water. "I've been meaning to tell you about a guy who's been in. He was in once last week, and he was back today."

"That Thai guy?" Claire asked, suddenly thinking of the man who came in for tea earlier in the day.

"Yeah."

"What did he look like?" Chai asked.

"Slight, maybe in his twenties, kind of handsome," Claire paused, "but also, kind of shabby. Like he'd come from the school of hard knocks. You know?"

"I got a picture of him!" Simone said and ran upstairs to get her phone.

Chai pulled out a chair and sat down. While he waited for Simone to get back, he pulled out his own phone and ran his finger across the screen, searching through his photos until he found the one he wanted. He held his phone up to Claire, showing a photo he'd surreptitiously taken without Aanwat's knowledge.

"That's him!" Claire confirmed.

"Wait!" Simone interrupted. "I want to see." She peered over Chai's shoulder at the screen and gasped. "Yes, that's him. Look!" She held out her phone, and there, too, was Aanwat's photo. It wasn't as good as the one Chai had gotten, but it was undeniably the same man.

"Does he speak English?" Chai asked, cop tone in place.

"A little bit. Heavy accent," Simone answered.

"Yeah," Claire said. "I tried to chat with him but couldn't understand much."

Simone added, "He seemed nervous."

"Yes!" Claire said. "Definitely nervous. Shifty maybe."

"Fuck," Chai said, and then quickly, "Sorry . . . sorry. I didn't mean to swear. Hazard of the job."

"Don't worry about it," Simone said.

"Yeah, I say it all the time," Claire told him, and Simone shot her a look.

"What?" she asked feigning innocence to Simone's nonverbal scolding

Simone watched Chai as he ran his hands across his face. His expression was grave, and it scared her. His mind was clearly processing the information they'd just given him.

"Okay," he said after a minute. "The fact that he's been here could be just a coincidence, but that seems farfetched. The man you've just identified is in fact Aanwat Chamrueangdej."

"That's a mouthful," Claire said.

Simone looked at her with an expression that said, *Really? Now's the time to be snarky?*

"He's the one who pimped out Suda and is now here looking for her," Chai admitted.

"Oh, my God," Simone closed her eyes for a moment, attempting to gather herself in front of Claire.

"That weasel," Claire said. "I should have put poison in his tea." She crossed her arms across her chest.

Simone sat down next to Chai. "If it is him, what does that mean, practically speaking? What do we need to do? Should we move Suda?"

"I think it's time for me to involve my captain."

"Will you be in trouble?"

"Probably, but it was worth it to get Suda out of there."

"Maybe we should make a plan before you talk to Suda. I don't want to terrify her. And I don't want her to end up in a detention center for illegal immigrants while it all gets sorted out. Because, as you said, it could be a coincidence, right?" Simone asked without a speck of belief in the probability that Aanwat just happened to go to Hope Bakery to get a cup of tea.

"Here's what I'm thinking," Chai said. "I want to talk to Suda to get more information on him, but let's not mention to her anything about him coming into Hope Bakery for now."

Simone and Claire both nodded their agreement.

"But, ideally I would like one of the two of you to be up front when the bakery's open, if possible, so if he comes in again you'll recognize him. If he does, call me immediately," he paused and then added, "and 911."

"I don't have your number," Claire said and handed him her phone.

As he added his number into Claire's contacts, he casually asked, "Do you have any weapons here?"

"What? No!" Simone said.

Claire pulled the knife she kept in her pocket and flipped it open. "I carry this."

"*What?*" Simone said again, looking at Claire as if she were a complete stranger.

"Don't judge me, Simone," she said. "If I ever see Nick, I can't guarantee I won't plunge this into his heart."

Chai looked at Claire. "Okay, you and I are going to talk about that later, but for now, keep the knife handy." Then he looked at Simone. "Sorry, Simone."

"Fine," she agreed, tight-lipped. Perhaps she'd put one of her chef's knives behind the counter as well, although she hated the thought of violence and would do everything in her power to prevent it.

Just then, Simone's phone buzzed in her pocket. "When it rains, it pours," she said, pulling the phone out. She looked at the screen, frowned, and answered.

"This is Simone," she said in her professional voice, which put both Chai and Claire on alert. They stood silently while Simone listened. "Oh, no," she said and then closed her eyes. "Is she alive? Thank God." She paused and listened. "Okay, yes. Thank you. Keep us posted." She slid her phone back into her pocket and then breathed in deeply and exhaled. "I'll be right back," she told them. "I need to talk to Grace for a minute."

As Simone walked out of the room, Claire and Chai looked at each other. Both speculating, but neither saying a word.

"Be right back," Claire told Chai and then silently slunk off in the direction Simone had gone. Claire knew Simone wouldn't tell her what was going on. She was strict about "protocol" as she liked to call it, but Claire didn't like being kept in the dark. After she left Chai standing in the kitchen, she snuck farther down the hall and listened to Grace and Simone quietly talking in what they jokingly called *the office*. The small space was really a desk and several file cabinets shoved alongside the washer and dryer in the laundry room, but it served its purpose.

But when Claire heard what was being said, she backed slowly away, horrified. The whispered words were *Hailey* and *overdose*. She had done nothing to stop it.

Claire

CLAIRE WASN'T KIDDING ABOUT THE FACT that she might plunge her knife into Nick's heart if she ever saw him again. She assumed he was long gone because the police had looked high and low for him when she finally came forward, but he couldn't be found. She'd had too little information to give them. His name, Nick Sinclair, was one of hundreds in the area and might have been an alias at that. He had moved into their apartment and started paying the rent with a cashier's check rather than from a personal bank account, so the landlord didn't know it was no longer her mother paying. The landlord had probably been relieved rather than inclined to ask questions, because the rent was finally being paid on time.

She imagined Nick must be in another state now. She hoped that he wasn't doing the same thing he'd done to her to some other girl. The thought of that sometimes kept her up at night.

He didn't have a car because, according to him, the parking was too much of a pain in the ass in San Francisco, and it was easier to take public transportation. In hindsight, Claire realized it was probably so he couldn't be traced through a vehicle. They didn't have a landline, and when Claire gave the police Nick's cell number, it turned out to be to a burner phone with no phone plan.

When Claire thought back to everything that unfolded after that horrible morning when she woke up naked in a strange hotel room, she could never understand, in retrospect, why she hadn't gone to the police immediately.

She and her therapist had gone over and over it, and all she could come up with was paralyzing humiliation in the beginning, which gradually became terror for her own life and her friends' lives once Nick had her in his control. Threatening to hurt her friends was one of Nick's favorite tactics to get her to stay in line. Then once he had her addicted to Percocet, it was over for her. At least that's how it had felt. The sweet contentment she got from the opioid was the lovely reprieve she needed to keep on going—until the police had picked her up and gotten her to finally talk about what had happened to her.

But before that came a long and irretrievable journey into isolation and hell. She would never forgive Nick for stealing her life from her. For using her, humiliating her, beating her. She had felt like an empty person for so long that she wasn't sure whether she was capable of happiness or love anymore. Protectiveness maybe. That's how she felt about Suda.

She had been annoyed by Suda's presence at first, but she was so skinny and pathetic that Claire couldn't help feeling a little bit sorry for her, too. Then she was always so relentlessly cheerful. How could that be? Claire had no idea. Like getting up at the crack of dawn and making bread was God's gift to her.

Maybe it was, Claire realized, contemplating the alternative.

Still, Suda jumped at the slightest provocation and was constantly looking over her shoulder, waiting for someone to grab her, but Claire could tell that she was so incredibly appreciative of being somewhere safe, it was becoming just the smallest bit contagious. And bread. That girl loved bread even more than Simone did. But the very fact that she could love anything, even a type of food, didn't escape Claire's notice. How could she be so resilient? And she smiled big, genuine smiles. Claire didn't think she, herself, had genuinely smiled in years.

After school let out the day she'd woken up to her new reality, Claire had hidden in the library. She'd crouched in the stacks at closing time and had fretfully slept, hugging her backpack under a table that night. But she was cold, hungry, and frightened all night, and she knew that wouldn't be a long-term solution. And Nick had relentlessly texted her. He promised that it had been a mistake and that he truly had thought she was having fun and wanted to be with them. He insisted that he hadn't drugged her, and she got so confused that after a while she started to believe him. Finally, exhausted, hungry, and tired, she let him pick her up and bring her home.

He'd been on his best behavior for a few weeks after that, and Claire was almost lulled into thinking it would never happen again when Nick came home late one night, hopped up on some drug, and grabbed her out of bed. He'd thrown open the door, and before she even had time to sit up, his fist hit the side of her face.

"You selfish little tease," he'd screamed at her. "You think you can pull something over on me?"

Claire screamed and held her hands in front of her face. "I don't know what you're talking about! I haven't done anything," she cried.

"You expect me to feed you, take care of you, put a roof over your head, and you give nothing in return. I should throw you out."

"I . . ." Claire didn't know how to answer.

"Give me your phone!" Nick yelled. "You don't pay for this phone. I do. You don't deserve a phone. You think you're so precious."

Claire's instinct was to hide it at first, but Nick saw her phone on her desk, grabbed for it, and jammed it in his pocket.

"You don't deserve to live here, sponging off me."

Nick grabbed her arm and yanked her out of bed. He pulled her out of her room, opened the front door, and shoved her out into the hall.

"Nick!" Claire cried. "I didn't do anything."

"Exactly," Nick said and then slammed the door in her face.

Claire stood in the hallway of her building, stunned, face pounding with pain where his clenched fist had contacted her cheekbone. She put her palm to her face and felt the blood on her fingertips. What had happened?

She didn't know what to do. She was barefoot and wearing only a sleeping shirt and undies with no phone, no money, and nowhere to go. The tears streamed down her face, and she sat down hard on the dingy carpeting. She tucked her knees into her sleeping shirt and hugged herself tightly.

Time passed. She didn't know how many hours she'd been in the hallway because she hadn't known what time it was when he grabbed her out of bed. How long had she been asleep before he came home? She curled herself into a tight ball in the corner and tried to rest while simultaneously trying to stay alert to anyone coming. Their apartment was in a dicey neighborhood, and she was only marginally less afraid in the hallway than she would have been outside. If she had been dressed, she would have left and tried to walk to Kate's apartment, but there was no way she was going outside wearing only a nightshirt. She might as well pin a sign on herself saying, "Rape Me!"

She was fitfully sleeping when Nick opened the door the next morning and looked at her. She sat up and averted her eyes, not knowing what to expect.

"Hungry?" he asked.

Claire nodded.

Nick opened the door, and Claire stepped inside.

"Here," he said and handed her a white pill. "This will make your face stop hurting."

She reached out, and he placed it in the palm of her hand.

Lately, Claire had been thinking about the feeling of contentment that pill had given her. She'd been trying to write a poem about it, but so far the words she needed had eluded her.

And now Hailey. She knew she'd been sneaking pills. She even suspected Hailey realized that Claire knew she was taking them. Once, sitting at the table before dinner was served, she had looked at her with an expression both pleading and defiant. But Claire had done nothing. She hadn't talked to Hailey about it, and she hadn't told Grace or Simone. She hadn't gotten involved.

How could she have not said anything? The remorse almost overwhelmed her. She slid into bed facing the wall and tucked her head beneath the covers. Her throat tightened, and she clenched her jaw against allowing tears to slide down her face. She tried to push away the vision of Hailey slipping unconscious onto the floor, but it replayed in her mind over and over again, forcing sleep to elude her.

Aanwat

SUNLIGHT BARELY MAKING ITSELF KNOWN, **Aanwat** hunkered down, hidden in the shelter of the doorway across from the bakery—a blanket obstructing most of his face so he appeared to be a homeless man still at rest in the early hours of the day. He found it to be a good way to become invisible and stay warm at the same time.

His goal was to learn about the place where Suda was sequestered. He wanted to discover when employees arrived and left each day, but to his surprise, no one came in or went out before the "open" sign was turned in the window. Did they all live there? Was it a brothel that covered as a bakery? Aanwat didn't know, but he wanted to find out more before he initiated a plan.

He wasn't sure how he was going to get Suda out of the place and wondered when Tea would come through with the gun he'd promised him. Worst-case scenario, he thought, was to just go in and point the gun at whoever was at the counter and insist that she take him to Suda. He would then get her into the car and take off before the police could be called. He wondered how long it took the police to show up to a call in San Francisco. Hopefully at least five minutes, but probably more, he guessed. Maybe ten minutes. That should give him a long enough lead time to get away.

As he lay on the cement in the doorway, contemplating how he was going to steal a car, he glimpsed a familiar figure walking up the street and shrank back, stunned. It was Tea.

Aanwat's heart started to race. Was he coming for him? How had he known Aanwat was there? Had Tea been following him? For how long? Aanwat tried to steady his breathing and slipped further into the shadow of the doorway's overhang. He peeked out, hearing his footsteps nearing. Should he be ready to run? Would Tea grab him? Aanwat had no idea what was about to happen, but what occurred the next moment was the last thing he would have imagined.

Instead of coming for Aanwat, Tea crossed the street and went into the bakery. Aanwat sat up. He didn't notice the blanket falling away in his amazement. That terrifying thug was in the bakery ordering coffee and getting food.

Aanwat was mystified and stared intently at the window. What was going on? He had no idea.

As far as he could tell, Tea seemed to know the woman behind the counter. They were smiling at each other, talking. That in itself was a shock. Aanwat had never seen the man express anything other than a chilling stare.

The woman handed him a cup and a plate with some food he couldn't make out, and he walked to a table and sat down. In a few minutes, the woman joined him.

What was happening? Maybe he was right. Maybe the bakery was a front for a brothel, and they were all taking him for an idiot. They knew Suda was there and had been lying to him about her being missing. But why? What would they gain from it? He would have to tell Gan. He would know how to handle it. Those smug Americans. They had something coming. Aanwat gritted his teeth, thinking of the weeks he'd spent searching for her when they'd known all along exactly where she was.

Aanwat continued watching and saw Tea take the hand of the woman who sat across from him. It was the woman with the light brown hair who had helped him the first time he had gone into the bakery. What were they up to? He didn't know, but they seemed like a couple. Maybe they were in on something together that Chakrii didn't know about.

Aanwat ran his fingers through his hair, stunned. The offhand comment he'd made to Chakrii in his hotel room had been correct. He'd blurted the first thing that had come to his mind in the moment, but he now realized it was true.

It changed everything.

He was suddenly in the power position and Tea, whom he'd feared from the moment he'd met him, was the one who was vulnerable. Knowledge was power. He just had to figure out how to play it.

Aanwat stayed in the doorway, hidden until long after Tea left Hope Bakery. Aanwat didn't dare follow him for fear that he would be discovered. Until he understood what Tea was up to, Aanwat knew it was a good idea to keep his distance. They were due at a meeting down at the dock later. Aanwat was interested to see if Tea would show up and wanted to observe how he acted. Aanwat believed in his bones that Tea wasn't who he said he was, but he certainly wasn't going to go in and start pointing the finger until he found out what was going on.

Or not. Maybe, he told himself, he should just get the gun he'd been promised, get Suda, and then escape. What was the difference really? Either way, the guy was dangerous. But now, he had a bargaining chip in his pocket, in case he needed one.

Chai

CHAI HAD DECIDED NOT TO MENTION to Simone and Claire that Aanwat had asked for a gun. He didn't want to scare them more than they already were, and his plan was to give him a faulty one that wouldn't fire anyway. In the meantime, he would behave as if he knew nothing but keep a closer eye on Aanwat until he figured out what he was up to.

How had he found Suda? Chai had no idea. Simone said he'd first gone to Hope Bakery weeks ago. That meant Aanwat had been playing it cool with all of them, telling them he had no idea where she was. Chai realized he'd underestimated Aanwat. If he was capable of making them believe he'd had no luck in finding Suda, what else was he capable of? And why hadn't he told them? What was his play? He would try to find out more at the meeting Chakrii had called for that afternoon.

Chai walked into the warehouse and found Aanwat already seated at a table, apart from the others. He looked up when Chai approached and, for the first time, looked him in the face. Chai stared back at him impassively. His light brown eyes locked onto Aanwat's darker ones. Finally Aanwat looked away for a moment but then turned back and ushered Chai over to him.

"Tea," he said putting his palms together and bowing.

Chai gave a small bow in return.

"Do you have the gun for me?"

"I do, yes," but Chai made no move to hand anything to him. "Do you know how to use it?"

"I'll figure it out," Aanwat assured him.

Chai passed a package toward him. "Don't do anything stupid," he said before releasing it into Aanwat's hands.

Aanwat laughed nervously. "I won't."

"How is your search for Suda going?" Chai questioned.

Aanwat shook his head, "Badly. She has disappeared. I think she's maybe dead."

"Hmmm," Chai grunted. "Maybe she is. How long are you going to keep looking?"

"I'm not sure. I have to check in with my boss in Thailand."

"You do that, Aanwat," Chai said and put his hand on the smaller man's shoulder. He turned and went to sit with the others.

Aanwat looked around nervously, feeling dismissed and being angry for it. He was tired of being intimidated and treated like a nobody. He had a gun now. And information. While the rest of the group was talking about strategically moving drugs, Aanwat stared out the window at the loading docks. It was time to get Suda and go. He just had to finalize his plan. It was ugly here, he thought. Shipping containers upon shipping containers stacked up on faded, cracked asphalt. The water beyond was blue, but as he understood it, prone to having sharks swimming in its depths. There were small islands off in the distance, including the famed Alcatraz. It looked disturbing, even from across the bay.

His eyes once again alighted on the containers, and then he had an idea. He looked at the man he knew as Tea and smiled coldly.

Simone

EARLY MORNING WAS one of Simone's favorite times of day. The kitchen was warm and smelled of fresh coffee, baking bread, and sweet scones. The radio was cranked up just enough to keep the girls energized while they went about kneading dough and cutting layers of butter into flour in order to create perfectly flaky croissants. Tendrils of fog heavily blanketed the city, but the oversized bakery windows allowed in the emerging sunlight.

She hadn't seen Chai in a couple of days, but his texts assured her that he was working and just couldn't get away. She was surprised to realize how different the mornings felt when he didn't stop by. She had to admit she was becoming attached. She took a pan of baguettes out of the oven while she contemplated that fact.

She stacked the warm loaves and shuffled through the items on her mental to-do list. It was a farmers market day at the Ferry Building, and she planned to head there soon. She went religiously to get the best fruit for her scones and tarts. The market stalls were bursting with fresh-smelling stone fruit, berries, jams, jellies, local honey, vegetables, and all sorts of organic miscellany. The tourists often joined in the shopping, but the earlier part of the day was usually given over to the locals and chefs. First, though, she had to run by the bank.

"Hey," Simone said to Claire. "I'm heading out to do some errands. Will you head to the front and flip the sign to "open" when it's time? You're in charge of covering the front, okay?"

"Will do," Claire said, pulling her apron over her head and walking toward the display counter. Simone had noticed that Claire had become much more agreeable of late. "I could use another cappuccino to get me going," she told Simone. "Hey, Suda," she turned, "want me to make you a Thai tea while I'm up there?"

Simone smiled. She thought it was interesting the way Claire always spoke to Suda as if she were a fluent English speaker, neither slowing her speech nor simplifying it. Yet, somehow Suda usually got the gist of what Claire said.

She looked over her shoulder in time to see Suda nod, confirming her belief. The two women seemed to have formed a strong bond. She wondered if Claire felt protective of Suda and guessed that she did. They all did, Simone realized. Suda was small and looked delicate and vulnerable. Simone hated knowing what Suda had been through. What all the women at Hope House had been through. Sometimes when she thought about it, it almost overwhelmed her. She tried not to allow visions of it into her mind and instead focused on keeping them safe and allowing healing.

Simone closed the door of the bakery behind her, turned, and walked up the street toward the bank, intending to deposit the receipts from the previous day at the ATM. She deeply inhaled the foggy air and saw the first thin rays of sunlight through the breaks in the mist. The street was quiet as it was so many mornings. The Haight was a funny neighborhood: late to bed and late to rise. It didn't get going until the tech workers and the corporate crowd sleepily emerged from their apartments and houses and headed for the bus stops. But the wee hours were for the few hale early risers. The calm before the frenzy of a city day. She smiled, thinking about what fruit she would choose for the scones this week.

Her attention suddenly shifted to a sound that caught her ear. A shuffling right beside her, and she turned, startled, just as the metal gun impacted the side of her head, and she went down.

Disoriented and lying on a cold surface, temple painfully throbbing, Simone woke in darkness. She looked around, frantically trying to understand what had happened. Fear and confusion ran unchecked across her heart. She got to her knees to feel around for something familiar, and a wave of nausea passed through her as searing pain engulfed her shoulder when she tried to move her left arm. She moaned and lay back down for a moment. She cradled her arm across her stomach to keep it stable and then gingerly worked her way to her knees again.

"Hello?" the sound echoed back quickly in small space. She yelled more loudly, panicked. "Is anyone here?"

She could see small lines of light around what she assumed was a door, so she got to her feet and tentatively shuffled toward it.

She felt her way with her right hand to a wall but found that it wasn't a regular smooth surface. It was metal and ridged. Where was she? She felt all around the door for a handle or any way to open it but her searching fingers came up empty. She went back to her knees, crawled along and felt for her purse, her phone, anything that could help her, but there was nothing, and a sob escaped her.

"Stay cool, Simone," she told herself. She had watched enough true crime shows to know that it was the people who stayed calm and used their brains who had a better chance of getting out alive.

She listened at the door. What sounds was she hearing? A distant banging, she thought. And something that sounded like the thrumming of a loud machine. Or maybe a freeway. Had she been brought to a storage unit facility? She heard that criminals sometimes used them. But why? Was this about Suda? Or was this a fluke because she was out alone and someone grabbed her for the money. But then why take her somewhere? Her heart raced. If she was going to die, she hoped it would be quick.

"Stop it," she whispered. "Be strong. Figure it out."

Think about what you know, she thought and then mentally listed the little she could glean from her exploration of the space. It was ridged. It was metal. What else? It was cold. And then Simone stopped—her mind refusing to acknowledge what she suddenly but certainly understood.

She was in a shipping container and the door was sealed from the outside. A ship's horn blared from afar as if to confirm her realization.

"No!"

She banged on the side and yelled for help. She hit the side wall over and over until her palm felt like it was on fire with pain and she couldn't take it any longer. Her shoulder pain intensified as her body jarred with each blow of the door with her good hand.

What time was it, she wondered. How long had she been there?

She tried to discern the noise in the distance, but she couldn't tell what it was. Machinery maybe? She wasn't sure. Was she at the docks? The cold realization that she could be anywhere hit her. Perhaps she was on a ship and wouldn't be found until she arrived at another port, dead.

No, she told herself. She would be able to feel the motion if she were on a ship and took small consolation from that. She tried not to panic, but terror sliced through her like a dull hatchet working the trunk of a tree.

She felt dizzy and lay back down, but the cold metal chilled her. She switched to her side and tucked her knees up for warmth. Her teeth began to chatter, but she couldn't tell if it was from her body temperature lowering or from the fear coursing through her. Maybe it was already evening. Maybe she'd been gone for a while. She got back to her feet and, crouching, methodically felt around the floor again in case she missed anything. In the corner, her hands found a bucket, and the thought of Chai's description of Suda trying to throw the bucket of waste at him flashed across her mind. How had it come to this? Now she was in a shipping container and would soon need to use the bucket. She was both horrified at the thought and relieved that there was at least a bucket inside to use. But there was no water and no food. She wondered whether that meant that she would be moved quickly or simply left to die.

She tried to remember what had happened, but her mind was blank. One minute she was walking to the bank, and the next she was locked inside this cage with a fierce headache, a back that felt bruised and battered; a shoulder that felt broken. Had she been dragged to a car? Was it Aanwat? It must have been, but why would he grab her instead of Suda?

She tried to think. When she didn't come back from the bank and the farmers market, it would be noticed. Claire would have told Grace, and Grace would have called Chai. Chai would get help. She would be all right, she told herself, and tried to do some deep breathing.

"Help me; help me," she implored God. They would find her. She had to believe that.

She sat with her back to the wall to think. The more she thought about it, the more sure she felt that this had to be about Suda. The question was whether her assailant was Aanwat or whether somehow Chai's cover had been blown and they had come for all of them. But again, why? Were others hurt? Were they in nearby shipping containers at that moment? Or was she wrong, and it was just some random psychopath? Not knowing was more torturous than the pain. She hadn't been there to protect them. That was the most important part of her job, and she'd failed. Were they fighting for their lives? Were they being whisked away never to be heard from again? She felt useless and angry. She tried to remember how long people live without water and recalled three days was the limit. Would she still be locked in here in three days?

She was grateful she'd dressed warmly against the foggy morning chill—but even with a sweater and jacket, she was cold. She wrapped her good arm protectively over her left arm, which she'd tucked across her stomach to try to keep it immobilized. And she prayed. She asked for help. She wished she'd been better about memorizing Bible verses, so she had something to get her through this moment, but she'd never been good about that. She tried to focus. She thought about God saving Daniel from the lions, but then again, Stephen was stoned to death, so this situation could go either way. She decided to just pray for peace and remember that, no matter what happened, God would be with her the whole way.

Aanwat

AANWAT HAD BOLTED THE DOOR, sealing Simone in not long before she regained consciousness. He leaned his back against the shipping container's outer wall. He was breathing hard; his heart racing. He was sweating profusely in spite of the chill air and had to bend over, hands on knees, to ward off nausea.

Simone was as tall as he was and probably weighed more, so getting her in and out of the car had been a struggle. It had taken all his strength to pick her up and hoist her onto the back seat. He'd then had to shove her farther in and tuck her legs up so he could close the car door. Once she was in, he went around to the other side, opened the door nearest her head, and tied her wrists together in case she came to while they were driving. But, to his surprise, she was still out cold twenty minutes later when they arrived at the very end of the dock, the most deserted section he could find, where the freight containers were loaded and unloaded at the Port of San Francisco.

Once there, he'd opened the car door and tried to lift her out, but he didn't have the strength. He stood up and frowned as he peered into the car and contemplated his next move. He tried lifting her one more time by sliding his hands behind her back and pressing upward. He grunted, but got her only a couple of inches off the back seat. Her body was annoyingly floppy. He scratched his head, thought about his options, and then took her by the bound arms and pulled. She thumped to the ground harder than he'd intended, and he cringed at the sound he was sure was the snap of a bone when her body hit the cement. At that moment, he was grateful she was unconscious, but the fact that the pain didn't wake her shook him. He'd never hit anyone at all, let along hit someone on the temple with a gun. He'd been afraid one blow wouldn't be sufficient, so he'd put all his strength into it. He realized now, maybe that had been too much, given that guns are surprisingly substantial.

To get her into the container, he'd again pulled her, this time by the legs, taking care to be as gentle as possible with her head as her body bumped over the transom and across the floor until she was all the way inside. The woman was breathing when he left her, he told himself. She would be fine. People hit their heads all the time and didn't die. Besides, he could do nothing to help her now. He'd had to do it, he told himself, because she was somehow connected to Tea, and he couldn't risk having her at the bakery when he went in. He would just have to keep going and hope the rest of the plan worked.

The important thing was that he needed to get her away from Suda, and he had done it! And, he'd been lucky. As far as he knew, the only person who saw him was a vagrant, and he hoped that even if the guy reported it, the police would be skeptical if they believed him at all.

Having never planned a kidnapping before, he was pleased with how things were progressing. Next on his list was grabbing Suda, and then finally, he would get that smug annoying thug, Tea. He would especially relish that. He wished he could get to him first, but he wasn't sure where he would be until later that afternoon, and he wanted to get to Suda soon, before anyone realized something had happened to the bakery woman and became suspicious. The trickier part was how he was going to get Tea, given that he was always on alert, but he had a solid idea of how he would do it. He just hoped it worked because that guy was big and terrifying. If it did work, though . . . Aanwat smiled at the thought.

His eyes darted furtively around him before he moved away from the container and back toward the car. His hands shook as he opened the car door and got back behind the wheel—adrenalin still coursing through his body.

Claire

CLAIRE RAN HER FINGER ACROSS the screen of her phone as she scrolled through Craigslist looking at apartments in San Francisco. Everything was so expensive; she couldn't imagine being able to afford anything, but it was nice to imagine for a while that she could someday live in one of the light-filled apartments in the Marina with bay windows and built-ins. She would paint everything a clean, breezy white. She would walk along Chestnut Street with all the rich people and along the walking path with the view of the Golden Gate Bridge.

She sighed and put down her phone, allowing the present to intrude on her reverie. The dingy, beige, threadbare apartment she had shared with her mother had bordered the Tenderloin and had been about as far away as a person could get from the architectural beauty of the houses she dreamed of. She loved living in Hope House—the windows were large, and the old Victorian definitely had charm with its odd hodgepodge of industrial and comfortable farmhouse style—but it wasn't, and would never be, her own. She was passing through on her way to somewhere. The problem was that she had no idea where to land. Where was she on her way to? She didn't know.

Grace was always getting on her to go back and get her diploma, which she fully intended to do, but the thought of going to some dreary night school felt too bleak. She had to figure out another plan. Maybe there was some online school she could attend. That might be better. For now, she just kept her nose in a book, usually with her lanky, faded-jeans-clad legs curled up on the window seat in her bedroom, wrapped in a light blanket to ward off the chill. Her dark framed glasses on, baseball cap pulled low, or hair twisted into a messy blond bun on top of her head. It was her most peaceful place.

When the police had allowed her back into her apartment to gather her things after Nick had "fled the scene," as she liked to think of it, she had boxed up all of her and her mom's books and had unpacked them in her bedroom at Hope House.

Simone had taken pity on her piles and stacks of teetering books and had picked up two used bookshelves she'd found at a secondhand furniture shop to hold them. Together they had chosen a light powdery gray paint for the shelves, which anchored the colorful book spines. Still, they overflowed, and she had extra piles here and there, including a double-wide pile she used as a nightstand by her bed. It gave her comfort. And she sometimes felt that at least she'd gotten something from Nick. After all, she and her mother had bought most of their books with the account Nick had foolishly opened for them at the bookstore before everything turned to shit.

She shook her head thinking about it. He had no idea how much damage two serious booklovers could do in a short time. At least she had her mom's books to remember who she was deep down. Of who she could have been if she'd never started drinking and taking pills. It was a cautionary tale. She felt she was getting to know her mother a little bit better from the books she had chosen, and she felt a link to her when she opened the covers and immersed herself in the stories. Her mother definitely loved mysteries and thrillers. Claire pretty much liked any good book with a smart heroine who knew how to handle herself in a sticky situation.

She especially loved the book *Across the Nightingale Floor* by Lian Hearn. In one satisfying scene, the heroine saves herself from being raped by jabbing a needle into the eye of her attacker. When Claire had read that scene, it had stopped her in her tracks. She wondered if she could have done that, even if she'd known to. It was both horrifying and empowering to think so.

She wondered what her mother would think of the attempts she'd been making lately at writing poetry. It made her sad that she had no idea. Still, they shared the love of reading, so maybe her mom would have liked poetry, too. Claire remembered that she often sang songs when Claire was little—usually badly and off key—but still. Claire recalled the song lyrics she had sung most often were the ones that told a story. Claire mused, probably of love betrayed.

Claire suddenly grabbed for a scrap of paper and a pencil and then scribbled the word *preternaturally*. She had no idea what it meant, but she had heard it somewhere and liked the sound of it. It sounded a little creepy to her ear. Next she reached for her phone and opened the dictionary app and keyed in the same word. *Beyond what is normal* was the definition that came up. Claire snorted. That was certainly fitting for her life.

She had a poster on her wall of a colorful Matisse print she often stared at while she daydreamed. She desperately wanted to go to France so she could see the world Matisse, Picasso and the Lost Generation of writers had lived in. She loved the beauty and color of Matisse's art, but felt more as if she were trapped in a world created by Salvador Dali.

Hope Bakery had been unusually quiet in the morning but had picked up as lunch approached. She'd expected Simone back already, but since she was nowhere to be found, she called up to Grace for some help, only to find that she was out with Hailey at a therapy session. Claire was happy Hailey had started back toward recovery. She was in a more restricted home for now, but maybe someday she could come back to Hope House.

Claire sighed in frustration as the line for service grew, but there was no way she was going to let Suda come up front, so—annoyed—she determined to get the job done on her own.

She tried to keep up with business and at the same time contemplated this Aanwat character who had come into the store to look for Suda. She wondered how he compared to Nick. Had he hit her? Beaten her into submission as Nick had done with her? Had he forced her to have sex with him as Nick had taken to doing to Claire when he was drunk or in an especially foul mood? Claire had learned to ignore her body during those times, fixing her mind somewhere else, often running through math equations until it was over. $(x + 5) / 4 = (x - 3) / 2$, $4(x -3) - 3(x + 2) = 5 + 2(x + 2)$. Over and over to push away her reality. She tried never to think about her favorite words, or about books she loved, when that was her reality because she didn't want to taint her favorite things by mixing them in her mind with what was happening to her body. Instead she stuck with numbers: they were utilitarian, necessary even, but not beautiful.

She wouldn't let Suda be subjected to being prostituted again, just as she wouldn't allow herself to. "Solidarity," she told herself. It had been one of her favorite vocabulary words as a kid. That and *pandemonium*. She had no idea why she had especially liked those particular words, but she had. Something about the cadence of them. She had learned both words in third grade—Mrs. West's class. Back when things were easier, and her mother was alive. Back when being a hungry girl with an irresponsible mother was the biggest problem she had.

It was during the first lull in early afternoon that he came for Suda. Claire looked up from restocking the display case to find a gun trained on her chest and realized the knife she had folded in her pocket wasn't going to provide the help she needed.

"Suda, run!" she screamed.

She heard footsteps running toward her and realized the error of her plan. Suda's English wasn't strong enough to understand that she was telling her to flee. Instead, she rushed up front to see what had happened to Claire and then stopped short at the sight of Aanwat.

"No!" Suda gasped, imploring him to leave her alone.

Aanwat yelled something Claire couldn't understand, and gestured toward the door with his gun, making it clear to her that he wanted Suda to go with him.

"Don't go," Claire told Suda.

She looked from Aanwat to Suda and back. He was yelling at Suda, but still pointing the gun at her. Claire realized Aanwat couldn't keep the gun trained on both of them and acted quickly—and in hindsight, recklessly—thinking she could hit the gun out of his hand. When he turned back to Suda, heart skipping a beat in her chest, Claire lunged across the counter.

The commotion startled Aanwat, and he jerked his head back toward Claire. His eyes bulged out in surprise, and before he realized what he was doing, Aanwat fired.

The bullet hit Claire in the thigh, and she screamed in pain as she hit the worn wooden floor hard.

"Fuck that hurts!" she yelled at him but wasn't about to give up. She tried to stand but he walked to her and pointed the gun at her forehead.

"Do what I say if you want her to live," Aanwat said in Thai, his calm voice chilling Claire in spite of her lack of understanding. Suda nodded. She believed he would kill Claire as he said, so she slowly walked toward the door when he gestured again in that direction. She wouldn't be the cause of Claire's death. She would go with him.

"You, too," he said to Claire in English. In truth, he wasn't willing to kill her, but he also wasn't willing to let her stay to tell what happened. But he couldn't let Suda knew that. If she thought he would kill her friend, he had leverage. So with them she would go. That way, he figured, he could point the gun at her head whenever Suda even hinted at resisting.

Claire gritted her teeth against the pain and tried to get up. Aanwat took her by the top of her arm and yanked her to her feet. Claire frantically looked around. Where was everyone when she needed them? Where were the customers? He made them go out the back door into the alley instead of out the main door. There were people down the street and others across the street, cars passed, but no one registered a problem. The three of them just looked like people getting into a car, and Claire was too afraid to scream for help, having already been shot once.

"Don't say a word," Aanwat told her when he noticed Claire searching the street for nearby people.

Maybe she should scream. It might save them, but then again, he might shove her away if she was screaming and just take Suda. She couldn't let that happen.

He said something to Suda, and then repeated it in English for Claire. "Into the car," he told her, gesturing to the ancient Honda hatchback idling in the red zone at the back of the bakery. The small backseat passenger window was shattered, and Claire guessed he had stolen it.

The pain in her thigh was intense, and she took a quick look at it. There was a hole in her jeans where the bullet had entered along with a corresponding hole in her flesh. Blood was spreading on the fabric, but she could tell by the fact that her leg was able to move her toward the car that the bullet must not have hit bone. She wondered if it passed through the meat of her leg or if it was lodged inside. She wondered how much it was bleeding and whether she could make it stop before she bled to death. She didn't feel frantic or afraid, just calm and angry. She set her jaw and shuffled as slowly as she was able toward the car, trying to buy a little time, looking around for someone to help them.

Suda started to cry when she saw Claire's leg. "I sorry," she told Claire in English, the sadness on Suda's face expressing her feelings of terror and pain. Claire waved her away.

"It's all right, Suda. Don't worry," she told her.

As she approached the car, Claire felt for the knife and was relieved to find it was still in her front pocket. She would bide her time and then use it on Aanwat the first chance she had.

She felt for her phone but realized it was no longer in her jeans. She closed her eyes in frustration. Someone could have used that to trace them. She wondered if it had flown out when she careened across the counter. She looked back into the bakery and saw it, abandoned on the floor. If only she had realized and grabbed it on her way out. She looked up at the surveillance camera Simone had hooked up, hoping it would catch what was happening. At least then, Grace would know what to tell the police when she got back and found the store abandoned and blood smeared on the floor.

Aanwat opened the back passenger door and shoved Claire inside. Pain shot through her leg when it hit the front seat on the way into the car. Aanwat then opened the front passenger door for Suda, and she dutifully climbed into the seat.

Suda seemed resigned, Claire thought. But sometimes her expressions were indecipherable. Claire hoped this was one of those times and that instead of resigned, Suda was ready to act if they had a chance to escape. As the car pulled away from the curb, Claire tried to assess her leg. The most immediate thing she had to do was stop the bleeding, so she took off the flannel button down she had over her tee-shirt and wrapped it tightly around her thigh, using the arms to tie it in place. The pressure of it helped, and she tried to breathe normally and think.

She was determined to figure a way out for both of them. She was damned if she was going to get killed now, after everything she'd been through. She had survived Nick; she was going to survive this, too.

She caught sight of Aanwat looking at her in the re-view mirror and glared at him in return. She was livid. She would allow herself to be frightened later, when she and Suda were both fine. At least she hoped they'd be fine. She tried to think of a way to get in touch with Chai—or any police for that matter—but nothing came to mind. If they drove by an officer, would she have the courage to yell for help? She wasn't sure given that Aanwat had a gun and had shown that he wasn't afraid to use it.

She looked down at her leg. The blood was seeping into her flannel shirt, but it seemed to have slowed, so at least that was a good sign, she supposed.

Suda and Claire

SUDA SNUCK A QUICK LOOK over her shoulder at Claire and saw that she was incredibly pale and clearly in pain, yet her expression was intense and resolved. Her Giants baseball cap was pulled low on her head, and her blue eyes were fixed. Claire glanced back at her and Suda attempted to convey reassurance.

"I didn't mean to shoot her," Aanwat said in Thai. "She startled me when she jumped over the counter and I . . . I don't know what happened. I accidentally pulled the trigger."

"We have to take her to a hospital," Suda said in Thai. "She's bleeding."

"No," he said. "She should have kept away. There's no way I'm taking her to a hospital."

"We could drive by and let her out. We don't have to go in with her. Just leave her in front of a hospital."

"No," Aanwat shook his head emphatically. "We're getting out of sight. We have to hide. I'm not going to hurt you. I'm here to get you, and then we're going to leave."

"I'm not leaving with you. I'm not going back. I won't, Aanwat. Gan will kill me. Or I'll die from one of the men. I would rather die now. I would rather jump from this car or step in front of a bus."

"It won't be like that."

"I've done what I was told to do my entire life, but I won't do this. There's another way. I can work in the bakery. Don't you see? I would rather live here and be free or die, but I'm not going back to working in a brothel."

Aanwat looked over at her, amazed at the difference in her since he knew her in Thailand. Her strength and determination surprised him.

"Life isn't supposed to be a sacrifice to be endured," she told him. "For you either. You don't have to do this, Aanwat. You can let us go. Then you can go, too. Somewhere else, away from Gan."

Aanwat shook his head. He would tell her the plan later, but for now he gripped the wheel, focusing intently as he drove, not used to the traffic or the road signs in English. He had studied the map ahead of time and traced the route he would use to go from the bakery to the new motel he'd rented, but in real time, having to heed traffic, watch for pedestrians and the hulking busses that ran on the electric cords, it was overwhelming. He wished he had a phone with navigation, but those were expensive, so he'd had to use the tourist map he'd picked up to create his route.

Suda sat as far from Aanwat as possible, hunched against the passenger door. She would have flung it open and bolted at a stoplight, but she couldn't leave Claire. She wouldn't have believed Aanwat would kill anyone, but he had shot Claire once—even if it had been an accident—and said he would kill her if Suda didn't do what he said, so she couldn't take the risk of bolting.

The city went about its business. Men and women were out—business people walked to or from lunch back to their offices. Bicycle messengers delivered packages; life happened in their midst. And yet no one was aware. She was another girl being moved from one place to another. *Trafficked.* She had learned the English word for it, and it evoked an image that haunted her in its accuracy. Girls, children, people—like so many cars on a highway, being delivered for other people's use like objects. She visualized a crowded road, full of girls like her, and it made her want to weep. The fact that human beings used others for their bidding—whatever the bidding—was an offense.

Aanwat's voice broke her thoughts.

"I'm not taking you to the boss. I'm taking you away. We'll live in Bangkok. There are so many people there, we'll never be found."

"What are you saying? That makes no sense."

"I'm not taking you back. We'll escape. Both of us."

"How? I can't fly, Aanwat. I have no papers."

Aanwat looked at her stupidly for a moment. How had he not thought about that? He pounded his fist against the steering wheel, swearing in Thai, and Suda jumped.

"Fine," he said, gaining control. "We'll figure out a different plan. I got a motel for us. We'll stay there until we decide what to do."

Aanwat looked back at Claire and thought about what to do with her. She was an unexpected complication, but he would decide what to do with her later. He turned back and focused on the road in front of him.

Suda saw Aanwat glance at Claire and looked back at her as well. She had no idea what would happen next. She was still in disbelief that she was sitting in the car with Aanwat and that Claire had been shot.

"How did you find me?" she asked.

They had been so careful. She had both feared it would happen and disbelieved that it would, given all of the precautions they had taken.

"I have been here looking for weeks. I was about to give up, but then I saw you. It was luck. I was walking to my hotel, and you ran outside and got into a car."

"But I look different. How did you recognize me?"

"At first I wasn't sure it was you because of your hair, but I waited and saw you when you came back. It was you. I couldn't believe my good fortune." His face animated, expressing the excitement he had felt when he'd found her.

"And my bad fortune," she said and turned to look out the window. She couldn't stand to look at Aanwat for another second.

She believed she was cursed. Born poor, no papers. Her parents died and sweet Ploy, too. Her aunt sold her. She suffered humiliation after humiliation. Each affront played like a film in her mind. She was forsaken. She was nothing but a thing to be used. Her life was only to be endured. How could she have believed for a moment that there would be anything but pain for her? She pressed her lips together and used the palm of her hand to wipe a tear that escaped.

She sniffed, and Aanwat saw that she was crying.

"We can be together now, Suda. I always wanted us to be together."

"You *sold* me, Aanwat. Over and over to men who beat me, who used me, and it was nothing to you."

"I didn't want to. I tried to get you the ones who weren't as bad. I told you to eat. I told you to be careful, but you didn't."

"You shoved me into a shipping container. I almost died. You should have seen me when I got here. I was skin and bones. Sick. Filthy. I was out of water, out of food."

"I'm sorry. I had to do it, or the boss would kill me. He still might if I go back, which is one of the reasons I'm not going to Chiang Rai. The other is you. I want us to be together."

He looked over at her with an expression of hope. His eyes asking for forgiveness.

"If you care about me, don't do this. Don't take me away. Bring me back to the bakery. I'm safe there. I like it there."

"It's too late. Now Tea knows about me. Who is he anyway? An informer? A cop?"

"Who? I don't know anyone named Tea."

"The big guy, with the arm tattoos."

Suda guessed he must mean Chai, but she didn't want to give him any more information than he already had. She smiled internally though, realizing the name play Chai had used. Chai tea. It worked in either language.

"Aanwat, I was happy there. It's like a family at the bakery. A good family like when I was young. And I love baking. Take me back. You can take Claire back, too. It will be as if it never happened, and you can go away without me. I have no papers. I will hold you back. We'll get caught; don't you see?"

The car turned into the parking lot of a small, dingy motel, and Suda felt trapped. Her life was again controlled by a man who wanted her for something. He pretended he was keeping her safe, but he would put her to work; she knew it. And Claire? What was going to happen? Had the bleeding stopped?

And where was this God that Simone and Grace talked about? Where was He for them?

She remembered Chai telling her that Jesus had suffered. That he understood what suffering was. That he had been beaten, stabbed, and betrayed, too.

So, maybe He understood, but she needed more than understanding now. She decided to try to pray and sent a silent plea for help. She did find it comforting in the midst of everything to feel that maybe their God was with her. Even in this.

Aanwat parked the car in front of one of the first-floor doors of the motel where he had rented a room. He took the gun off of the seat where he had rested it while they drove and turned to Claire.

"Don't be stupid, you understand?" He said in English. Claire nodded.

"I'll let you in first," he told Claire. "Suda, you stay here, or I will shoot your friend again. It doesn't matter now."

Aanwat got out, quickly moved to the trunk, and pulled out the same rope he'd used on Simone. Then he opened Claire's door and pulled her out. She gasped when her leg had to move, but she was able to limp into the room. Aanwat pulled out the desk chair and told Claire to sit in it. She lowered herself down but kept her injured leg straight instead of bending it at the knee in an effort to manage the pain. She felt herself sweating and felt nauseated. She wanted to close her eyes and go to sleep—even just for a moment—but there was no way she was going to check out and leave Suda to this guy.

She had miscalculated when she jumped at him back at the bakery. It had been a mistake, but he was small for a man, and she had thought she could knock him down. Now her leg was throbbing, and she was bleeding. But she was also furious. And determined. She wasn't going down without a fight.

"Don't move."

"As if I could," she said, not being able to resist pointing out the stupidity of his command.

He glared at her, tempted to inflict pain on her just because he could. Instead he turned away and went out and opened Suda's door.

Suda shakily got out of the car and made her way into the motel room. Her eyes immediately scanned for a phone but she didn't see one.

"Don't bother trying to find the phone," Aanwat said, seeing her eyes moving around the room. "I took it."

Suda frowned, angry with him but also with herself for being obvious.

Claire looked from Aanwat to Suda, wondering what they were saying, but she couldn't understand them. She looked down at her leg. The pain hadn't eased up at all. At least the pressure of the flannel shirt she'd used to tie around her leg was doing the job. That was something. She hoped it would stop bleeding soon.

She looked around the dingy room at the stained carpeting and a lime green bedspread that had seen better days. She shuddered at the memory of being in rooms like this when she was still with Nick—a vision of herself drugged and with men invaded her mind against her will. She refused to die in a room like this. The sounds of the city were loud around them. Cars honking, buses hissing as they lowered and raised up to let people on and off. Yet here were Suda and Claire: invisible. In the shadows. Ignorable.

Ironically, a dingy motel like this one was where she was rescued. A hotel clerk had seen her coming in and out with men too many times and realized what was happening.

When the cops grabbed her, she was seventeen years old, and at 2:00 a.m. when they picked her up, she already had been on the street for five hours that night. She was wearing a miniskirt and a little cropped top in spite of the cold night air, fog, and wind. The early days, when Nick was holding down a better job and just selling drugs on the side, had been the honeymoon phase. As Nick's road had become more and more rocky, so had Claire's. The hotels became squalid, the clientele became dingy, and then finally she ended up on the blade—walking her block until she was summoned to a car. Maybe once or twice a week, Nick still came up with a hotel room, but mostly her world had narrowed to a city block and men in cars.

When she'd gotten her first venereal disease, Nick had made her take a long shower, keep her face clean of makeup, put her hair in a ponytail, and tell the doctor that her high school boyfriend had been sleeping around and given her an infection. It worked then and kept working with each doctor they visited over the next three years, because her wholesome looks invited trust, and Nick, as her concerned father, was always waiting for her in the waiting room. But by the end, Nick had stopped even helping her with that, and being with men had become even more painful.

She had long ago stopped going to school. She had become too tired to get up in the morning, and to say that the quality of her homework had slipped was an understatement. She was no longer the golden student. Her teachers and then eventually the school counselor had asked her repeatedly if there was something wrong at home. She'd noticed Claire's sallow face, and she had become skinnier than before, but Claire wasn't about to say a word. By then Nick was her lifeline to the Percocet that she desperately needed to get through the day.

Her lying had become expert, and she had dressed the part of the conscientious student when she was there. Her friends tried to engage her, but eventually gave up. The library became her only connection to normalcy— and books her only escape.

When she finally did get picked up by the police, three years into her ordeal, she was more afraid of Nick and what he would do to her if she talked to the police than she was of being on the street, so initially she was determined to bluff through being questioned. She had no identification on her, after all. Nick kept everything back in the apartment in case something like this happened. And he took the money she made after each customer, so as of the moment the police grabbed her, she had nothing except the way she was dressed that gave any indication that she was working.

Because Nick kept his eye on her, Claire knew he had seen her get picked up and was already fuming. He would believe she was in on it and that she had willingly gotten into the police car. He would beat her when she got home. And she already dreaded it. But better a beating that would be over, she figured, than ending up in a detention center. Nick had told her how terrible they were.

A woman police officer had been on the scene and had gotten into the back seat with her. Claire stared down at her hands, refusing to look at her.

Her beautiful blonde hair was drab and oily; her face was covered in heavy makeup. But still, the officer could tell how young she was. It had taken her hours to convince Claire to give them Nick's name and the address of their apartment, but by the time they got there, he was gone.

Claire looked up, blinked away her thoughts, and made herself focus on the current moment. The leg pain was making her mind wander, so she tried to concentrate. She wondered if Grace had returned to Hope Bakery yet. Had she discovered they were gone? She hoped the bakery surveillance cameras had captured a good shot of them being dragged out of there, and caught the make of the car. If they had that, they had a fighting chance. She thanked God for the camera; knowing that it might have caught them on film gave her hope.

"I have to go out for a while, but don't think of trying to escape." Aanwat reached into his duffle bag and pulled out two rags.

"What? Where are you going?" Suda asked.

He paused, contemplating whether to tell them he had taken Simone and was going to get Tea, and then decided to tell a partial truth. The corner of his mouth turned up slightly, showing that he was pleased with himself. And he was. His plans had gone better than expected. Soon he and Suda would get out of San Francisco.

"I have an errand to do. It's important to keep us safe." Aanwat told Suda. The timing was bad, but he had to take Tea out of play while they got away. And he had to do it now because now was the only time he knew exactly where he could find him.

He went to the bed, where Suda had been sitting and bound her hands together and then looped the rope around her ankles, making it impossible for her to get up without forcing her to bend in an unnatural, painful angle. If she stayed still, she would be fine. Then, he lifted her head and as gently as possible, pushed the rag into her mouth. He then moved Claire from the chair where she had been sitting to the bed and repeated the process, but more deliberately and forcefully. They were both on their sides, bound, immobile—wrists and ankles wrapped in rope.

"Don't try to get out," he told Suda first in Thai and then repeated it to Claire in English.

"I have the bakery lady."

"What?" Suda tried to ask, confused. Her mouth stuffed with the gag so she couldn't get the words out.

"The bakery lady," Aanwat said again, agitated. "And I know you don't want me to have to hurt her. I will though, if you make even one noise."

"S'mo?" Suda tried to say Simone's name, but it came out muffled.

"The one in charge," he said. "The one working with Tea."

Claire tried to follow what was being said. Was Suda trying to say "Simone" or just something that sounded similar in Thai. Inwardly she screamed in frustration but had to content herself with simply glowering at Aanwat instead.

Aanwat tucked his gun into the back of his jeans and zipped on his jacket. He had been watching a lot of American television while he had been in town and he liked feeling as if he were in one of the shows he had watched.

"I'll be back," he said first in Thai and then in English and shut the door behind him.

Chai

CHAI HAD BEEN FEELING a heightened sense of impending change for days. He could tell Aanwat was up to something. He pondered that fact as he sat at the table in the office near the San Francisco cargo port and watched men pack heroin into bags of rice and then slip the packaged rice into cardboard boxes, which were then packed into wooden crates. If only he could find out the name of the man behind the operation, he could arrest him and get out. He felt stymied and filled with self-doubt. Was he missing an opportunity? How could he infiltrate further? This case needed movement soon. He got up and walked out the door, needing to stretch his legs and get some fresh air.

He looked toward the edge of the port and was surprised to see Aanwat himself walking toward him. He squinted his eyes menacingly at him as he got closer and was surprised to be met with a reciprocal stare. The guy had surprised him; that was for sure. He had more grit than expected.

"Tea," Aanwat said in passing and kept going, walking toward Chakrii's office.

Chai nodded in return and then walked toward the water.

He paced outside for a long while, breathing in the mixture of air and ship fumes; thinking over his next move and realizing he didn't have one. It was just a waiting game until something broke and that could be weeks, months, years. He couldn't stand the thought of continuing the charade. The smell of the exhaust combined with oil was a distinct scent he knew he would remember long after this assignment was finished. He hated it. He thought of Simone and Hope Bakery with its inviting smells of coffee and bread. He stared out over the water to the horizon. It was blank and gray—indistinct, like the progress he was making.

The water was choppy and the wind whistled around the containers. The noise of the loading gear ground out the noise of approaching steps as the massive machines lifted containers weighing thousands of pounds onto awaiting ships.

He was about to turn back when he felt the unmistakable pressure of a gun against his spine and froze.

His mind flashed. Who was holding the gun? Was it an organization man or was it Aanwat, whose gun he knew wouldn't fire? Had his identity as a police officer been discovered? If so, his life was most likely over.

"What do you want?" Chai asked, hoping to discover the identity of the person who held the gun.

"Come with me and you'll know soon enough," he heard Aanwat's voice speaking in Thai. Relief flooded through his body as he realized who it was. He mistakenly believed that the weapon being pressed against his spine was the gun he had provided for Aanwat, which he'd purposefully jammed to prevent a bullet from escaping the chamber.

"Aanwat," Chai said, "what are you doing?"

"I know about you. You've had Suda all this time."

"What are you talking about?" Chai stalled.

"I saw her, and I saw you."

"I don't know what you mean."

"Walk," Aanwat said and directed Chai to move toward the storage container where he had left Simone.

Aanwat clenched his jaw. This was the most vulnerable part of the plan. The walk to the container would take several minutes, and he knew Tea was well trained and brutal. He had to stay focused, and he had to keep the gun pressed against Tea's spine, or he might try to grab it. If they got into a physical fight, Aanwat knew he would end up on the losing side.

Chai compliantly walked in front of Aanwat, allowing the pressure of the gun to determine the direction they took.

"Two things to know," Aanwat told him as they walked. "I have your girlfriend. If you try to escape, I will kill her." He gave that a moment to sink in. "Also, you should know this gun isn't the one you got for me. This one will shoot."

"What do you mean? The one I gave you was fine."

"I went to a gun range. And it's a good thing I did because finding out it wouldn't shoot was valuable and worth every bit of money I spent. You . . ." Aanwat couldn't find the word he wanted, so instead he spit on the ground.

Chai's mind was now sprinting through all possible scenarios, discarding some, quickly filing others as possibilities. Who did he think was his girlfriend, and how had he discovered so much?

"Look, Aanwat, you're confused. I don't have a girlfriend, and I have never even seen Suda. You're mistaken."

"I saw you through the window. You were there, Suda was there, your girlfriend was there."

"Where?"

"Bread shop. I saw you. I saw her. I saw your bakery lady girlfriend."

"Did you follow me?"

"Yes," he lied, knowing that would hurt him far more than the truth. "And it was easy."

Chai clenched his jaw. How could he have missed Aanwat tailing him? A sense of shame washed through his body. And now he had Simone. Chai wouldn't be able to cope if anything happened to any of them because he had led Aanwat to them. How? He internally screamed at himself, but he wouldn't give Aanwat the satisfaction of seeing his emotions.

"Look, the bakery lady isn't my girlfriend, so you can let her go. She has nothing to do with this."

"She is in on it. Suda has been living there. You two have been hiding her there. Is the bakery a brothel? Has Suda been working?"

Chai paused, trying to gain some time to assess the situation. Should he say "Yes" and offer to cut him in or tell him the truth and see what happened? He wasn't sure which play to make, so he decided for the time being to simply continue being steered by the gun at his back. Time was what he needed. He wanted to get to Simone.

"How much farther?" Chai asked.

"Not far," Aanwat said. He stopped within sight of the shipping container but decided not to tell Chai which one it was so he could keep control of the situation. "Throw your phone over there." Aanwat nodded to an empty patch of cement between the rows of containers.

Chai's fury barely allowed him to do Aanwat's bidding. He clenched his teeth to keep himself from saying something to provoke Aanwat's anger, but his fingers formed a fist in hopes of having a chance to land a punch if Aanwat let down his guard for even a second. He told himself to keep his anger in check because Aanwat had Simone. He was the one who got her into this situation in the first place, and he would do anything to make sure she wasn't harmed for helping him.

He sighed, reached into his back pocket for his phone, and unceremoniously tossed it where Aanwat had directed.

"Now your gun."

Chai hesitated. This would be his last chance to gain the advantage. He visualized himself wheeling around and smacking the gun out of Aanwat's hand. But he had underestimated the man before and didn't want to do so again when both Simone's and Suda's lives were in danger.

He reached behind him, unclipped his gun, and then tossed it.

"There," Aanwat indicated a specific container, and they began to move toward it. He knew this was the moment it could all go wrong. If the bakery lady was dead, Tea would kill him, even without his gun. Aanwat didn't know how, but he knew without a doubt that it would happen.

"Open it," Aanwat said and nodded to the lever that held the door closed. He heard Simone begin to yell from the inside. Both relief and dread coursed through him. He was relieved he hadn't killed her, but he was afraid she would try to get out when the door opened.

Chai recognized Simone's voice screaming for help, and his heart froze. He really did have her.

His instinct was to turn and punch Aanwat in the face, but he couldn't be sure Aanwat wouldn't get off a shot before his fist landed. And with the gun trained on Chai's spine, he wasn't willing to risk it. Instead he slid back the lever and opened the door.

"Simone, it's me," he said before swinging the door open.

"Stop," Aanwat told him, indicating that the door was opened as far as he wanted.

"Chai!" Simone came forward. He took in her swollen face and the fact that she was holding her left arm in her right. His intense look told her that he was intently controlling his emotions.

"Are you okay?" he asked calmly.

"I think my shoulder is broken," she said quickly and frantically, "but aside from that I'm all right. My head hurts."

"Enough talk. Get in," Aanwat said.

Chai slowly began to step in, only to be shoved from behind, forcing him deep into the container. Before he could regain his footing, the door closed and the lever slammed into place.

Simone and Chai

SIMONE LET DOWN HER GUARD and started to cry from the pure, overwhelming relief of Chai's presence.

"I don't know why I'm crying now that you're here," she told him. "I was being brave before, but . . ."

"Shhh, it's all right Simone."

"I can't believe you're here," she told him. "I know I shouldn't feel relieved because now you're stuck here, too, but I do. I thought I was either going to die here alone or end up dead in some foreign port when the container got unloaded."

"Come here," he said and then wrapped her into a bear hug. "Neither of us is going to wind up dead," he reassured her, not entirely believing it himself but resolved nonetheless. "We're going to get out of this. I just have to think about a solution." She could feel his chin moving against her shoulder as he spoke. The feeling of his arms around her gave her a sense of security, and she forced herself to stop crying before she embarrassed herself by actually heaving out tears and snot. "Start by telling me what happened," he said.

She recounted the little she remembered.

"He clearly wanted to take us out of play," Chai noted.

"Do you think he has Suda?" Simone hiccupped, in the aftermath of her suppressed crying jag.

"We have to assume so."

Simone sighed. "I agree."

"Was Claire there when you left?"

"Yes. Hopefully she was able to call the police if Aanwat got to Suda."

"The fact that I didn't get a call before Aanwat took my phone tells me that probably didn't happen. Was Grace home?"

"She was when I left, but I know she had stuff to do today. I don't know when he showed up since I was apparently out cold."

"Listen, he won this round, but it's not over," he rubbed her arm. "How would you have known you were about to be attacked?"

"Still."

"It would make me feel better if I knew Grace had been at the house."

"Does this shipping container belong to the organization? Do we have to worry about them finding us here and killing us?"

"No, so that's one good thing at least. And it's not in the 'immediate loading' section of the shipping yard, so at least we're not in imminent danger of being put on a ship."

"Good." Simone attempted a smile, but it came out more like a grimace, which Chai could hear more than see.

"In the meantime, come sit with me," Chai said. He leaned against the wall and drew Simone back so she could lean on him for comfort.

She rested against him and breathed out some stress. She was angry and frightened for Suda, but she was no longer as frightened for herself.

They sat in silence for a while. Both thinking. The seconds ticked by like hours.

"How did you end up being a cop anyway?" Simone asked after a while, thinking about how crazy her life had become since he showed up at her door with Suda.

Chai chuckled, "It was either become a cop or end up in jail myself, I think."

"What?" Simone instinctively turned to look at him although he was only a dim outline in the darkened container.

"I was a bit wild when I was younger."

"That surprises me. I'm not sure I can see it."

"I didn't entirely fit in. Smoked a lot of weed. Tagged."

"*Tagged?* No. You?"

"Oh, yeah. I started blowing off school and hanging out with some kids who weren't going in a good direction. My parents were not having it, though. They made me keep going to youth group even when I fought it. My father walked me right to the door and made sure I went in. I was livid, but messing with my father, who was very strict, was never a good idea, so I went. In my junior year, I got paired up with a mentor who happened to be a cop. He got me on another path, and I never looked back. I went to college and then to the academy. I'm grateful. The life the guys in the organization live is bleak. Empty. I wouldn't wish it on my worst enemy."

"I can see how that would be the case. I think about that sometimes when I visualize the men out there trafficking girls. Not just the men, but also the women who recruit. The women who see other girls as commodities to keep themselves off of the streets. The whole thing."

"If we could just stop the demand," Chai said.

"If we could stop the demand," Simone agreed, "it would all go away." She rested her head back on Chai's shoulder and sighed.

"I wonder what's happening out there."

"I wish I knew. I usually check in with my department contact around now, and the fact that I haven't will set off alarm bells. He'll tell the captain, and hopefully the captain will send someone over to check on Hope Bakery. I talked to the captain after I realized Aanwat had been to the bakery, so she's in the loop, which I'm very glad about now."

"How did it go over?"

"Not great. The fact that I hadn't reported having Suda," he paused. "You can imagine. I'm on seriously thin ice, but she was happy Suda was taken out of play, so there was that at least."

"Your captain's a woman?"

"Yep, she's seriously badass. We all respect her. She's no nonsense."

"You kept Suda safe for a long time," Simone said. "You saved her life. That's got to count for something."

"It won't if Aanwat has her. Instead it will have been reckless for nothing."

"We have to have faith that she'll be all right."

"Yeah. You're right," Chai said, sighing and leaning his head against the container wall.

"Tell me about Claire," he said after a few moments of the two thinking their own thoughts. "How did she end up at Hope House?"

"We usually don't tell the survivor's stories, but I don't think Claire would mind, and this is an extenuating circumstance," Simone said. A vision of Claire when she'd first arrived passed through her mind. "You should have seen her," Simone began. "She was covered in bruises, hair dirty, and the most horrifically bad attitude I have encountered in any of the girls to date. Who could blame her? Her mother had either overdosed or been killed— Claire isn't sure which—and the poor girl had been being pimped out for years. It was heartbreaking."

"Did the police bring her in?"

"Yes, eventually. She had been evading the cops because Nick, the guy who pimped her out, had her conveniently terrified of getting put in the system—as if that would be worse than what she was going through, right? And she was hard-core addicted to pills by then. Percocet mainly."

Simone closed her eyes, seeing Claire as she had been then. "She was placed with us by a judge for her protection," she told Chai. "The man she had been living with—who had been her mother's boyfriend before she died—had been using her to get clients for his job, according to Claire. I'm not sure exactly what kind of job would require sex with girls, but that's what she understood."

Chai pressed his palms into his eyes and shook his head wearily. "How long ago was that?"

"She's been with us more than a year now. For a while, I thought she was going to be one of the ones who could never get past it—the accumulation of losses took a toll on her. Some girls are so emotionally damaged that they never really recover. And the addiction to the pills is so strong. But Claire has something. A resilience. And she's incredibly smart. Freakishly so. I kind of wonder if she's got a genius IQ. She comes up with stuff I can't imagine she's been able to learn, given her life and age. It's nuts. We'll get her going back to school one of these days."

A memory of Claire popped into Simone's mind, and she smiled, thinking about it, then recounted it to Chai.

"One day, not long after Claire came to Hope House, I was sitting at the table in the kitchen attempting to do a *New York Times* crossword puzzle. I was stuck, because I'm pretty bad at them, but have delusions that I'll get better with practice. Anyway, Claire came in, looked over my shoulder, and after about thirty seconds, she sighed loudly, said, 'Really Simone,' pointed to a line of boxes in the puzzle, and named the word I needed. She said, 'Maybe you should try the *People* magazine crossword instead,' and walked away."

Chai laughed.

"I know; right? She was such a smart aleck, but I filled in the word she suggested, and not only did it fit, it was the key to the rest of the crossword."

"How old is she? Claire's one of those people who could be seventeen or twenty-seven. It's hard to tell her age because she has a face that's seen too much, and it shows."

"Yes, I hate seeing the world wariness around her beautiful eyes. She's nineteen but seems older."

"How'd she get picked up?" Chai asked after a moment of quiet.

"A hotel clerk, thank God. Someone who saw something that was not okay and did something about it. She called the antitrafficking hotline, and they got in touch with local authorities. They sent a police car and picked Claire up kicking and screaming. She was terrified Nick would think she was going willingly and punish her for it . If the antitrafficking task force hadn't known better, they would have sworn she loved the life and that they were taking her out of paradise. Fortunately, the group is versed in handling that specific type of trauma."

"I'm sure they could tell right away what was happening."

"Oh, definitely."

"Sometimes it feels so bleak, as if nothing will ever change."

"All we can do is what we can do."

"I just wish it was more."

"She needed medical attention so badly, too. She had serious infections. Having sex must have been excruciating on top of everything else. She probably won't be able to have children."

"How does anyone recover from that?"

"Rehab, a lot of prayer, a lot of healing, a lot of therapy, and time," Simone responded. "Grace is a great example for the girls, too. They see from her that they don't have to own the shame. That what happened wasn't their fault and that they are survivors. Survivors, rather than victims. Survivors have power." Simone pumped her fist the way Grace always did when she said the word, *survivor*. She had ingrained it in all of them.

"Did the man who was pimping Claire get arrested?"

"Nope, he slipped away before they could get him. Claire is always looking over her shoulder because of it. We keep her close to Hope House and far away from her old neighborhood. As much as she complains about getting up early to bake bread, I know she's appreciative of being with us and safe."

"I'm sure. You've created an incredible place."

"I'm lucky I can do it. It was touch-and-go at the beginning, but getting a grant helped us get on our feet."

"Thank God for people who are willing to share money."

"No kidding."

Simone sighed as a vision of Suda invaded her thoughts.

"I can't stand not knowing what's happening out there."

"Me, too," Chai said, and the two fell silent as they contemplated.

Claire and Suda

HOW LONG AGO HAD AANWAT LEFT? Suda wondered but wasn't sure. Since then, the shadows had crossed the room, and the light had grown dim.

Her hands and feet had finally become numb, which frightened her, but it was at least a reprieve from the excruciating pins and needles she had been feeling before she completely lost feeling. She had scooted herself close to Claire, so the two were touching for comfort. Her mind had been spinning for what seemed like hours while she lay there. Did Aanwat really have Simone? Where? Was she here in the hotel in a different room? Where else could he possibly have her? Had he hurt her? Her mind wouldn't still. She was gripped with fury and fear.

At some point, Suda realized that Claire had been slipping in and out of consciousness. She wasn't sure what to do. Should she try to keep her awake or allow her the temporary relief that sleep brought? She decided on the latter for now. The blood from her wounded leg had dried to a crusty dark burgundy, which Suda imagined was a good sign. The size of the stain was no longer expanding fresh vivid and red.

Lying there, gagged, a sadness had settled into Claire. She had endured so much already, but this somehow felt different. She had people again. Simone, Grace, and Suda had become important to her.

I won't lose them. I won't lose them. Her mind wouldn't stop repeating the phrase, like a record skipping, and it both annoyed her and gave her strength. She didn't want to care about anyone, but there it was. It had happened in spite of her best efforts, so she might as well make damn sure she didn't, in fact, lose them.

She hadn't realized she'd drifted off but jerked awake when the door opened and Aanwat slunk back in. She caught a glimpse outside and noticed the sun was down and evening had come. What time was it? How long had she slept? She writhed against the ropes and tried to talk through the cloth that was shoved in her mouth.

"Stop," Aanwat told Claire. "And shut up, or I will leave you like that."

Claire complied and went still and silent. She closed her eyes seething, but she knew she had to get him to trust that she would behave. She needed to be untied or she wouldn't be able to accomplish anything. And, aside from everything else, she desperately needed to use the bathroom. And, if she could get him to let her go in there alone, she would be able to find something to use as a weapon, she was sure of it. He had found her knife, when he had tied her up, which had almost broken her spirit, but then her mind clicked into overdrive searching for possible weapons that could be created from the objects in the room. A pencil would be ideal, but in her furtive search, her eyes hadn't found either a pencil or pen. Maybe a nail file? Don't some hotels have little kits with stuff patrons need? Not that this place was of that caliber, but her mind was searching for any possibility.

Sleeping a bit seemed to have helped. She felt more clear and able to think about getting out of the situation.

Aanwat stood over the bed, his brown expressionless eyes assessing them.

"I took care of Tea," Aanwat told Suda, "so don't think he is going to help you."

Claire felt Suda's body stiffen next to her. What had Aanwat said to cause that? Claire looked between them to try to understand and saw anger flash in Suda's eyes. If only she could understand their language.

He reached over to take the cloth out of Suda's mouth.

"Scream, and it will go right back in," he said, and she nodded.

"What did you do to them? Where is Simone? And what happened to Tea?" Suda decided to use the name Aanwat used for Chai, hoping that the fact that he was a police officer was still unknown.

"It doesn't matter."

"It does matter to me."

"What will you do to keep them safe? Will you leave with me?"

"Yes," Suda said. "Just leave them alone." She couldn't bear the thought of Simone or Chai coming to harm after they had done so much for her.

"It's a deal then," he told her and smiled a boyish smile of delight. He had gotten his way.

"And you can't hurt Claire," Suda added.

Claire perked up when she heard her name among the rest of the Thai words being spoken. What had Suda said? She couldn't stand not knowing.

"I have no intention of hurting any of them, Suda. As long as you come with me. I'm not a bad person. You know that. I only want what's best for us."

"Where are they? What have you done with them?"

He smiled at his own cleverness.

"I locked them in a shipping container . . . just like the one you were in. By the time they're found, we'll be long gone."

"A shipping container? On a boat? Like me? Where are they going?" Her voice filled with panic, and Claire again hated the fact that she had no idea what was being said.

"They aren't *going* anywhere. It was empty. Down at the dock. Smart, huh?"

"Who have you become, Aanwat? You're not the boy I knew in Thailand."

"I had to grow up. Kill or be killed; right? That's what they say here."

"Take the cloth from Claire's mouth, okay? I promise I won't cause a problem."

"As long as she keeps quiet," he said and then reached for Claire's gag.

As soon as it was off, Claire inhaled deeply, savoring a deep breath of air. "I have to go to the bathroom," she said.

"Fine," Aanwat said and untied her ankles. "But these stay on," he told her, indicating the ropes around her wrist.

"That's ridiculous," Claire said. "Where am I going to go? I can barely walk."

"They stay on."

"Fine," Claire told him, desperate to get to the bathroom and to find something—anything—to use as a weapon.

"Where will you take me?" Suda asked after Claire limped into the bathroom and closed the door.

"How about Los Angeles?" Aanwat asked. "No one will find us there. We can get work. We'll get lost in the crowd."

"I will never go with men again. I'll kill us both before doing that."

"I won't ask you to," he told her, taking her hands. He began to unbind her feet, to free her, and then he paused, adding, "Unless it's an emergency."

She looked up at him, her eyes meeting his, and she knew, beyond any doubt, that he would sell her again. More men, more pain, more shame. It already was an emergency. She looked away; said nothing. She would let him think she was happy to go with him and then escape. She would make him believe in her so he would let Simone, Chai, and Claire go. Then, once she had a chance, she would sneak away and call for help. Simone had made her memorize all of their phone numbers, and she had been reciting them over and over like a mantra while she lay there, waiting for whatever was going to happen. She would call them, and they would get her. She was sure of it.

She needed to communicate her plan to Claire, but how?

Just then, Claire opened the bathroom door and met Suda's eyes. Claire had a look of determination on her face, and it worried Suda. What was she up to now?

Suda held her eyes and subtly shook her head. She tried to tell her not to try anything. That she would take care of them both.

"I go," Suda told Claire in her minimal English and held out her hands to Aanwat to unbind them.

"No," Claire said emphatically.

"Stop talking," Aanwat told them, left Suda's side, and walked toward Claire with the cloth he'd used to gag her in his hand. He would shove it back in her mouth and leave her there when they left. The motel cleaning people would find her soon enough, he assumed. By then, she wouldn't be his problem.

Claire stared at him with abject hatred, and when he was within reach, she lifted her still-bound hands and screamed as she lunged at his face with the tail end of the toothbrush she'd found in the bathroom. He looked at her in horror, and then he yelled and hit her hands away just as she was about to make contact with his face. He grabbed her and tried to wrestle the toothbrush out of Claire's hands, but she was not going to give up her makeshift weapon without a fight. She grasped it as tightly as she could.

"Let go!" he said through clenched teeth and dug his nails into the skin of her hand while trying to pry the toothbrush from her grasp. She could feel her resistance weakening and tried to hang on with all of her might. Aanwat took hold of her wrists where they were bound and banged her lower arms and hands repeatedly against the doorframe, splitting the skin covering Claire's knuckles, but she refused to drop the toothbrush. Adrenaline coursed through her, and she was hardly aware of the pain in either her leg or hands at that moment.

"Stop!" Suda yelled at Aanwat. She tried to pry him off of Claire, but he shoved her away. She ricocheted off the edge of the bed onto the floor but got up immediately and tried to jump on his back, just as he landed a punch on Claire's face. Blood sprayed from her nose, and she screamed in pain and dropped the toothbrush. Suda also screamed when she saw Claire's face and jumped again onto Aanwat's back. She managed to get her bound hands looped over his head, and she yanked back with all her might to try to choke him. He turned, trying to pry her off, then in desperation threw himself and Suda against the wall.

Focused on getting Suda off of him, Aanwat didn't see Claire grasp the toothbrush again until she was upon him, arms back, hands over one shoulder, wielding the toothbrush like a sharp stick. And then she lunged.

The sickeningly soft, excruciating feeling of the toothbrush being thrust into his eye socket caused Aanwat to let go of Suda and cover his eye. Blood squirted from the entry point and splashed down his cheek. He held his hands in front of his face and screamed at Claire in Thai. Suda's arms were still looped over his head, and the two of them fell to the floor.

Claire shuffled to Suda and tried to untie the ropes around her wrists while Aanwat writhed. Claire's hands shook as she worked the knot, but finally it released. She pulled Suda to her feet.

There was a loud banging against the wall from the adjoining room. "Shut up!" someone yelled. Aanwat continued screaming in pain.

"Come on!" Claire pulled Suda out the door and started yelling for the police as soon as the door opened to the parking lot.

The slight, sweater-vest-wearing, aged clerk was out the office door and coming toward them to see what going on. Taking in Claire's bleeding face, blood-soaked, torn jeans, and split knuckles, as well as the loosened ropes still around both her and Suda's wrists, he immediately lifted his phone and dialed 911.

"What happened?" he yelled to them, waving them over and ushering them into the office while relaying the location to the police dispatcher.

"We were kidnapped," Claire said. "He was after her," she pointed to Suda, "but I stabbed him in the eye with a toothbrush. You better tell them to send an ambulance, too."

"Oh, my God!" he said and then relayed it to the 911 operator. They could already hear sirens coming. "Is he in the room?"

"Yes."

"Chai, Simone!" Suda said emphatically. And then repeated it. Claire looked at her and tried to understand what she meant. "He got! Aanwat got!"

And then Claire understood what they had been saying in the room before she went to the bathroom and her blood turned cold. He had Simone and Chai. But where? Had he hurt them?

"I think he has two of our friends, too," Claire relayed. "And one is a police officer."

One police car, followed by a second tore into the parking lot, sirens and lights on. Claire ran out of the office, waving her still-tied hands at them.

"He's in there," she yelled. "Room 5! He has a gun!"

Guests peered out the windows, curious and shocked at what was unfolding, and onlookers stopped on the sidewalk and crouched behind cars, peeking out when curiosity overtook common sense. Two officers moved to the sides of the door, while a third used the megaphone to advise everyone staying in the motel to remain indoors.

Between the sirens and the speaker, the sense of chaos was surreal. A fourth officer tried to lead Claire back inside the office, but she wasn't having it. She was determined to stay and watch Aanwat be taken out of the room.

"I stabbed him in the eye," she told the officer, "and then we ran."

"You were brilliant," he told her. "Brave, quick thinking."

"I wasn't going to let him take her," she told him. No stopping the flow of words. "There was no way." Claire was amped up and filled with adrenalin as the officer untied her wrists and then finished the job Claire had begun of untying Suda's ropes as well.

"They'll get him," the officer said, just as the other two broke through the flimsy motel door.

Grady. Claire noticed the name on his tag. Officer Grady.

"Bang! Bang!" Suda said to him, pointing to Claire's leg.

"Were you shot?" he asked, seeing the torn pants and the blood.

"Yes, and it hurts like a bitch," Claire said, but smiled for the first time. "I jumped across a counter to try to stop him, but it turns out that wasn't the best idea."

He spoke into his radio.

"An ambulance will be here soon."

"We'll need two, because I am not riding with him," she said as she watched Aanwat being led out by the two officers.

Suda sat down weakly, her legs no longer strong enough to hold her up.

"Does she speak English?" the officer asked.

"Only a little. She's Thai, here visiting me," Claire stammered, realizing Suda could get detained and deported. "We're friends with Chai. Do you know him? He's a cop." She hoped dropping Chai's name would keep them from asking too many questions about Suda. Claire gestured with her chin toward Aanwat. "He said he has Chai, and our other friend Simone, too."

"What?"

"Yeah, we told the hotel guy to tell the dispatcher. He has them somewhere, but I don't know where."

Suda heard Simone and Chai's names and understood that Claire was telling the officer that they had been taken, but she had no idea what the English word for "shipping container" was, so she pointed to herself.

"Like I here."

"What?" Claire asked.

"Like I," Suda said again and mimed a box.

"I don't understand."

Suda frantically mimed a box and pointed to herself.

"What's she saying?" the officer asked.

"I don't know." Claire stared at Suda intently, trying to understand.

Finally Suda took Claire's hand and brought her to the desk, grabbed a pen and paper, and drew a boat and a box on top.

"A shipping container! A shipping container," Claire yelled and turned to the officer. "He has them in a shipping container."

"Wait here," he said and then strode to his car and spoke into the radio and to the other officers, gesticulating intently.

It was then that the first ambulance arrived on the scene, and Aanwat, barely conscious from shock, was loaded in. An officer climbed in beside him, and they pulled away.

The second ambulance arrived while Grady was conferring with the other three policemen on the scene. When it pulled up, two EMTs—one a beefy red-haired man and the other a ponytailed woman—jumped out of the cab and then, after a quick word with him, strode toward Claire and Suda, stretcher between them. They helped Claire onto the stretcher, gently unwrapped the flannel shirt Claire had tied around the wound, and then cut open the leg of her jeans to see what they were dealing with. It was jagged and covered in blood, which began flowing freely again once the makeshift bandage had been removed. Claire paled at the sight, and they laid her back and then loaded her into the ambulance.

"She comes with me!" Claire insisted, taking Suda's hand. She wasn't about to leave her here to end up in police custody.

"Of course," the female helped Suda climb in and told her to sit on the small seat while the other EMT started an IV.

"This will help," he told Claire and reassuringly squeezed her arm. "Do you know whether you're allergic to any medications?"

"No pain meds!" Claire said, jerking her arm as if to rip out the IV.

"It's okay. Don't worry. There are no painkillers in there. Just saline to get you hydrated and help with shock."

"Okay," Claire relaxed and laid her head back. "I was addicted to Percocet," she explained. "I can't have anything with opioids."

The EMT noted it on a clipboard attached to the gurney.

"Got it," she smiled at Claire reassuringly. "You're going to be fine." She leaned over Claire and looked closely at her nose but didn't touch her face.

"What happened?" she asked.

"Got punched," Claire said matter-of-factly.

"I think we can safely say it's broken, but they'll fix you right up in the ER."

"Thanks," Claire said and took Suda's hand, but her mind was on Simone and Chai more than on her injuries. "But we have to help them find our friends."

"The police are on it now. You can rest," she told her. "Just rest."

"She can rest soon," Officer Grady said. Climbing into the ambulance, he sat next to Suda. "First, though, I need her statement. We can talk on the way to the hospital."

Claire took a moment to assess him to determine whether he was trustworthy. His short-cropped salt-and-pepper hair showed on the sides of his police cap, and he had deep smile lines around his eyes. But still, plenty of men she would have guessed were safe had picked her up and paid for her services. How could any-one tell anything about anybody? It was impossible. But Chai was a cop, and the officer who finally convinced her to get help from the police was a cop, so she decided to trust him, and she poured out the whole story, hoping she'd be in good hands.

Simone and Chai

"IT'S AMAZING HOW SLOWLY TIME PASSES when a person is stuck in a small dark space with nothing to do but fret," Simone said and tried to stretch out her stiff legs. After hours of sitting on rigid steel, her butt hurt almost as much as her shoulder did, and her eyes hurt from trying to see in the dark.

During the day, a hint of light had seeped through the crack encircling the large, swinging door, but now that it was night, darkness infused the space, entering into every inch—so much so that they couldn't even see the faintest outline of each other.

"But," she continued after a pause, "there's something good about entering into the suffering together. We're still experiencing part of what's happening with Suda—but from afar. Still, somehow being cold, being frightened, worrying about her—feels like we're a part of it. Does that sound odd?"

"I think I understand. It's what you do; right? You enter into the suffering that the women have been through. That way they're not alone. You fight for them."

"You, too. You go down into the trenches to help get others out. It's painful and difficult."

"And frustrating," Chai added.

"Sometimes it feels like rowing upstream," Simone agreed.

"Yeah, against the wind."

"I think we've both counted the cost and are willing to be in it. The suffering, the cost that comes with living life in the way we are. Weirdly enough if feels like a privilege, don't you think?" Simone asked. "We get to live our lives with people who have been through so much, and we get to at least do a little bit to help."

Simone paused and was quiet for a moment, then continued. "And there's joy, too. For sure," she mused.

"What do you find the most joyful part?" Chai asked.

"The joy that comes from the hope, I think. The girls get to have hope for a different future. And that's real. Not just daydreaming about a better life but getting tools to live it. And help; you know?"

"Mmmmm," Chai agreed. "It's real. And the moments when you're all around your dinner table—I see joy there. The bond between Claire and Suda. Did you notice how protective Claire was of Suda when I told the two of you about Aanwat?"

"I did. She was right in it. Ready to fight for her although they have known each other for only a matter of months."

"She doesn't even know it yet, but I think Claire has a heart of gold."

"Don't tell her that. She would hate it and would probably just say something snide—and most likely profane, too," Simone said, but Chai could hear the smile in her voice.

"It's our secret for now."

"I'm starving, and I feel like a jerk for being hungry and bored. What if we never find her?"

"Inhale and exhale. We'll just be here for the moment. breathing and praying is all we can do."

"Yeah." Simone shivered. The temperature was dropping. "But I actually suck at praying. It's not my strength at all. I'm a doer, and praying takes a still mind."

"I get it. It's difficult. I'm around so much ugliness and have thoughts that are no good and say stuff that's no good that half the time I'm trying to pray, it consists of saying, "Sorry, God . . . sorry, God . . .'"

Simone laughed. "I do that sometimes, too. I'll say, 'shit,' pause, and then add 'Sorry, Lord!' I like to think He's got bigger fish to fry than my bad language."

"Let's hope so, or I'm in serious trouble. But, hey, at least we're in communication, right?"

"Knowing that it's okay to be flawed is such a gift; isn't it?"

"Huge."

"Here," Chai took off his jacket, felt his way to her in the darkness, and then wrapped her in it. "In the meantime, at least we've gotten time to get to know each other better."

"That's been nice," Simone smiled in spite of herself and thanked him for the use of his jacket. "Tell me if you get too cold. We can trade off."

"Is it okay if I just tuck my hands in for a minute?"

Simone opened the jacket, and he wrapped his arms around her, tucking his cold hands inside to warm them up. They rested that way for a long moment, each savoring the warmth and the comfort of each other.

"What if she's dead?" Simone said softly, her head resting against his chest.

"We can't think that way."

"You're right," Simone concurred. They both paused, listening to the silence for a moment "What time do you think it is now?"

"I'm guessing somewhere between ten and midnight," Chai shifted, trying to get comfortable.

Simone jerked her head up and turned toward the door. "What?"

"Did you hear something?" She thought she had heard a sound that didn't fit in with the silence her ears had adjusted to as the dock noises had gradually receded with the light of day. She strained to hear beyond the layered quiet.

Chai sat completely still and listened, trying to distinguish any distinct sound. "I don't think . . ."

"That," Simone said, staring into the darkness of her surroundings, as if the sound itself would manifest. "It might be the crackle of a radio."

Chai listened again. And then he heard it, too, and then again, as it seemed to increase in volume as someone drew closer. He put his finger to his lips, which Simone could just make out in the inky surroundings.

"Why?" Simone barely whispered.

"Let's see if we can figure out who it is before giving ourselves away."

Chai stood, walked quietly to the door and angled his ear toward it. The sound came again, this time accompanied by a voice.

"Nothing seems out of the ordinary here," he heard a man's voice say.

Who was it? Chai wondered. Something about the tone and the faint radio sounds made him think it was police, but he wanted to be sure before he banged on the door.

"I see no signs of foul play, Sergeant," the voice said, and that was enough for Chai to believe his instincts had been correct, so he raised his fists and began to pound.

"We're in here," Chai yelled.

"Help!" Simone shouted.

Chai took off his heavy, black leather belt and used the solid metal buckle to create a clang that caught the attention of the man outside.

"Grady," they heard the voice say. "They're in here!"

"Chai?" Officer Grady yelled through the door.

"Yeah, I'm here. Simone Williams is here with me."

"Hang tight. We've got bolt cutters," he yelled.

Time seemed to move in slow motion as they held their breath until a sharp snapping sound signaled their freedom, and then the door hinges creaked open, allowing a whisper of fog to enter the container.

"Grady," Chai started speaking before the door was all the way opened, "there's a possible abduction in progress. A woman, Asian, slight, about five feet, maybe a hundred pounds. Long, bleached hair. Brown eyes." Chai was rattling off Suda's stats in a matter-of-fact tone.

"Suda Hwan? It's okay; we've got her."

"You've got her?" Simone asked. Her fear and stress felt like it blew out of her body, leaving her feeling limp.

"She's fine. Her associate was shot in the leg and has a broken nose, though. She was taken by ambulance to San Francisco General."

"Who?" Simone frantically asked. "Who got shot?"

"A young woman named Claire," Officer Grady said, remembering only Claire's first name. "She was amazing. Single-handedly took out the perp. Stabbed him in the eye with the handle end of a toothbrush."

"A toothbrush?" Chai asked.

"She stabbed him in the *eye*?" Simone asked, grimacing. They had moved outside the container and were huddled against the wind coming off the bay.

"She told us that she read it was the easiest way to kill a person in some novel."

"Is he *dead*?" Simone asked, shocked.

"Not dead. At the hospital in police custody."

"That's so Claire. Only she would learn the best way to kill someone in a book," Simone said, attempting but failing to stop herself from inappropriately laughing. "Sorry," she mumbled, embarrassed, and covered her mouth. "I don't know why I'm laughing. It's horrible."

"Don't worry," Chai squeezed her shoulder. "You're just reacting to the shock. It's not uncommon."

"It was a smart move, actually," Grady said. "It may have saved both of their lives."

"Listen, Grady," Chai said. "We've got to get Simone to a hospital, too. Either her shoulder is dislocated or her clavicle is broken, I can't tell which. She needs an x-ray."

"I see that," he said, taking in the way Simone was cradling her arm. "Ambulance or a ride in the back seat of our patrol car?" he asked Simone.

"Back seat would be fine. Thank you," she said gratefully.

"C'mon," he said and steered them both toward the black-and-white SUV while he spoke quickly into the radio attached to his shirt at the shoulder.

Chai helped Simone get into the back seat and then slid in next to her.

Once they were in, Grady passed back two bottles of water. Chai opened Simone's first, handed it to her, and then drank deeply from his own.

"They're safe," Simone said to Chai. "Thank God."

"Yes."

"What's going to happen now?" Simone whispered.

"I'm not sure." He turned to her and said softly, "It depends on whether they've realized that Suda isn't here legally."

"They won't deport her; will they?" Simone whispered.

"Not if I can help it," he said.

Simone reached for Chai's hand, entwined her fingers with his, and leaned her head against the back of the seat, eyes closed. The SUV's heater combined with the relief of being out of the container had infused her body with warmth. Suda was safe. Claire was safe. She would soon know what had happened, but the details almost didn't matter. What mattered was that they had stopped Aanwat from taking her. She wondered about the rest of the organization Chai was working in and whether they would give up and leave Suda alone now, but she would have to find out about that later. For now, she would happily put herself in the hands of a competent doctor, but first she wanted to call Grace.

Grady passed his phone back to Simone so she could make the call.

"Grace! It's me," she said when Grace picked up.

"Simone!" Grace shrieked, hearing the familiar voice. "Where are you? Are you all right?"

"I'm fine," Simone said, although Chai heard a wave of emotion in her voice now that she really was fine and talking with Grace. "A little banged up, but nothing too bad. The police found us. I'm with Chai. We're on the way to the hospital."

"I'm at the hospital with Claire and Suda. Call me when you get here, and I'll meet you."

"Yes, I will." Simone said and paused. "Grace . . ."

"Yeah, Sy?"

"Nothing. I'm just . . . I can't believe this all happened." Simone felt heat behind her eyes but pushed her fingers against her lids, refusing to give in to crying again.

"I know. It's going to be all right, though. Everyone is okay."

"Yeah, you're right. See you soon," she said and then hung up, inhaled shakily, and passed the phone forward. She thought of Claire and Suda safely together with Grace and whispered, "Thank you, thank you, thank you."

Chai

"WE SUSPECT YOUR COVER'S BEEN BLOWN, but there's a bright spot," the captain told Chai the next morning, after calling him into her office and closing the door. Chai sat in one of the uncomfortable plastic chairs that faced her desk, which was barely visible under stacks of paper. The morning sun slanted through cheap metal window blinds, leaving a striped patch of sun on the industrial light green wall of the office. It felt good to Chai to be at the precinct. It had been months since he had been in, and it felt like coming home.

"What's that?" he asked, his face giving no indication of his feelings about the matter.

"We have Aanwat in custody, and I'm thinking we can flip him." She ran her fingers through her short brown hair—flecks of gray beginning to add streaks through it. She had a frank, no-nonsense face, neither pretty nor unattractive, old nor young, but intelligent, animated. Her shrewd eyes penetrating and watchful. "We send him back with the caveat that he reports in regularly. A member of our counterpart in Chiang Rai will be designated to be his handler and voilá—our combined task force will have a man on the inside. We basically swap him for you. That could give us the breakthrough we need."

"I'm out?"

"Afraid so. You've done amazing work though, Chai. There's a lot to be proud of."

"I made too many errors. A couple that could have cost lives." The memory of Aanwat telling him he'd been followed had been eating at him all night. How had he let that happen?"

"What errors are you referring to, exactly?" the captain asked.

"For one, putting Suda in harm's way." Chai cast his eyes to the grungy linoleum floor. He didn't want to admit what had happened, but he knew he would feel like a liar if he didn't tell her his part in Aanwat finding Suda.

"In what way?" she asked.

Chai clenched his jaw and then admitted it. "He followed me to where she was staying. And then he saw Suda at the safe house."

"Really?" the captain paused and looked at her desk. She lifted a stack of papers and then slid a notebook out from another pile after spying a protruding edge. She flipped it open. "That conflicts with the statement Suda made. She informed us that he saw her getting into a car and then waited until she returned to confirm it was her."

"What?"

"Look," she passed the notebook to Chai who began reading it.

He looked up and smiled, shaking his head, giddy with relief. "He told me he followed me."

The captain raised her eyebrows. "Sounds as if he was turning the screws."

"I'm so relieved I'm not even angry," he paused. "Still, I didn't get to the top. I wanted that name."

"I know," the captain put her hand on his shoulder, "but someone else will have to pick up where you left off. I can't send you back in if you're compromised. You know that."

"But we don't know I've been compromised."

"My gut is saying that you have been, and I'm not willing to take the chance. We don't know what Aanwat said before he got you into that storage container. We can't be sure, and if I'm not sure, you're being taken out."

"Understood."

"How do you feel about going back to detective work?"

Chai paused a moment to reflect then said, "Ambivalent. A little relieved. A bit pissed."

"I get it," she said. "But I think it will be best. Your old desk is waiting for you."

"And Suda? Will we be able to get asylum for her?"

"She can certainly prove her life is in danger if she returns, so I'm guessing yes. But," she looked at Chai while she scratched the back of her neck, "it will be a process. You know that."

Chai sighed again. He had hardly slept and felt bleary eyed, having first gone to the hospital with Simone and then having been in questioning until the wee hours after leaving her x-rayed, splinted, and safely checked into her room to spend the night.

"But she can stay at Hope House for now?"

"Yes, but we had to notify our friends at ICE."

"Ugh."

"Sorry. It's protocol. And I would get her a good immigration lawyer."

"Will do," Chai said and stood to leave. "Thanks."

Chai climbed into his white Prius, placed his hands on the wheel at ten and two, and then laid his forehead at twelve o'clock. He couldn't deny feeling a sense of relief to be out of the game. It was ugly on the inside, and he hated the way it was seeping into his very being. But he had failed to get what he had been after and that gave him a deep sense of dissatisfaction.

He gently thumped his forehead on the top of the steering wheel a few times then sat back up. He thought of Simone and what it would be like to simply go by her bakery and not have to worry about being followed or about hanging out for as long as he wanted. And, he had to admit, he wanted to spend as much time as he could with her. She was a truly exceptional woman and going through the ordeal they had just experienced together only served to confirm his high opinion of her. He started the car and headed in the direction of the hospital with a stop planned along the way.

His shoes squeaked on the shiny hospital floor as he walked past the nurse's station, down the hall to the room Claire and Simone strategically shared. He arrived, a bag of fresh glazed donuts and hot lattes in hand for the invalids. Chai was surprised to find Simone up and dressed in fresh clothes, eagerly awaiting her release. The light dusting of freckles shone up stronger than usual against her pale skin. Her eyes looked tired but animated.

"Hey there," he said when he came through the door. "It looks as if I got here just in time for you to be leaving."

"I'm ready. Just waiting for the word." She spied the donut bag and smelled something sweet. "For us?" Simone asked taking a latte and reaching into the white bag and finding a donut. "Oh, my gosh, they're still warm!" she said, biting in. "Claire, you have to have one," Simone handed the bag over.

"Coffee and donuts? Isn't that awfully *Hawaii 5-0*?" She reached in to take a circle of puffy, sweet dough from the bag. "Thanks, Chai."

"You're welcome," he said and lifted the coffee cup to Claire with raised eyebrows.

"Yes, please, sir," she said, accepting the cup. "The coffee here sucks, and they woke us up about ten times during the night to check on us."

"What's the prognosis?" Chai asked, taking them both in.

"Simone here gets to fly the coop," Claire answered. "Whereas I have to remain in custody for another day or two, according to the doctor."

"In *custody* is putting it a bit melodramatically, isn't it?"

"She has to stay in the hospital for a couple of days at least because she lost a lot of blood," Simone explained. "But because the bullet went through the muscle and missed the bone, the healing process should be pretty quick."

"Thirty-four stitches," Claire nodded, eyebrows raised proudly.

"Impressive," Chai said. "And how's the nose?"

"Hurts almost as much as my leg, but aside from all the cotton shoved up there, they don't have to do anything to fix it."

"How are you?" he turned to face Simone.

"She's good," Claire said before Simone had a chance to answer. "Busted collarbone, but that's it. Nothing as exciting as being shot."

"And, in solidarity with Claire, I am not taking any pain meds aside from Tylenol."

"You two are impressive, I'll tell you that." Chai lifted his latte in a salute to them.

"I can't believe you guys were in a shipping container the whole time," Claire shook her head. "Kind of ironic; right?"

"No reason to look smug," Chai furrowed his brows as if to look angry. "How's Suda?"

"I'm anxious to get home and find out," Simone said "I've talked to Grace, and she said she's quiet but seems pretty good. She'll see her therapist today to process, but still. I want to be there."

"They're not going to deport her, are they?" Claire asked.

"I don't think so. We should get a good lawyer for her just in case."

"I'll marry her if it'll help. Same sex marriage is legal, now."

"That's sweet, Claire. Not a bad idea. I'm going to give that some food for thought," Chai nodded

"Or, hey, you could marry her," Claire said. "Or Simone. Either of you could."

"Actually, we can't," Chai loosely put his hands over Simone's ears, but she could hear every word, "because I intend to marry Simone, which will take us both out of the game. But don't tell her." He winked at Claire.

Simone's head snapped toward him, "What did you say?"

"What? Nothing at all. I didn't say a thing."

Claire looked almost as shocked as Simone did but was, for once, speechless.

"Are you ready to go? I could give you a ride home," Chai asked, as if he'd said nothing shocking.

"Yes," Simone said, still not at all sure how to respond to what Chai had just said. "Could you just give me a minute with Claire?"

"Sure, I'll wait for you in the hall. See you soon, Claire," he waved and then stepped out.

"Did you hear what he said?" Claire whispered excitedly as soon as Chai was out the door.

"Yes," Simone answered, "but I'm sure he was joking because of your suggestion of marrying Suda."

"I think you're wrong. I think he was dead serious."

"I doubt it," Simone laughed. "Will you be all right if I leave you here for now?"

"Yeah," she said, looking out the window. "No problem."

But she found that she, in fact, did mind. She was worried that they would slip from her grasp if she didn't have them all in her sight. A feeling she found both thrilling and disturbing. She wondered whether the terrifying aspect of belonging was how it felt to be a part of a family and smiled a little bit in spite of herself.

Suda

SUDA LAY ON HER BED in Simone's small living room and contemplated the word *hope*. She said it aloud in English first and then in Thai. *Hope*. It was an elusive thing. How could it be defined, really? Wishing for something that might be possible? Kind of. Maybe it was more the expectation that something *could* happen. Something good actually could come to pass.

The pillow and mattress were soft, the comforter thick down wrapped in a white duvet. She felt safe, clean. The sunlight streamed in the window she was no longer afraid to stand in front of. She pulled back the curtain and looked out at the day and drank in her new sense of freedom.

She thought of the contrast between this bed and the many others she had lain in at different times in her life: The low pallet of her childhood, where she felt protected and had no idea of the future; the thin, hard, mattress where she worked and slept in the brothel; the bare mattress she'd clung to in the dark, frightening shipping container crossing the ocean from Thailand; and finally the dingy mattress she'd been on in the motel.

While she and Claire had been lying side-by-side, tied up on the stained blanket covering the uncomfortable mattress, Suda had—oddly—felt a sense of hope. It was not the hope that Aanwat had changed and would take her away, or that they would live happily ever after. Not that her circumstances would even be okay. After all, she had been laying tied and gagged, in a run-down motel room. Still, she had a sense that life was more than what was happening in the moment. She had a sense of peace, and the only reason she could conceive that it had happened was that it was somehow tied to the hope that Simone had been talking about. She didn't understand the whole Savior thing, but she realized she felt that she wasn't alone. How did it work? She was unclear. Yet there it was again— a sense of hope.

And she had come through it, with the help of Claire and the police. Now, she was determined to stay in this country that was so different from hers. She again thought about being in the shipping container—crossing the deep, tumultuous ocean. She had traversed windswept, choppy waters that threatened to drown her, and yet she had come out on the other side at last in spite of the many hands that had shoved her beneath the surface. She was now bringing air into her lungs. Alive, not drowned. The tears that slipped down her face were the same saline as the sea and would be a constant reminder.

She heard the downstairs door click, and Simone yelled up to her as she climbed the stairs.

"Suda?" Simone's American accent still didn't get the tone right, but Suda loved the way her name sounded coming from her.

"Here! Hello!" She responded in English, just as Simone and Chai came into the room.

Simone dropped her stuff on her kitchen table and then as best she could, wrapped her arm around Suda.

"Suda, Suda, Suda," she said. So happy to have her right there, accessible, touchable. "I was so scared. I prayed and prayed. I can't tell you how happy I am to have you back."

Chai translated while Simone kept her arm wrapped around her.

"How are you?" Simone asked her directly.

"Good," Suda smiled and nodded, speaking in English. "I am good." She said each word individually and distinctly.

Simone turned to Chai, "Will you ask her how she really is. Dig in there in Thai and find out please."

Chai sat on the couch and motioned Suda to sit next to him, and while Simone made a pot of Thai tea for them all, Suda and Chai talked. She recounted everything she could remember from the moment Claire yelled her name until Grace picked her up at the hospital.

"What will happen to Aanwat?" Suda asked. In spite of everything that had happened, she wanted to know if he would go to jail here for what he did, or whether he would be sent back to Thailand. They had both come from hill tribes and had understood each other because of it. She felt only pity for him now. And sorrow.

"He'll be deported," Chai said, but left out the fact that they would be using him to get to the man who ran the brothel she'd been kept in. It would be better to let her move on without adding that worry to her mind.

"Will I be sent back?" She looked at Chai, trying to read his expression.

"We're going to make sure you don't," he said and squeezed her shoulder.

"Were you afraid?" Simone asked, and Chai translated, while she brought tea and set it on a tray for them to share.

"Yes, but it was a different kind of fear. When I was brought to the karaoke and told what was going to happen, that was the most frightening moment of my life. Maybe even more terrifying than when it actually happened. I refused, and they beat me," she looked down. "They beat me so many times. This was a different kind of fear. I felt calm in spite of what was happening. And Claire was with me. She was bleeding, and I was more afraid for her than for me. At first I thought she would die, and if that had happened because of me, I wouldn't have been able to stand it."

A tear slipped down Suda's cheek, and she wiped her nose. Simone grabbed the box of tissues for her.

"I had a plan, though," Suda continued. "I had decided to go with him and then call you as soon as I could."

"I'm relieved it didn't come to that, and I'm glad you knew you could call us, no matter what."

"I thank you, Simone," Suda said in her limited English and then began crying in earnest. "I think hope. Thank you, Chai."

Suda hugged him, touching him for the first time since he had carried her into Hope House months ago. He felt honored by her trust and hugged her back.

"I think maybe your God was with me. I felt a sense of peace I couldn't explain," she said. Chai's expression made Simone wonder what Suda had said, and when he told her, Simone gave Suda an extra squeeze.

"Are you hungry?" Simone asked.

"Yes, and you know what?" Suda asked in the midst of her tears, "For the first time in so many months, I am in the mood for Thai food. Maybe pad thai and some spicy curry soup?"

"You got it, sweet girl," Simone kissed her cheek and walked to the phone to call her favorite Thai restaurant.

Claire

GRACE GENTLY KNOCKED ON THE DOOR to Claire's hospital room before entering. It was dim inside, and at first she thought Claire was sleeping, but then noticed her sitting up in bed, statue still, gazing out the window at the darkening sky.

"Hey," Grace said softly.

Claire turned toward her, surprised out of her dark musings, "Hey, yourself. What are you doing here?"

Grace thought she looked especially thin and vulnerable in her bed, propped against the pillows, silhouetted in the window, her hair pulled back in a ponytail. The bandage on her nose overwhelmed her face. With her standard issue Giants baseball cap absent from her head, Grace could see the delicate bones in Claire's face.

"Came to check up on you."

"Oh," Claire said, tucking her arms protectively across her body.

"How are you? Does your leg hurt too much?"

"I've experienced worse."

"Always our tough one."

Claire shook her head, with the corners of her mouth turned down, and looked out the window.

"Are you all right?" Grace asked.

Claire shook her head again but still didn't speak.

"What is it?"

Claire sniffed, biting back tears.

"I was just thinking about the fact that I'm ruined. My body is ruined. My life is ruined."

"Not ruined, my sweet girl. Just interrupted. You'll get back on track."

Claire shook her head again. "Polluted with disgusting men and drugs. It'll be with me—a part of me—always. It can never be undone, and I hate it. But it's *me*; don't you see? So, I hate *me*. I'm *rancid*." She said the words with such vehemence that Grace could physically feel her emotional agony and self-disgust.

"Oh, Claire," Grace came and wrapped her arms around the fragile young woman who worked so hard to appear hardened and uncaring.

"What brought this on?"

"Simone and Chai. He loves her so much, and it's because she's good through and through. Anyone can see it. But I'll never have that." She paused and shook her head. "Because I'm *not* good. I'm . . ." Claire paused, but no word came to mind.

"Listen to me," Grace said. "Simone is good, no doubt, but she is flawed *and* still lovable. She's both. Just like I am flawed and still lovable, and so are you."

"Did you know that the Bible is full of prostitutes, compromised women, screwups, murderers, adulterers, liars and God *loved* them. He could see into their hearts and know the good in spite of all the bad. And, I've got some news for you, Claire. There is so, so much good in there. In addition, nothing that happened to you was your fault. It happened to you."

"There were fuckups in the Bible?" Claire asked, and Grace decided to give her a pass on dropping the F-bomb for once. "I assumed everyone was perfect."

Grace burst out laughing. "I assumed that, too, before I actually got to know what's in the book. It's opposite, as it turns out. It was a bunch of people bumbling along for the most part, interspersed with a few amazingly great people. So, yeah, the Bible has some Simones in there, but, for the most part, the people who God loves are like you and me. And some others who are worse, way worse."

"Huh," Claire paused and gave that some thought. "Maybe, you could tell me about some of the badass Bible chicks some time."

"I will. But in the meantime, know that you are loved, you are pure, you are beautiful, and you are clean." Grace took a hold of Claire's hand, and they sat there quietly together for a bit. "You might want to get baptized someday, too. Ceremonially wash away any remnants of filth you feel and come back up sweet and clean just like before any of this happened."

"Thank you, Grace," Claire whispered after a while.

"Don't thank me. I'm just the messenger."

Claire must have dozed off after that because the next time she opened her eyes, it was the middle of the night, she was alone in bed, and a nurse was in checking her IV. Once the nurse tiptoed out in her quiet-soled shoes, Claire slipped back into a contented, restful sleep.

When she peeked her eye open again, sun was shining in the window, and she felt as if she couldn't stand to be in bed for one more moment. She swung her legs down and, along with the IV pole, made her way into the bathroom that adjoined the room. When she reemerged, the morning nurse, cheerfully dressed in blue polka-dotted scrubs and a bouncy brown ponytail, was writing notes on her whiteboard.

"Can I go home today?" Claire's voice came out more whiny than intended, and she flinched.

"The doc will be by doing rounds in a few, and if she says you can go, then you can go. I think the news will be good," she winked at her patient. "Want some breakfast? You must be starved. You slept right through dinner last night. You were out cold."

"I don't know. Is it something gross?"

"Not too bad actually. Scrambled eggs, sliced apple."

"I'll try it," Claire said, wondering when someone from Hope House would be in. She decided to give Grace a call to see if she could entice her to bring some good coffee.

Simone

IT WAS A MONDAY MORNING, and Simone was in the bakery's kitchen, humming to herself, a sunbeam spilling through the window onto the worn hardwoods. She was pulling scones out of the oven, when she heard the bakery door chime and Chai's voice. Her body became aware, and she could feel his presence even from the other room. She knew Grace had the front of the house covered, but still, she wanted to burst up there to see him, but checked herself.

Chai hadn't said a word about the comment he made to Claire about "marrying Simone" when they were leaving the hospital. She was starting to feel a little jumpy around him. Still, if he could ignore the topic, she could ignore it harder.

She set the scones down and deliberately placed them on a cooling rack one at a time. She heard Grace chuckle at a comment Chai made, but Simone was too far away to decipher the words. She stood still, rhythmically tapping her fingers on her lips while she pondered and then turned and picked up a tray of croissants. She couldn't resist emerging from the kitchen, as if oblivious, carrying the tray on a fake errand so she could see him. When she came through the door, there he was, clean-shaven, looking fresh and somehow vulnerable, hands in his pockets, concentrating on the display counter. He wore a crisp long-sleeved button-down, and it felt as if she were seeing someone she had become intimately familiar with anew. He looked up, caught her eyes, and smiled. And then he was familiar again. Chai. And she knew she was his, and he was hers without anything being said.

"I just met with my sergeant," he said. "I'm officially back to detective work, new cases."

Simone searched his face to see how he felt about that fact but found his eyes unreadable.

"How does that work?" she asked. "Do you have to move and switch precincts so no one will see you as a police officer?" She kept her voice light but was holding her breath, wondering what it would mean for them.

"No, but it will be a bit tricky. I'll meet with a couple of other guys I know who made the transition and see what's what."

"How are you feeling about it?"

"Ambivalent."

"I'm sure."

Grace placed Chai's coffee on the counter between them and turned back to the espresso machine to start on the coffee order for the next customer.

"Thanks, Grace." He reached for it and took a small, tentative sip, checking to make sure it wasn't too hot while watching Simone over the top of the cardboard to-go cup.

"I'll still be involved peripherally because I'll be Aanwat's handler."

Simone chuckled and raised her eyebrows. "He's gonna love that."

"Yeah," Chai drew out the word slowly. "He was none too pleased to see me walk into the room when they were negotiating a deal."

"I bet."

"Hey, how's Claire doing?"

"It's interesting, actually. I think she turned a corner. Like somehow fighting—and winning—the altercation with Aanwat gave her a renewed sense of control in her life. Every day she seems a little bit lighter than the day before. Startles less easily, argues less, seems more engaged. Smiles even."

"I can see how that could be. In a way, she got to fight the physical manifestation of her fear."

"And get this," on the way home from church yesterday, Claire said, "'What the fuck, I guess I finally get it. I'm in with Jesus. Team love, right?' Her tone was sarcastic, but she had the biggest smile I've seen cross her face. Happiness actually reached her eyes."

"Wow."

"Yes, and then she said, 'I'm dragging Suda along with me. She and I discussed it. She's in, too.'"

"I love that they 'discussed' it. I don't know how they communicate so well given the language barrier, but they seem to."

"I know: right?

Chai wrapped Simone in his arms. "You're good with them."

"I love them, even though they can be a huge pain in my tush."

"I know you do," Chai paused. "And so do they."

Aanwat

THE AIR ON THE 747 HAD MADE HIS EYE SOCKET DRY, so Aanwat dropped some saline onto his prosthetic eyeball and blinked so the moisture could sooth the scratchiness he felt inside. Another hour on the plane, and he would be back in Chiang Rai. His last weeks in San Francisco had been a blur of physical and emotional pain. Over and over, he relived the combined agony and terror of that girl plunging the toothbrush into his eye socket. It had happened so fast, and the unexpected searing pain had been intense. He imagined it would have felt the same had his head been sliced in half with a machete. He flinched even now thinking about it. He was sure he was going to die on the way to the hospital. When he awoke from the anesthesia after surgery in police custody, he almost wished he had. Even more so when he learned that they were unable to save his eye and had to remove it. Then there were the relentlessly boring weeks spent in the crowded, noisy infirmary of a holding facility while he healed enough to put in a permanent fake eye before he was deported. And they had been stingy with the pain meds.

He looked at his face in the mirror and practiced getting his new eye to track using his muscles so that it looked natural, even though he could see only out of his one remaining healthy eye. He still got dizzy and had headaches but at least the socket had stopped itching. That had driven him to distraction. His hair had grown long during the months he had spent in San Francisco, and when he looked at himself, he hardly recognized the man who was looking back.

He made his way from the airplane bathroom back to his seat and turned to look out of the window at the lush, green landscape below. He was relieved it was almost over. The entire trip had been one calamitous nightmare. He rubbed his hands across his face. If only he could go back to being the guy who cleaned the karaoke as he was when Gan first took him in. He sighed and shook his head subconsciously when he thought about everything that had happened since.

When Tea had showed up in his hospital room with a police badge hanging around his neck, Aanwat had known it was over and he had lost Suda. When the police chief informed him of their intention for him to be their inside man in exchange for his freedom, he understood that he had also lost the ability to get out of the organization. He knew he was trapped and always would be.

Now, his job was to try and get in farther. He was to find out who was above his boss and then send the information he collected to the local police who would relay it to their counterparts in San Francisco. He figured he would eventually be caught and killed, and the thought of it froze him with fear. He would try to figure out a way to escape once he was back. Assuming Gan didn't rip out his other eye when he learned that he had never found Suda and that he wasn't paid a dime for her. It was a complete loss. There was nothing he could do about it, and he had nothing left to lose, so whatever happened, happened.

In the meantime, he decided to live in the moment. He looked around the plane. The flight attendants were beautiful, and they spoke Thai, which was a relief. He was tired of having to think in English all the time. If he never heard the language again, he would be fine with it. He would eat the mango sticky rice the lovely flight attendant had placed in front of him and relish the idea of being back in a warm climate.

It would be nice to be around the women in the karaoke again. He had missed them while he'd been gone. The people coming and going, the drinks. He had been lonely while he was away. Maybe he would go with one or two when he was back. Sample the pleasures of the karaoke himself for once.

He might visit his family again and see if there was a little money to be made there. After all, he would need an extra source of income and connections if he was going to get away at some point. He could keep himself away from the heroin—though, he told himself. Maybe just deliver packages here and there if his brothers wanted him to. How hard could that be?

The plane touched down and taxied to the gate. The aisle filled with passengers, and he got up and took his bag down. He walked off the plane and into his new reality.

Hope House

"HOT PLATE COMING OVER," Simone said and then set a cast-iron skillet of steaming hot, homemade macaroni and cheese in the middle of the dinner table. Suda, Simone, Chai, Grace, Claire, and Nittha sat together to celebrate the news from Suda's immigration lawyer over dinner. She was now the proud recipient of a green card and would be able to work toward becoming a citizen.

"Cheers," Grace said, and they touched their glasses filled with sparkling apple cider.

"I thought we were going to have to marry her off," Claire said. "Seriously, it was a good idea."

"I have to admit: when you suggested that, my mind started cycling through friends who could help us," Chai told them.

"I would have done it. No problem." Claire held up her hands.

Nittha leaned close to Suda and whispered what they were saying to her.

"No, no, no!" Suda, waved her hand dismissively. "No marriage. Me only. Baking bread."

"Maybe once we're done with the program, you and I can move to an apartment together. Somewhere safe. And close by," Claire raised her eyebrows appraising her own idea and liking the sound of it.

"Speaking of the program, we are going to get a new resident in a few days," Simone told them.

"What's her deal?" Claire asked.

"I'll leave it to her to tell in her own time, but suffice to say, she's going to need a lot of love, understanding, and compassion."

"It's a journey," Grace said. "As it is for all of us."

Claire

Later

AS HER AFTERNOONS WOUND DOWN, Claire liked to stop by Hope Bakery. Her favorite table was tucked into the corner by two large windows. The late sun, slanting through the panes, warmed her and caught the blonde strands that were no longer hidden by a baseball cap.

Before Claire had a chance to ask, Suda set a cup of coffee next to her.

"The foam art still isn't as good as yours used to be," Suda looked at the cup critically, and Claire glanced at the tulip swirled on top of her latte.

"Overly modest as usual," Claire told her and poured two packets of sugar into the cup, swirled the milky-brown latte and took a sip. "Delicious, thanks." She smiled at Suda.

Her friend was still slim but had long since lost her frail appearance. Her hair was back to a shiny black and had been cut into a fashionable chin-length style. She again wore black-framed glasses—no longer to disguise herself—but because she'd become nearsighted. They had a tendency to slide down her small nose, so she was forever pushing them back up.

Six eventful years had passed since Claire and Suda moved out of Hope House and into an apartment of their own, but still, the bakery was Claire's favorite place to write.

"Was the bakery busy this morning?" Claire asked. "I'm surprised there are any croissants left."

"I'll get you one," Suda popped behind the counter, put one of the flaky pastries on a plate, and brought it to the table.

Suda's love of all things bread and her devotion to Simone hadn't waned, and getting up long before sun up had become as much a routine to Suda as it was to Simone. Claire on the other hand, had studiously avoided the wee hours required of bakers since the day she left.

"Mmmm," she inhaled the scent of buttery croissant and tore off an end. "It's so good," Claire chewed, "but I don't miss having to make them. I just never got the knack. I think it takes a softer touch and more patience than I've ever had."

"How were your classes?" Suda asked, kindly avoiding commenting on Claire's true self-assessment of her pastry skills. "Did you finally turn in that paper?"

Not long after "the Aanwat incident" as they all called that crazy day, Grace had convinced Claire to set aside her pride and finish high school through a combination of online courses and local night school. Claire had surprised herself because she not only didn't hate being back in classes, she adored having a reason to study with a purpose. She found that keeping her nose in books was the perfect way to avoid both people and the reality of her situation. Books were safe. They were consistent. They never betrayed.

"I did turn it in, but I'm afraid it was kind of rushed. Not my best work. Maybe sucked."

"You always say that, and then you get an A, so . . ." Suda shrugged, having long understood that Claire was her own worst critic.

After she had her high school diploma safely tucked among the books on her shelf, Claire had applied for college and qualified for a federal grant to attend University of San Francisco.

"How is it?" Grace had asked her after her first day of classes.

Claire paused, trying to express the feeling she'd had in the midst of all the other students.

"I think kind of like being a foreign exchange student," she mused. "I spent the day with a bunch of people who couldn't have had more different life experiences than me. It was like being thrown into another country."

"How did that feel?" Grace wondered aloud.

"Weird. A bit like I was faking it."

"You're a student. They're students. Just keep that in mind. You're not pretending. You're worthy of being there as much as anyone else."

"Thanks, Grace. On the upside, the buildings are beautiful. I love the atmosphere."

The students had smiled at her, included her in class discussions and study groups as if she belonged. But stranger than being around peers, who seemed endlessly carefree to Claire, was her realization that in spite of her feelings that first day, over time she came to understand that they saw her simply as one of them—not a homeless girl—not a victim of sex trafficking, but as a contemporary. The P for "Prostitute" that she felt had been blazoned on her chest was visible only to her, and as the months and years progressed, it faded to only a hint of the torrid color it had previously held in her mind. She majored in comparative literature with a minor in poetry and felt that it must be somewhat akin to heaven. Not only was she able to read novels upon novels, but she actually got credit for doing so.

As for love, it was too soon to tell whether she would someday succumb. For now, she couldn't quite bring herself to trust another person enough to become vulnerable. But someday— who knew. Until then, she had four people who truly knew her: Simone, Grace, Suda, and Chai. And while she might never truly open up to others in person, she found she could do so on paper. So she wrote—often while sitting at a table at Hope Bakery, where she always felt safe.

"Hey," she said to Chai, who came through the door, badge over his tee-shirt.

"Hey, yourself." He squeezed Claire's shoulder. "Good to see you." He plunked down beside her and turned to Suda. "Has Simone gotten back from the farmers market yet?"

"Not yet," she told him. "Want a coffee?"

"That would be great. Thanks," he said and then reached into his bag. He held out a book to Suda, "Here's a novel Nittha thinks you'll like," he said, handing it over.

"Oh, thank her for me; will you?" she said, flipping through the pages. Her reading still wasn't as strong as she would like, but she was getting better, and luckily for Suda, Nittha had a weakness for young adult novels and always passed them on when she was done.

Chai had moved in after he and Simone got married. His undercover days were over, but maybe that was just as well now that they had a baby on the way. He still worked the sex-trafficking beat, but now he worked from the opposite angle. He was out on the blade, trying to convince the girls that they had a safe alternative. Some believed him and got help; others didn't fare as well.

"Are you up for working with me this weekend?" he asked Claire. "I can always use your help if you want to come with."

Claire sometimes went along and talked to the girls herself, but she couldn't do it too often because it brought up too many bad memories for her. Instead, she found that she healed through prose. It was cathartic to allow her thoughts to empty onto the page.

"Nah, I want to spend the weekend getting some writing done."

She had been working on a novel for the last year and a half or so. She reached for the coffee Suda had set on her table and opened her laptop. She had begun it with the arrival of a starving girl in a shipping container. She scrolled back to the beginning to get her bearings before she continued writing. Her eyes followed the lines of text that read:

The deep blue water pitched and churned—as if expressing distress while simultaneously protecting the ship's cargo: the girl was held in a steel box among stacks of the same. Desolate and lonely, she had only the sounds of seabirds and crashing waves as her company. The wind, which began as a warm breeze against the ship at the port of departure had turned cold and howled as the days passed, and then finally stilled before the ship reached its destination. Weak with hunger and deeply fearful of what was to come next, the girl journeyed across the deep ocean from Thailand to the docks of San Francisco.

If you or someone you know is a victim of human trafficking
please contact the Human Trafficking Hotline
at **1(888) 373-7888** *or* **humantraffickinghotline.org**.

WHAT IS HUMAN TRAFFICKING?

Human trafficking is a form of modern-day slavery.
This crime occurs when a trafficker uses force,
fraud or coercion to control another person
for the purpose of engaging in commercial sex acts
or soliciting labor or services against his/her will.
Force, fraud, or coercion need not be present
if the individual engaging in commercial sex
is under 18 years of age.

ACKNOWLEDGEMENTS

First and foremost, I would like to acknowledge
the amazing women I have had the privilege to get to know
and love in the safe house I am fortunate to be connected
with. You are a true picture of strength and resilience
in this sometimes-heartbreaking world and I am grateful
to be a part of your lives.

This novel would have been a mere shadow of itself without
the love and attention showered upon it by my strong,
wise, beautiful friend, Kate Canova. Special thanks
as well to Jeff Reed, who helped me learn the heart of a poet.

To my husband Matt McGuinness and to
Kim Carpenter, who both checked the character connections
early on to make sure the puzzle pieces all fit.
Gratitude to Cheryl Duncan, Bill Duncan, Chris Boral
and Natasha McCormick for giving a recent draft a read
and for the insightful feedback.

Appreciation goes to my homegirl Tracy Sunrize
Johnson for the beautiful design and for being such a delight
to work with, to Hugh D'Andrade for the amazing
cover illustration, and to Amy Bauman, copyeditor and
proofreader extraordinaire.

Finally, huge thanks goes to Jacqueline Mitchard,
Catherine Armsden, Jeff Reed and Cynthia Newberry Martin
for such kind words of praise and for allowing those words
to adorn the cover.

Each of you played an important role and I am truly grateful.

ALSO BY LISA MCGUINNESS

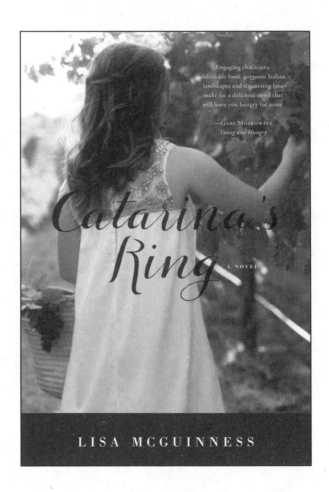

Engaging characters, delectable food, gorgeous Italian landscapes and simmering love make for a delicious novel that will leave you hungry for more.

—GABI MOSKOWITZ
Young and Hungry

Catarina's Ring

A NOVEL

LISA MCGUINNESS